THE DARK NETWORK

HELEN TREVORROW

For Louise

1

ANDREW MARLOW

I take a deep breath. My back's against the locked door of Andrew Marlow's bathroom. It is small and old-fashioned. There's a squared-off sink that looks like it's from the 1950s; it reminds me of the one we had in my mother's house and replaced with something modern. I'm sweaty, nervous, and I can feel my heart beating in my throat.

The metal taps, once shiny, are now dull. Andrew's mother's pink bathrobe is hanging on the back of the door and it brushes my face. It smells musty. The bath has a plastic tray that sits across it and resting peacefully within it is a crisp dried flannel.

I use the loo but I can't pee. I flush the toilet to make a noise. The toilet paper is tissue thin, a cheap brand, and the roll is thrown wonkily on top of the cistern. Inside the bathroom cabinet are Andrew's mother's potions and ointments: a pink powder puff, Cabotine de Gres perfume, three different types of talcum powder, face cream, haemorrhoid cream and Vagisil. My God.

Shining on the windowsill, cutting through the pink furnishings, gleams a long, curved cut-throat razor. A bone handle, perhaps ivory? A four-inch blade, slimmer at one end and adorned with tiny Arabic script. I want to take it. This object slices straight through the suburban mediocrity of this house. I know that it belongs to Andrew.

I step out of the bathroom and I'm tempted to sneak a quick look in the bedrooms. I suspect that if I open a wardrobe all of his mother's clothes will still be there. As I head for the master bedroom, Andrew Marlow steps onto the landing as if he has been waiting for me. Which, of course, he has. I jump, startled. This could be it. He could overpower me right now and no one, not even Harry primed in his Ford Galaxy outside, could do a damn thing about it. He might kill me here and now, whether I'm a nurse looking for a date, or a journalist looking for a story, I am exactly the same thing to him.

"I've not had a chance to clean out my mother's things yet," he says. "I don't have many visitors."

I'm an idiot for putting myself in such danger. But I want to expose the truth, and I am so close to it. I know one thing: even if Andrew Marlow is innocent, he is an oddball, so I am vindicated, I am right.

"I like your mother's things," I say, walking down the stairs. He follows, his body only inches from mine. "I lost my mother recently, too," I say.

"Then you know how it feels," he says, and moves awkwardly around me, leading me to the foot of the stairs and then further into the house. To the front is the lounge, immaculately presented chintz, as if it were the scene of a retro music video, with doilies on the back of the sofa and pink rose-adorned cushions, black and white china dogs, and brown flock wallpaper.

"I don't really use the good room," he explains as he leads me into the back room down the hall. It's large and runs along the width of the house with a kitchen at one end and what is supposed to be a dining table at the other.

The table is pushed up against the wall and on top is a

computer. There are three screens, a hard drive that glows red, white and blue, and a mouse that's like something from *Star Trek*. This is what I'm supposed to interact with? Harry's plan is never going to work. I won't be able to turn it on and even if I can, I won't be able to figure out how to get onto the internet, never mind install the spyware Harry has set me up to download. It's crazy. I might as well just turn around and walk out while I still can.

In the middle of the room where the table should be is a beaten-up piece of gym equipment, a bench press with large weights, and a bar for pull-ups. The leather pads are worn. There is an NGK spark plugs sticker on one beam, on another a West Ham football team logo. A poster of the Spice Girls is tacked to the wall above his computer.

On the kitchen surfaces are large canisters of protein powder, and a pile of cucumbers and avocados. A black duffle bag gapes open on the floor with clothes spilling out, and Andrew quickly kicks it shut so I won't see the contents. This is a single man in his alpha pad. I've never seen anything like the juxtaposition of the immaculately preserved in soft pinks of his mother's things and the cold stark blackness of Andrew's stuff. Everything of his has sharp corners.

"I would have tidied up if I thought someone was coming round." There is a desperation in his voice, a loneliness. I don't know why but it warms me to him. I look around this place and I'm reminded of myself: alone and living in my dead mother's house in Willesden.

"Who's your favourite Spice Girl?" I ask, more as myself, Dolores O'Rourke, and not me acting as a made-up honey-trap nurse. He could easily be me. Or I could be him. I look at him and think, this could be my life. Is this what I am heading towards?

He studies his poster of the Spice Girls, screwing up his eyes, imagining.

"Definitely Baby Spice, Emma Bunton," he says. "She's really pretty, and innocent."

Of course it's Baby Spice, the dirty bastard. His answer pulls me back to the task at hand. We are nothing alike. He is a pervert. He's been phoning a fifteen-year-old girl.

I look at the clock. I don't have long. I need to get him to switch on the computer and enter his password before there is a knock at the door. I have to move fast. I have to put aside my feelings and persuade him to do what I want.

"So, what do I need to set up a basic CB radio?" I ask. "Can I buy it online?"

"Let me show you," he says, suddenly energetic. "Sit here." He pulls up a large gamer's chair. It swivels on wheels and has speakers built into it. I sit down and he leans over me to shake the mouse. The computer is sleeping and at his bidding it rears into life with a big whooshing noise as the hardware fires-up. I knew it had a big RAM and a big memory with an element of self-build customisation.

"This is some computer!" I say.

"Do you like it?" he asks, looking intently into my face.

"Oh, yes. It's very cool."

"It's my thing. I love computers, radio, tinkering with them. I game, sure, I game, but it's messing around with hardware that I really love."

"Me too," I blurt out, hoping that he doesn't pry too much and catch me out. I need to focus, to keep my mind on track, to stop myself from going crazy, losing it. I feel a bead of sweat trickle down my spine and I hope panic isn't visible on my face.

"Really?"

"No, I mean, I would really like to learn more about it." I correct myself so I can't be tripped up later.

"Well then, you need to get kitted out!" He types an address into his web browser.

Good, we are on the internet. At long last. We are getting

where we need to be. This is so hard. This is above my pay grade. Why am I not walking away? Then I look up at Baby Spice and I think, no, I need to know. I can't walk away now. I need to know the truth about this guy.

"The best website to buy CB radio equipment from is CB World, because they do great quality second-hand kit. You get guys like me trading up to more sophisticated hardware, and so a lot of us sell it on here."

"Okay, cool," I say, feigning interest.

"This is for computers. What computer have you got?"

"Just a laptop."

"What make is it?"

"HP."

"What RAM?"

"I don't know, it's silver," I say, and he laughs.

"Are you *really* into computers?" He is still laughing, and then he glances down at my breasts. Clear as day.

The doorbell rings. I jump. He doesn't react.

"Isn't that someone at the door?" I ask.

"I don't answer the door." He puts a finger to his lips.

Why isn't he answering the door?

"It might be something important," I say. "Or don't you want anyone to know that I'm here?"

He leaves the room to see to the caller. I have only thirty to forty-five seconds. I have no time to make mistakes, to fumble over the keyboard. I click open a new browser page. I pull up my sleeve. Harry had created a TinyURL, a shortened link to a webpage, that was easy for me to remember. I spring into action. My fingers are shaking. I can hear men's voices at the door. I can hear the top line of the conversation; a man is telling Andrew that the council is proposing to make the road one way. I tap in the URL address. His system is fast and the page springs open. I click 'download' and the computer whizzes into action. Andrew is trying to pull away but the man, who in reality is a friend of

Harry's, is trained to keep him talking and keep him at the door for at least 120 seconds – two minutes – which is seemingly all it takes. The installation is an RDP, a remote desktop protocol, that will allow Andrew Marlow's computer and all of its contents to be viewed from afar.

I hear the front door close. There is silence again underneath the slow crunch of Andrew's boots on the once soft carpet that is now silvery with years of dust and debris. The tiny roundel on the screen comes full circle and clicks to one hundred per cent. A file pops open. He's coming. I double click on the file to open it and complete the installation but he is already back in the room. He is in the doorway as I watch the computer screen through my peripheral vision and see the software silently ping in completion and automatically close, deleting any trace of itself.

I hold my breath. Has he seen? Was there a reflection in the glass of the back window? Is he onto me? Will he now attack me? Hit me with something? I glance around for a weapon of my own, something normal and innocent with which I can catch him off guard. They teach you that in self-defence – how to weaponise lamps and ornaments to fight off men.

"They're trying to make the street one way." He tuts and I stand up slowly, the chair on wheels pushing out behind me.

"I better go, I've got an early shift tomorrow," I say, needing to get out as quickly as I can.

"No!" he snaps, aggressively. "You've only just got here!"

There's a pen and a piece of scrap paper, an insert from a local newspaper.

"Can I take your number?" I ask before he asks me, before I have to give him the number that will later turn out to be false, and arouse suspicion.

"Have I done something wrong?" he asks.

I shake my head.

"I've got some cans in the fridge, I thought we could have a drink," he says.

"I'd like to see you again, I really would, but right now I better be getting back."

He takes the pen, pinching my fingers around it so he's got hold of the tips.

"Isn't it the man who should be asking for the phone number?" He speaks in a slower, deeper drawl than the voice he had been animatedly talking about computers in. He quickly glances at the screen and narrows his eyes.

"Can I see you again?" It feels like the only currency I have to keep it nice, to keep it civil, is the promise of another date. He screws up his eyes and squeezes my fingers hard. It hurts. I pull my hand away. I take the pen and write 'Claire Halliday' and the fake phone number that I always use and will just ring out if he ever dials it.

I push past him and head out to the hallway. He is right behind me, his heavy boots, his height, his muscularity weighing over me. I move to open the front door.

"Give us a kiss then." I have to turn the angle of my body to open the door and he presses up against me and holds it closed with his arm while his mouth goes to mine. His tongue in my mouth is hard, brutal, not nice. I push him off me.

"That's enough." I prise the door open and squeeze through and down the short path, out through the gate with its innocent sing-song metal lock. I notice the green framework of the tiny leaves in the hedgerow, the uneven paving of the path. I cross over so as to not be on the side of his local pub where I met him, the Red Lion. I head into Chatham town centre. I pass a bin and bend to vomit. I am sweating; I am dizzy.

10 YEARS LATER

2

————

FERRY

osie drops a pink jelly baby into the frothy Irish Sea, and wrestles her hand free from mine to grab for it. I snatch her other hand and pull her back, away from the railings. I shake my head. On this cold ferry deck there is nothing around us, not a single soul, only the sea.

My name is Dolores, but everyone calls me Doll, except for Rosie who likes to call me Mummy Doll. It was a joke at first but it has stuck.

If we are going to make it through our first rural Irish winter in decades then we will need to upgrade our winter coats. I didn't have time to plan outfits. In the end I didn't even have time to pack before we jumped into the car and drove away.

The angry wind makes salty tassels of Rosie's hair. We are patiently waiting for land to appear in the slit where the grey padded sky meets the grey rolling sea. Rosie tries to pull her hand away again. She's a determined little girl. People say she's just like me, and I am often delighted by her tenacity.

She'd like to run around this deck but I pull her tight to me, cheek to cheek. My knuckles redden in the cold. Rosie's skin has a luminescence in this light. Her new front teeth make her look so very grown up, but the big gap between them is cute. I was astounded when I discovered that the new teeth have sharp crenellations that will be worn smooth over time. No one ever told me that. Rosie's cheeks are juicy and strawberry red and she spouts giggles. She's eight but she's still my baby. Once we set foot in Ireland she will be safe.

"Mummy Doll, look!" Rosie shouts, pointing at a large seagull who keeps pace flying alongside us. Over the engines we can barely hear each other. There's a welcome warm blast of wind from the ferry's chimney, and it swirls around the deck and disappears. My hair is plastered across my face, an annoying strand sticking in my mouth. I tug at it desperately, spitting it out, trying to tuck it behind my ear.

"Naughty hair." Rosie tells it off with a pointy finger. Rosie loves to play hairdressers. She plaits the nylon strands of her doll's hair over and over again to get it smoother and tighter. My eyes water, either from the wind or from my aching heart. We are travelling west. We are going back, returning to the safe haven of the little island of Ireland in the Atlantic Ocean. We are closing our family loop and going back to a place steeped in magic and simplicity. A place where I can stop pretending to be something that I'm not, and just be Rosie's mum.

I taste the sea salt on my lips. Could this work out? Could we start over? I imagine my worries floating away out of me and blowing across the sea.

Breathe.

But instinctively I tighten my grip on my child, and slip my arm around Rosie's waist. I can't help it. I won't let her be torn from me, not by the brutal wind, and not by any person. Rosie crumples up her brow in disgust and readies herself to complain.

"Mummy Doll!" She thinks she's a grown-up. She is growing up. I know that. On cue she shouts, "I'm a big girl!"

"Yes, you are," I say. "But no one stands at the edge, not even the ship's captain." She is disappointed. She wobbles her jaw slowly as if she might cry. I know this won't be the last time that I disappoint her. One day she'll know everything that I have done. I kiss her head. "You taste like seaweed," I say, and I laugh and try to coax her into a smile. I conceal my fear from her. I don't want to contaminate her with my anxiety. My thumbnails are bitten down to the quick. Rosie looks at me. She's reading my mind. I can't help but think she knows everything anyway and chooses not to let it show.

"Don't be frightened." She puts her small arm around me and rubs my back like I was *her* little girl.

"I don't want you to fall in and drown," I say. "Where would I be then?"

She winds her hands up around my neck and kisses me. "Guess who I love?"

"Who?" I ask, playing along.

"You," and she rubs the soft palms of her hands on my cheeks. Something wet, either rain or waves, spatters our faces.

I feel a vibration over the engines, under the wind. My mobile is buzzing inside my coat pocket. The phone holds me, it paralyses me, my stomach flips over with nerves. He's calling. I try to ignore it, to push it down. It stops ringing but immediately starts up again, and with each ring bile rises in my throat.

I take it out and look at the number. I feel a queasy sensation and I clutch my sides. Bent double for a moment, a quick and sharp pain rears through me. I straighten up, sweating. I don't want to let Rosie see the fear in my face.

I lift my hand and point out the emerging hazy tip of land, jutting out into the sea. "Look. Ireland," I say.

"Where? Where?" she screams. I point again. It is almost imperceptible at first, like a ghost shadow of land and then it grows, it morphs, and it becomes textured and real.

"That's where we're going to live." Rosie clenches her jaw in excitement. I let her go for a moment. I step toward the starboard side and I take out the still ringing telephone. I drop it from my open palm over the side of the boat and into the Irish Sea.

The screen flickers as it spins and the phone quickly disappears into the dark grey water. It is absorbed into the cold ocean. No trace remains.

We are starting over, just me and my daughter. We are starting life all over again. We are going to live a simpler life. We will be happy.

Rosie jumps up, realising that I have dropped something.

"What have you done, Mummy?" Rosie asks, alarmed, her wide eyes panicked.

"Nothing, baby," I lie. "I haven't done anything." She should never know the truth.

"Play," she commands, holding up her hands. We put our hands together and swipe and clap against each other in a game that she has taught me. Rosie sings the song because she's the leader, and I join in.

"Tick-tack-toe, give me a high, give me a low, give me three in a row," and then Rosie speeds it up and beats her little fist into the palm of her hand. "A bunny got shot by a UFO, and landed in a marshmallow, and got eaten by a Haribo…" We clap our hands and recite the words so fast they fall upwards as gibberish into the air. We laugh.

"I don't like the bit about the bunny getting shot," I say, and I shiver thinking about guns and all the things that I have seen and done in my life that could hurt her.

"Let me tell you something," Rosie says, like an ancient philosopher, "it happens."

I know it happens. I've seen it. But I can't think about dead bunnies, or think about Rosie thinking about dead bunnies. I won't let myself remember. I won't let him find us. We are starting again.

3

HOLY CROSS

"You've made good time in that old banger!" my cousin Connor says, shaking my hand. He's been waiting in his expensive-looking silver BMW. The engine is off, but inside the car smoulders in a soft orange glow. He is film star looks in estate agent clothes.

"Thanks for waiting, Connor." My real car is still parked outside my house in London. I've borrowed this from a mum friend at the school. I smell musty after the long drive with the heating on, my hands are clammy and jeans sticky from hours in my seat. Rosie is fast asleep, though she rarely naps these days. She had been so excited, but when I turned around to tell her we'd crossed into Limerick her eyes had closed, her little head nodded over the bumps and turns. At each junction her eyes flickered as though she might wake up.

"Welcome home." He peers into the back seat excitedly. He has never met my daughter. "Look at her! She looks like you, Doll."

"She has the biggest brown eyes."

"And the O' Rourke mouth."

The O'Rourkes all look alike. We are compactly built with

males and females having the same, some might say dense, genes. In a room full of women, I'm the one who gets given the jar to open. We are dark haired. My mother had lashings of jet-black hair. We're the sort of people who get mistaken for Spaniards when on holiday in Spain.

"She'll be so upset she missed us arriving!" I throw my arms around him.

He has lines punctuating the skin around his eyes but they only make the good-looking bugger look even better. I once looked younger than him, but now I don't. He must have been going to the gym and working out. He probably hasn't contended with as much deception, as much death and as many sleepless nights as me.

"You can leave her sleeping there for a second while we open up."

"Leave her in the car?" I ask, astonished, because I see *him* everywhere. In the shadows. In the passing figure of an unknown man. I see *him* everywhere.

"She'll be fine. It's not London. There's no one dodgy round here."

I look around us in the darkness. I can see my own breath. I see the light from the pub next door. The blackness is so inky and luminous that it shimmers. I'm dizzy from speeding through a labyrinth of dark lanes. It was so familiar to me but I'm a stranger here, much more comfortable in London's constant half-light. Will I ever get used to this cold and dark?

"For a minute, then," I say, bravely, and against my better judgement. We go to the door of the house and Connor takes out the keys.

"It's stiff." He turns the key in the lock. "I meant to come earlier to put the range on."

"Is it the right key?" In my dreams this moment was warm and sunny with birds chirping and Rosie's hand in mine. A lovely old cottage with rambling vines and warm suppers.

"Of course it's the right key. I do this for a job. There," he says, generating a hefty click. "It's an ancient lock. As old as you are."

I push him. "You're older than me! I'm the baby."

"Where'd the time go, huh? Take me back to 1998." The door opens and the cold air hits me. It is colder inside than out! There is a stale smell of damp, dusty masonry, and of green flower stalks and cat's pee. I sneeze. The garbled noise of the adjacent pub grumbles through the wall. We step inside, slipping on a shallow pile of envelopes. Connor bends to pick them up.

"Your new home." He laughs, his face illuminated by a dim bare lightbulb hanging in the hallway. Boom! I am hit with panic. Drab is the word to describe the place. In fact, drab is an understatement. What on earth am I doing here? It would be fine if I kept telling myself over and over again, don't look a gift horse in the mouth.

At this country crossroad there is nothing but this cottage and the pub. This junction is called The Holy Cross. One fork leads up to the small parish church where my granny is buried, and the other winds on for a mile, ending up at the local tourist attraction, Lough Goren. The pub, Powers Bar, is a run-down one-room affair frequented by ghosts.

"Your pal is back next door," Connor says, squeezing past me in the hallway, pointing at the wall, and it panics me again.

"Who?" I snap.

"Herself. The sister in the pub, Katherine Power."

"Katherine." It seems strange to say her name. I'd thought about her while driving here, how could I not? This was her home, after all. The pub was where she grew up.

"She's back from New York. You couldn't have timed it better."

"I haven't spoken to her in years," I say, absent-mindedly tracing my fingers along the door frame. The floral hall wallpaper is peeling in the corners, and where the paper is supposed to meet, it gapes. There are framed photographs all over the wall. In the first photograph I see myself. I must have been nine years old. That's the age when this house was most real to me. That is the age, I think, when my memories took shape. School photographs of me sent from London show me every year, delicately ageing in a primitive time lapse. I go from long hair to short. The length of my collar reduces, as does the hue of my navy school uniform. In one image I remember the reddened cheeks from having just run in from the hockey pitch to have my picture taken.

Without any action from me, all of these photos are here because my godmother, Sheila, loved me. Because she loved my mother. I never did anything for it, nothing for her, didn't even visit her for years. For reasons that I don't fully understand, my godmother left me this house.

In the sitting room the older photographs near the front window are faded. In some of the pictures the photographer didn't put in the correct acid and they have lost their colour. I knew about photographs from work. The pictures have aged, but still they remain, suspended here, while the people in the pictures have gone – Sheila, my mother, and Donal. Their faces full of smiles and their heads full of dreams, all lost and gone to heaven, where I tell Rosie they reside, without believing it myself.

Rosie.

"I'll get Rosie," I say, panicked.

"I'll go out and wait with her," Connor says. "Have a look round. I'll sit in the driver's seat. And don't drink the tap water. The tank is off. I've put bottles of mineral water in the fridge."

"Thanks." Though I don't intend to leave Rosie for long; I'm just being polite. I walk into the back room, the kitchen. It is dimly lit and flickers between brown sepia, darkness and light. It buzzes with sad memories. I tap the bulb which fizzes and then brightens to a stark white light. Uncle Donal used to sit here peeling potatoes for dinner, stripping the skin away around a plume of hot white cigarette smoke. The carpet was threadbare in places making the floor feel uneven under foot, exposing patches of cold damp cement underneath. Donal had not kept the place in good condition. He'd let it go to rack and ruin, but I could fix it up. It was perfect for Rosie and me.

Rosie. I can't leave her any longer. I rush outside. Connor is leaning against the car smoking a cigarette.

"She's fine," he says.

"Of course, I'm just…" I didn't want to offend him, not after him being so kind. Not after everything he'd done. I didn't want to insinuate he's a pervert.

"You're just being a good mum. That's what good mums do."

I used to laugh at women who glorified motherhood, but then suddenly it was all that I wanted. There was a time I'd have argued with Connor about his sexist, backward views about women but I was terrified of losing it – of losing being a mum.

"You should sell it, you know. There's a new bungalow up for sale by Ma's that's much nicer."

"I think she'll wake up if I move her," I say, ignoring him. The last thing I needed was a house sale and a mortgage application. The whole point was that I could move straight in without any checks and paperwork.

"You can't sleep here, Doll, that's crazy." He snorts, blowing two plumes of smoke from his nostrils. "It's Halloween for feck's sake!"

"I don't give a shit about Halloween, Connor. We'll be fine." I pull out our sleeping bags from the seat beside Rosie. "It's the living you should be afraid of, not the dead."

"It's freezing and it smells. No. You can stay with Ma." He flicks his glowing cigarette end into the black unknown night.

"We're going to sleep in our own house tonight," I retort. Whatever shape it is in, it is mine. It is ours. No one else's. I undo Rosie's seat belt and kiss her on the forehead gently waking her. Her eyes flutter and then open wide, taking in the scene.

"You're not really going to live here, are you?" Connor asks, looking shocked, and seeing my conviction shakes his head. "Jesus, Doll. It's a tip!" He couldn't be clearer that he wants me to sell it. That makes me sit up, I mean what's it to him where I live? Why the hell would he care?

"Are we here?" Rosie asks, stretching. I help her out of the car. She's in a flannel onesie.

"Have you got BunBun?" I ask. BunBun is her toy comforter that she's had her entire life. He's the one thing we could not leave behind.

"Yes, Mummy," she says and I lead Rosie into our new home. She is mine. The house is mine. I lead her around the rooms. I don't care what Connor thinks. Nor what my aunt thinks. Rosie is heavy but when I hold her in my arms the feeling is the same as when I first held her as a baby. Honestly it is. It is less surprising but still true and pure. It grows more every day.

"What do you think?"

"It's kind of smaller than I thought it would be, but it's nice," she says.

My Rosie is very kind. Much kinder than me. Immediately after she was born, when I first held her in my arms, I knew that I didn't love my husband. I knew his purpose – he'd given me this beautiful baby, but I didn't love him. In an instant I knew.

I lay my child down safely to sleep on the threadbare rickety sofa. I wave Connor away at the door, and lock it behind him. I unzip the ends of the sleeping bag to make a blanket. I snuggle into her. I close my eyes and fall asleep.

4

BALLYMAURA

Auntie lifts up the heavy cast iron lid of her Rayburn with a metal lever, and throws her still smouldering cigarette butt into the fire. She flexes the muscle in her forearm, still sinewed and strong. She is seventy-five years old but with the strength of someone much younger. There is a luxurious whiff of peat burning in the stove. She fixes her lipstick in the oval mirror above it, a habitual action I used to copy when I was a child. I think of her whenever I put lipstick on. I take pride in the notion that people say I resemble her. I look more like her than I do my own mother. It hurts to look at her, because she is a tiny living piece of my dead mother.

She straightens her silver hair, still streaked with black, with the tips of her fingers and turns to me, braced for a fight. Bruce Springsteen plays in the background. It's always Ryan Tubridy on the radio.

Auntie exudes the weary tolerance that people who have lots of children have. (For the record it's seven.) She's not excited by me (or anyone else), and there's little that will shock her. She's amused by my focused dedication to Rosie. She thinks I'm spoiling her. "Let her be!" she says.

But Auntie is traditional, and she understands that life, like water, finds the path of least resistance and flows in one direction only. She believes that to stand any chance of happiness you have to go with the flow, and not fight against the current. For that reason, rather than morality alone, she detested deviation. There was a rod of steel running through her.

"It's nothing like the place you had in London." She has never been to my place in London, and in all likelihood a cousin had exaggerated its size and sophistication. Though it was a beautiful house, more than I ever imagined I would own. I miss my desk and book-lined shelves and my walnut worktops. I miss my own bed, and the sound of London air at night humming through an open window. I miss the scattered cushions in a mess of colours that I had collected from a life, a good life. I have left it all behind.

"It's fine for us." I was starting to get annoyed with the inference that I was a princess incapable of living in modest surroundings. My godmother had lived there her entire life. Was I so removed from my roots that I could no longer live the way that they had? Is this what growing up in England made you? Soft? There was a cousin on the other side of the family who had grown up in Connecticut, USA. When she visited they cleaned for weeks. They got out the best linen, and the best china. I hope they weren't doing this for me. I hope they were just behaving normally with me. But how could I tell? Was I on the inside, or was I on the outside?

"When you phoned, I thought you would come in summer. I didn't expect you to come straight away."

"It was half-term holiday. I just thought we'd go for it. Seize the day." But it was the message I received from *him* telling me that he was being released from prison that made us run the very next day. I wanted to take it to the police but my husband wouldn't let me.

"I suppose it could be a holiday cottage. But whatever you think it's going to be like, know that it's going to be a lot harder, especially in winter. You'll hear the noise from the pub next door and it will keep Rosie awake."

"London houses are tiny, even the poshest ones are all crammed together. I'm used to hearing my neighbours. I'd feel weird if I couldn't," I say, proudly.

"But the noise from a pub is completely different. Your godmother never got used to it, even after a lifetime."

"I'm surrounded by fields. You have so much space here. I love it. I love my new house, and I'll be able to help you out."

Auntie puckers her entire face at me.

The walls are adorned with Auntie's artwork. She paints the landscape and the lough in watercolours. It is her hobby, taken up after six children had left and only a young Connor remained. The paintings hang messily around an ancient shotgun slung up and mounted on the wall forever, since I could remember.

"You? Help *me* out? You haven't been here for ten years, Doll. Ten years and not so much as one visit!" Her eyes are wild and her voice pitched high and shrill.

My cheeks redden. I wasn't expecting her to be so candid. I didn't think that she would care. I want to apologise, but I don't know how to talk freely or honestly with her. I certainly never spoke to my mother like this. I was more used to a delicate nuanced dance. We would skirt around the crux of the matter, never daring to dismantle our defences. I squirm in my skin. I don't know why I hadn't visited her. I wish I had. Many reasons kept me busy; one big reason kept me away. Time had moved so fast then, but now it moved so slowly. The clock ticks. The Rayburn growls. A coarse silence grows between us.

"I was just so busy," I say, fumbling for the right words, and unable to find them. It might have been a decade for my aunt but for me it was like ten minutes had passed, my career had taken off, I had a baby, I got married, my mother died, and I bought the house. Everything that I had achieved in my life was crammed into those ten years, and my biggest shame. I hadn't been thinking about her, I just took it for granted that she, and this place, would always be here if I wanted it, frozen in time.

"I don't need help. Jesus. By the time I'm old enough to need help you'll be back in London."

"Actually, I've got something to tell you. I'm planning on staying indefinitely."

"Oh, you are, are you?"

"Like, forever," I say.

"Don't be ridiculous. I don't need help. I have seven children, and all of them bar Connor are away from here. Two are in America and four are in London. And tell me, Doll, why is that, do you think?"

"For work." I'm realising more and more that work is such a convenient blanket to hide underneath from all of your familial responsibilities. Although my cousins lived in the same city as me, and though I mentioned them frequently in tales of pregnancies and children and illnesses acquired, I never actually saw my cousins in the flesh. Connor is the first one I've seen in years.

"Because this is a washed-up country run by crooks and corrupt priests and dotcom bastards. The church still has hold of this country, and until we get new blood in we're not going to get anywhere." She runs the tap to fill the kettle. There's a sweet aroma of meat roasting in the oven. A red pot boiling with vegetables. I sense Rosie spying behind the door, I hear the scuff of her feet.

"What about your husband?" asks Auntie, and I rush over to open the door, flustered. I don't want Rosie listening to this, but there she is, statue-still, wanting the answer herself. What about my husband, her father? She wants my response. But I am not ready to give it. I shoot my aunt a look. *Not now and not in front of Rosie!* There's an intimacy in arguing with those closest to you which we haven't yet established.

No, my aunt would not be able to handle, nor understand, the truth. Rosie has told me that she thinks it's rather quiet here, and "like the olden times." My Rosie grew up on the Tube and got taken to the Natural History Museum weekly. She was a city girl, like me. It would take us both time to adjust.

"Now then, let's see what toys we have for you to play with," my aunt says, walking over to a large cupboard. She opens the doors wide. It is full of boxes of cars, Lego, board games, and musty old things that so many children had pawed since the 1970s.

"Have a little play, Rosie, and after lunch the cows will be up in the back field. I'll take you out there and we can see them, and wander down to the lough." I'm desperate for her to like it here. She does like the cows, and the animals. It was years since my aunt had her own cows and so she rents out her fields to the farmer, Peter Crowley. The cows come right up to the back of the house much to Rosie's delight. My aunt has acres of fields stretching right down to the banks of Lough Goren.

My aunt holds out an old long truck, modelled on the type of tanker that collects milk from the farms. Rosie holds it. It is almost rusting; I can still smell its metal from when I had played with it as a child. It doesn't seem that long ago. It isn't something that Rosie would usually play with but she'll do whatever my aunt says. Rosie looks at her suspiciously. I can tell that Rosie finds her hard. Perhaps she is hard but I just can't see it. All I can see is the soft part of my aunt, no matter how much she tells me off.

"There now," my aunt says. "The TV is on in the front room. I'll call you for your lunch soon. Have a little play."

Rosie's big brown eyes plead for me to come with her. If we were on our own she'd beg me to play with her, and I would play what she wanted. But in front of my aunt, she doesn't dare ask. Rosie slopes off back around the door and into the front room.

"It breaks my heart that your mother can't see her." Auntie

shakes her head and opens the cooker, bending down with the heavy pan of meat. I stand up to help.

"I can manage!" She spoons cooking juices over the gammon joint and kicks her small white dog, Mr Todd, away from under her feet. "There'll be nothing for Rosie here. Mark my words she'll be away back to London as soon as she's sixteen, and who can blame her?"

"That's a long way off," I say, but my aunt is so familiar with people leaving that she actively drives them away to soften the blow. I can't think that far ahead. For now I need to concentrate on surviving the next six months.

"You might get back together." She slams the meat back in the oven, ignoring me, and straightens up to stir the pot on the hob. "Did you have an affair?"

"Shall I lay the table?" I ask, flattered that she assumes I would be the philanderer, and annoyed that this is what everybody thinks. I rifle through the cutlery drawer that houses the same old-fashioned sterling silver forks that my aunt used to lever and repair bicycle inner tubes with.

"What about your job?" she asks. "Your mother was so proud of your career. It's hard, you know, being a mother with nothing else. You have to put a whole part of yourself on hold, the part that carries your own dreams, and you can never go back to it because it'll be too late when you do."

"I'm having a career break. A kind of adult gap year," I say, setting out the same thin silver knives and forks that I'd eaten from as a child.

"Peter Crowley's son had a gap year. He went to Australia. He's nineteen years old." She slams a drawer for dramatic effect.

But I was done with work, though not ready to disappoint my aunt by falling from that pedestal. I was through with my career whether I wanted to be or not. I'd been chewed up and spat out. The most shocking thing of all was realising how much importance people had put on my job. It was as if they didn't want to hear that I was no longer me, or that I had never really been me. If I didn't work then I was not myself, or I was somehow lower in people's estimations.

"What time's Connor coming?" I ask.

"He's not. He's got a council meeting. He's big in the council, running their errands. Has he asked you to sell up yet? You were always such a bright child, Doll. You always stood out. All that talent."

I squirm again. Had I wasted my life?

I realise that all the meat, the piles of potatoes and cabbage and gravy are all for Rosie and me. My aunt still cooked for eight people and pecked over her own portion like a bird, eating little while being scathing about people who didn't eat a lot.

"Once Rosie's settled in at school I might get a job around here." I could do something else. I could work in a pub or tutor children in English literature. I could do something that helped people in the community.

"School?" barks Auntie.

"I thought you might introduce me to the headmistress, or headmaster?"

"The priest, you mean. You need to speak to the priest about getting a child into the school."

"The priest then."

"The newspaper here is tiny, Doll. You'd have to go to Dublin or maybe the *Limerick Leader*. You could be a Mummy Blogger, but sure, there's no money in that. Around here it's who you know. If your uncle's in the police, then you can get in the police. If your father is a town councillor, then you'll get into the council. Crooks, the lot of them. Doing what they like, polluting the water, and ruining the land."

"I'm sure it's not like that now." I want it to be different. I want it to be perfect, like when I was a kid. But the truth is, whether it's the city or the country, whether it's in the past or in the future, the hustlers hustle and crooks rise to the surface.

Most people don't set out to commit crime, they just end up out of their depth, knee deep in trouble. When they start to drown, pray that they will float.

"It is so! Look what's going on down at Lough Goren. In front of our eyes!" I smirk slightly at my aunt's dramatic turn. This enrages her. "It's true!"

"Sorry, I didn't mean that," I say. "I'm listening."

"They sold the dairy and the new owners released pesticides or something into the lough to get around EU regulations. Chemicals. They've poisoned the water. You can't swim there, and if you do, you get all sorts. Been going on for five years, and not one person will do anything about it. The council is covering it up."

"Really? I'm sure that's not true."

"It is true. The toxins that are a byproduct of pasteurisation. There's a limit which they exceed, so they dump it. Over and over again. The dairy has quadrupled in size and there's been no investment and," she ran the tap on full, "they flush the waste into Lough Goren when they produce more than they can dump legally."

"Really?" I ask, smelling a story that I can't possibly do anything about.

"They're killing people. And they're killing animals."

"Who's they?" I ask, my interest piqued. I believe my aunt, although she was well known for being a conspiracy theorist long before conspiracy theorists were a thing. Raising seven children on your own tends to make you a little bit more cynical about the world. But it was the first time that my mind was interested in anything other than my own troubles, and shielding Rosie from those troubles. It's working, being here, away from London, just with my daughter. It is going to work out, it really is.

"Peter Crowley's dog ate something down at the end of the fields there and it died. Just a few days ago."

"Who bought the dairy, Auntie?"

"Call Rosie for dinner. The dairy is owned by Americans. A big corporation. The Golden Vale sold out. The main councillor here has shares in it. It's been covered up."

I went to the door and shouted for Rosie.

"Why would local people cover it up?" I ask as Rosie appears. My lovely, beautiful girl. She squeezes my hand as she passes me. I am so lucky to have her.

"Money of course! The dairy employs the whole town."

Rosie climbs up to the long table. I put a cushion underneath her bottom to raise her up and she looks disappointedly at the potatoes, meat and cabbage. My aunt pats an empty chair next to her and Mr Todd jumps up and sits at the table like a human. In the olden days the dogs slept outside and ate scraps.

"I know," I whisper," but it's good for you." I wink. I'd take her to Supermac's tomorrow and buy her a burger and chips. "What does Connor think of all this?"

"Sure, he thinks I'm a crazy old lady."

I wonder if my aunt considered herself a good mother. I don't think her generation graded themselves on maternal performance, like we do. We never went to ballet, or the Outdoors Project. Our parents never felt bad about not taking us anywhere.

"Eat this, it'll make you strong," I say, trying to encourage Rosie along. "And are you?"

"Am I what?" asks my aunt.

"A crazy old lady?" I suddenly regret it. She pauses to light another cigarette in front of a half-eaten plate of Sunday lunch, while the gravy still steams. She must be one of the last people left in the world who still smokes at the dinner table. I dare not point out that it is bad for her, and bad for my child. I quell my desire to join in and light up myself. Rosie's mouth is agog. She has never even been in the same room as someone smoking before.

"Connor would say that, wouldn't he?" She throws a salivating Mr Todd a large piece of thick pink meat. He catches it in his mouth and with a series of big seizure-like gollops moves it down into his gullet.

"Why?"

"Because Connor's making a hell of a lot of money out of it all."

5

THE LOUGH

My editor at the newspaper, Julian Harper, used to say: "We can never be silent," and he meant that we can't just watch things happen and not report on them. Silence is inaction, cowardice and weakness. Julian is a first-class bastard, and he completely screwed me, but he is right about this. I shouldn't be writing this story and yet here I am. It is who I am.

Even though I'm supposed to be in hiding I find myself at the lough. The scene of summer swimming, picnics and paddling. The binoculars feel loaded in my hands. They are my version of a pistol. Small and powerful. I've borrowed them from Connor. Luckily the camera has a long lens. I used to use binoculars all the time, and once to see the wedding of the actor Kate Winslet from my vantage point on a neighbouring hotel balcony. Celebrities were fair game then, complicit in their cat-and-mouse tussle with the media. I'm not so sure I still believe that.

Now, I only use binoculars for stargazing with Rosie. We are on a hill overlooking Lough Goren. We have hiked up a well-trodden path. Rosie took ages. It might be the longest distance she's ever walked. The path side is facing away from the wind so it isn't until we get to the top that we realise how gusty it is.

There is no ledge, no vertiginous drop for me to fear and for those few moments my anxiety leaves me because we have truly escaped. Up here so high no one would find us, no one would come after me asking questions. We are free.

In front of me the lough curves in a horse-shoe shape. It holds dark grey water and appears mysteriously deep. The banks are deserted. There's a row of old-fashioned boats, traditional Irish coracles made from a stretched skin over light wood like willow. Rosie says they look like giant Oreos. Rosie turns over some freshly plucked clover in her fingers, starting an imaginary game.

"When's Daddy coming?"

I keep the binoculars up to my eyes, hiding my face, giving me time to think. Do you ever wonder if you are doing the right thing for your child? We're supposed to know, but sometimes I don't. Children see things in black and white. You have to be clear. Even when nothing is clear in your own mind. This is how we fuck them up as parents. I'm doing it right now.

"Remember I told you? He's got a lot of work to do at the moment."

"Can't he do it from here? You said that you're going to work from here."

"Oh, goodness no, he has to be at his office in London."

"Why?"

"He has important documents that can only be kept in his office," I say, and that part is true.

"I forgot."

This is a holiday for Rosie. I don't know if she fully understands that we are going to live here. I have to do what's best for her, even if it might not always seem as if it is the right thing to do. Making decisions for someone else is hard.

"Next time we'll have to bring Mr Todd with us." Rosie is silent. "Your dad loves you very much."

In the distance a milk truck, like the toy Auntie had given Rosie, climbs the far hill and pulls into the dairy. I've never been up on this hill before, looking back towards Auntie's fields, her bungalow tucked into a cleaving fold in the land. I thought I knew the area so well but the dairy seems to disappear from the road and the lough itself into a kind of dip in the earth where it remains busily working, quite hidden away. It's like looking into the inner workings of a watch.

It's ingenious because you can't tell it's there. I don't know about the processes of the dairy but I can clearly see it's a huge operation. Another milk truck arrives, one after the other.

The outside is beige corrugated steel. It sits in the lush green landscape like a gruesome battle scar. Six metal silos stand equally spaced along its perimeter, each at least fifty feet tall. There are a number of office buildings by the fenced entrance and behind that a series of hangars with docking areas for the vehicles.

But there is something wrong. Something incongruous around an indent in the bank of Lough Goren; an area of what should be grass is brown and muddy. I pull my binoculars away and speed-scan the delicious verdant banks of the lough. Everywhere else is spectacularly luscious with thick green grass. It stretches down and into the waterline itself. It can't be. It simply couldn't be this obvious. There is a two by three metre area of scorched earth, odd amongst the wet grass, where a large dirty pipe protrudes into the lough. When I say scorched, I mean chemically burnt.

"He's not coming here, is he?" Rosie asks.

I lower my binoculars. I make a mental note of the location of the pipe.

"He's not coming, is he?" she asks again, but what should I say? Should I tell the truth now and break her heart and change her forever? Or should I keep quiet and let her start school, and let things become easier, let her adjust, and let time pass.

"Have you ever fallen out with a friend?" I ask. "Like when you had an argument with Martha?"

"I miss Martha. I miss my bedroom. I miss my house."

My heart aches for her. My guilt flares up like acid reflux. We're better here, I tell myself over and over. I am doing what I have to do. She might miss him, but she would be devastated to lose *me*. That might sound trite but it was the truth. I couldn't allow myself to be taken from her. She reads my mind. She touches the tear in my eye. Does she know what I am doing is for us? Will I make her sad forever? I can never say anything bad to her about her father, no matter what he has done. I won't do that to Rosie. I won't be that woman.

"Me and your dad have had an argument and we've fallen out, and we're not friends at the moment. We've had a disagreement. We both love you. It's got nothing to do with you. We both love you very much. And we're going to work it out so that we're friends again."

Rosie hums. She has lost interest, or doesn't want to know any more. Or perhaps she is satisfied with something as close to the truth as I can get. Her father thinks I'm crazy, that I'm deluded, and paranoid, that's what he tells me over and over again. He made me sign a contract to silence me forever.

"I've got a wobbly tooth," she says, "at the back."

"The fairies are much better in Ireland." Her eyes widen. "More magic. More money." She nods. I sit with my arm around her.

Back in the car, I drive it around near to the entrance of the dairy. We stalk across the fields. Rosie is moaning and complaining. It takes ages to orientate ourselves to locate the pipe. When we find it, it is two metres in diameter. Rosie easily fits inside. Me too. It has been painted green, which has peeled back to reveal a copper-coloured rusting surface. Small stalactites have started to form around its opening. Rosie holds my bag open while I stoop down to scrape water and mineral samples from the pipe.

In the distance over the fields I can see Auntie's bungalow, and in the other direction, if I could look through the hill, would be the pub and our house. It is shielded by trees, now barren and wiry. The camber of the land seems to draw the flow down towards our house.

My eye is drawn to a lone hooded figure running atop the crescent of the opposite hill. He is running where we have just come from. His blue windbreaker balloons and then collapses as he moves, his arms are pumping. His body pivots as he jumps an old rock wall, and in that pivot I shudder. There is something memorable about that movement, a thin reflection, a memory of *his* body in the way that he ran. I'm paranoid. I'm seeing things.

"Can we go to Supermac's now?" asks Rosie.

"Yes!" I reply, gripping her hand.

6

LIMERICK CITY

eep. Beep. Beep. The machine flashes an 'incorrect pin' message. The air is thick with the early morning smell of burning turf. The fields are sodden with rain, and the sky a thick rich grey. In the reflection of the cash machine I can see my hair has tiny droplets of water blistering like those on a spider's web.

I tap in my PIN number again and turn behind me to look back into the car. My aunt sits in the front seat wrapped up conservatively in a thick woollen scarf. She is in full make-up including red lipstick. Her shoulder is turned inward and I can see that she is giving sweets to Rosie who is sitting in the back leaning forward conspiratorially alongside an expectant Mr Todd. It's nine in the morning. They catch me watching so I raise my eyebrows to disapprove of the sweets.

I look back at the small dark screen of the cash machine. It is blinking. Wrong pin. Inside the shop the cashier sits inside a hot steamed-up booth chewing something (pastries or sandwiches, I can't quite see) and listening to the chaotic buzz of breakfast radio.

My PIN was the first four digits of my parents' phone

number. It always has been. I'd never had recourse to change it. I'd had the same bank account since my first week at university, when I'd signed up to get a free student railcard.

I enter the number again. The machine slowly issues a series of scary noises, and swallows my card whole.

"No! No, no!" I slam the keypad with the heel of my fist. "Shit!" I kick the machine.

I should have brought more cash. I'd already spent two grand on food, and new furnishings. Two grand! How? I do a mental tally trying to work out how I've spent two thousand pounds in less than two weeks.

At least I have the credit card. I have online banking. I can set up an Irish account and transfer the money across. I could transfer to Auntie or to Connor and they could give me the cash. I start to breathe again.

Auntie rolls down the window of the car.

"Are you all right?"

I don't answer, instead I storm into the shop. The chap is in his sixties and looks like a farmer. He has red, full cheeks that ripple as he chews.

"It's eaten my card. Perhaps you've got a key for it?"

He shrugs his shoulders. "If I had a key that could open cash machines, do you think I'd be sitting here?" He chortles into the sandwich; his entire face breaking into a huge guffaw.

"Hi, all fine," I say, starting the car, pretending to be happy.

"What was all that about?" Auntie asks.

"Hi! All fine!" Rosie laughs, mimicking me.

"Rosie, I hope you aren't eating sweets?" I rub my hand against the windscreen. I turn up the heating and aim the flow at it.

"I can't hear the radio! It's Bono!" Auntie says, as if Bono should never be muted.

"I had one small thing," Rosie says in a coy voice. She can't lie yet.

"Well, you have to brush your teeth when we get back. Have you got your seat belt on, Rosie?" I put the car into gear and accelerate hard, throwing Mr Todd back up against the back seat.

"Mummy Doll!" shouts Rosie.

"Sorry, doggie," I say.

"Bono has glaucoma," my Auntie says, turning up the radio and pulling down the sun visor to examine her own eyes in the mirror. She pulls her bottom eyelid exposing thin red veins, and looks to the right nervously.

"What's the matter with your eyes?"

"Don't mind my eyes, what's the matter with you?" she asks.

"The cash machine ate my fucking bank card," I reply and she tuts loudly, and slaps the sun visor shut.

"I knew something was wrong." My Auntie never once told me off for swearing. It was as if knowing how hard life was, she was surprised that people didn't swear more frequently. "How will you get your money?" she asks as I put my foot down and pull away.

"It's fine," I lie.

"If you'd have gone on the main road like I told you, you would have gone to a better cashpoint machine and this would never have happened." Her logic is unquestionable, complex, and true.

"I'll survive."

I don't drive on the main roads in this car. *He* has got access to things like the ANPR system. We drove all the way from London without going on a single motorway. It was almost impossible but we did it. I stay on the back roads, the minor roads, just in case.

Twenty minutes later we pull onto the South Limerick ring road and pass by The Crescent Shopping Centre.

"You're going the wrong way!" Auntie shouts when I quickly pull off the road as it becomes the M7 – the main motorway heading for Dublin. They've changed everything. Improved everything. Made it faster, slicker, and more advanced with European grants. Why does nothing stay the same?

"This is a better way," I say. "Quicker." I haven't a clue but I follow my nose and as luck would have it after a mile the laboratory appears on the right-hand side of the road. "See!"

"Well, who would have known we have one of the most advanced labs in Europe right here on our doorstep." Auntie's bosom swells with pride.

The laboratory is a bog-standard two-storey corporate building made of brick, with white window frames and a brown awning stretching over the entrance. It could be any office in any town. I park in a small bay marked 'visitor'. I instruct them to wait in the car but Mr Todd insists he needs a wee, so I give them the keys and Mr Todd, Auntie and Rosie begin walking around the corporate flowerbeds.

"Isn't it lovely," she says, not expecting an answer.

Inside the brown-carpeted entrance I'm welcomed into a side room by the receptionist. Through the window I can see the three of them outside. Rosie jumps off a low wall acting something out. She's chewing. Auntie is feeding them from a small white paper bag. For God's sake! The dog smells the treat, takes it in his mouth, drops it on the floor, smells it again and then eats it.

"Wait in here, please, Mr Docherty will come to you," the lady says, and I take a seat at the long boardroom table.

"Jack Docherty," he says, as he enters the room.

"Hello," I say, "and thank you."

"Just call me Jack, but for matters of professionalism I have a PhD in organic chemistry, so technically Dr Docherty, but we do not stand on such ceremonies here so please do just call me Jack."

It suddenly occurs to me, why did Connor leave my fridge full of drinking water? I don't believe his story about old pipes at all. It doesn't make sense. I think that Connor left the bottled water because he doesn't want Rosie or me drinking from the tap.

"Now firstly, before we begin, there is the small matter of payment."

"Of course."

"In my notes it says that this order was to be charged to the *Irish Times* account."

"Yes," I say.

"It's for a piece in the *Times*?"

"I can't really say."

"But you're a journalist?"

"I am."

"With the *Times*?"

"Freelance."

He leans back in his chair and I get the vague, ever-so-nuanced impression that he knows something more. It's hard to pinpoint, but he's asking me too many questions.

"Can I ask where this sample is from?"

There you go, he's asking too much. He's just supposed to deliver the results, but I expect a big dairy like ours is going to have many tentacles around here.

"I'm afraid you'll have to pay before we release these results. We don't normally do individual jobs like this so we don't have an account with the *Times*."

Oops. That was a really blagging ruse, and I would be happy to pay and reclaim it. I reach down into my bag for my purse and then remember I don't have a card.

"Oh God," I say, "the cashpoint just ate my card."

"Do you have any other way to pay?"

"God, this is embarrassing." I'm wondering if he might simply share his results just to get rid of me and to end this awful stifling conversation. "Can't you invoice the paper?"

"No, I've been told no."

"Or invoice me?" I don't really want him to do that, I don't want him to know too much about who I am or where I live.

"No, I've been told by finance that I need cash or credit card payment to release the results of this test."

"Fine," I say, "wait there, I'll just get my aunt, she'll pay."

I bluster out through the door.

"Mummy Doll!" Rosie's mouth is full of something.

"What are you eating now?" Jesus Christ! "Can you stop feeding her, please?" Auntie looks hurt. I don't want to upset her right now. Not when she's got to pay 395 euros. "Actually, I'd love a sweet myself. Anyone got any sweets?"

"Here," says Auntie, "have one of these." She beams as she shakes the bag at me. I shove a strawberry bonbon in my mouth. I can't believe Rosie's eating these. She's never had one in her life. I'm a single mother, reliant on others for childcare and everything has changed.

"Well, is it poison?" Auntie asks.

"He won't tell me until we pay."

"But you said the paper will pay?"

"And they will, but…"

"It's a big butt!" Rosie giggles.

"But we'll have to pay now and then be reimbursed by the paper?"

"Yes." It's a small white lie. They are interested in the story, but I need this evidence and not just the paranoid ramblings of an old lady.

"Pay it then so."

"I don't have a card."

"Oh, Jesus." She realises what I need.

"I will pay you back straight away when we return home. I swear. I know it's a lot of money but we don't have any choice."

"How much?"

"Three hundred and ninety-five."

"Jesus! I'm a pensioner!"

"I know. I'm sorry," I say.

She throws me Mr Todd's lead and adjusts her handbag around her neck. "Hold her hand! This is a car park!" she shouts and I grip Rosie's hand and Mr Todd's lead and we start marching back across the car park to the main building. "It's all well and good running around. This is the first and last time."

"I won't do it again, I promise."

Rosie's mouth is agog. She's enjoying watching me get a bollocking from my auntie, who stops in the middle of the car park and turns to face me.

"If you're going to run around playing Erin Brockovich, don't expect me to pay for it."

"I'm sorry," I say.

We're through the double entrance doors and being buzzed in by the receptionist. "No dogs," she says.

"He's very clean," I say, hoping that he doesn't shit on the carpet. Dr Jack is already making a fuss of my auntie. He pulls out a chair for her. Auntie reluctantly pays using the card machine.

"This is a robust water toxicology report. One of the most comprehensive tests in Europe. We've tested for over one thousand known water hazards. The police should be notified if this is from an open water source."

"They will be," I say.

"I have an obligation to report this but if you assure me this is being dealt with, I will trust you to take it further."

"I can assure you, doctor, that this will be taken to the highest authority in the land," Auntie says, and I know she's thinking of Ryan Tubridy when she says it.

"Well then." He places the report open on the table. "Overall, we found unusually high and illegal levels of mycotoxins."

"What are mycotoxins?" I ask.

"They are present in animal feed and they transfer into milk. We found aflatoxins, ochratoxin-A, fumonisins, trichothecenes, zearalenone and cyclopiazonic acid amongst other compounds."

"Could they kill a small animal, like a dog, if ingested?"

Rosie covers Mr Todd's ears and pulls an angry face.

"It's possible. But the important thing is that they exceed the EU legal limit, so it needs to be investigated."

"An illegal discharge?" I pick up the report.

"Well, I don't know where the sample is from, but possibly, yes. The Environmental Protection Agency should be called in. We would want to look at the milk as well if this is from this dairy, and I suspect it is. We also found high levels of pesticides, and those can easily be fatal to a dog, and you would not want those around children or humans at all, and would definitely not want to be swimming in them."

"Right," says Auntie. "Can it cause cancer?"

"There would have to be prolonged contact with the chemicals. Is it from Lough Goren?" he asks, and Auntie is about to say yes.

"We'll let you know," I interrupt.

"Some of the most concerning aspects can't wait, they need to be reported now."

"Like what?" I ask.

"The source of the mycotoxins needs to be identified urgently. You might have cows eating contaminated grass, right now, today, and passing that on into the milk supply, so the original source has to be located as soon as possible."

"I can assure you that we intend to make this public knowledge, and involve the authorities," I say.

"Whether mycotoxins are in the feed, or in the fields themselves, we need to know. Going forward we need to ensure that legal levels are not being exceeded at this site, wherever it is."

"That is exactly what we are doing."

"Well, if this is correct then it is illegal and a criminal offence, never mind the possible illegal discharge into Lough Goren or wherever you got this sample from. I'm concerned that the cows may be being fed sub-standard feed and that is also illegal. At the site that this comes from I suspect they are testing levels in milk and then any batches that are high are being flushed away. So that's a long list!"

"I knew it!" Auntie beams. "Give us a week or so and you'll read about this."

Auntie was right. I bow respectfully at her and she levitates in her chair. I can't drop this story now, I just can't.

Back at her bungalow I pick up Auntie's phone and move into the good front room. It's immaculate and hardly ever used. I telephone the news desk at the *Irish Times* and ask to speak to Kelly O'Hagan, and much to my surprise she answers the phone with minimal fuss or gatekeeping.

"Hi, Kelly, it's Dolores O'Rourke from…"

"Doll! God, how are you?" I can hear the smile in her voice.

"I'm good. I'm good. How's the kids?"

"Grand. They're ten now. Ten years of twins. Mental. Jesus Christ. How long is it since I've seen you?"

"Eight? Nine years, maybe?" I say, thinking back. I know exactly how long and on what story, and where we went for her leaving drinks before she moved back to Dublin for good.

"Oh, it's a different lifetime, what a craic we had. Do you remember my leaving do?"

"How could I forget it?"

"You were doing so great, Doll, you were everywhere! So many stories. You never missed a beat."

"I had a baby."

"I heard that. Lovely, how old?"

"She's eight. She's called Rosie. She's gorgeous."

"And you married David, the dishy lawyer with the NDAs."

I redden. "Yes. Yes, I did."

"I'd have never seen that coming."

"I was pregnant."

"Okay, gotcha! Anyway, it's much easier here I find, being a mum and working in this job. I'm nine to five at my desk commissioning stories and then I go home to the kids. I wouldn't have been able to keep up in London. They make it deliberately difficult for mothers. You can't be out every night once you've got kids."

"Well, we're here for the foreseeable future, Rosie and I. We're living down in Limerick."

"Ah, you never are!"

"Yes, we are. And my reason for calling, Kelly, is that I have a story for you."

"Of course you do, Doll. Tell me. Tell me all about it."

7

WEST LIMERICK NATIONAL SCHOOL

Slung amongst the idyllic low hills of West Limerick, Lough Goren has provided sustenance for local communities since neolithic times, for 12,000 years; that is, until now...

I look at the piece I've written on Auntie's laptop. I'm well into the first draft, I've written half but it's still missing something. The general gist of the piece was how even in rural Ireland greedy corporations had ruined the land. In fact, it felt worse here. I was used to it in London, absolutely nothing surprised me there. I had seen it all. I was hoping that we'd find an oasis here, a place trapped in time. But already I'd seen my fantasy of the 'good old days' replaced with brand-new roads, increased pollution and technology company headquarters. Maybe these things were always here.

Auntie thinks I'm a fool. She doesn't understand what I'm running from, and what I need from Ireland. Ireland is an emotion, a dream, a hazy memory from my childhood, with those I love still alive and with me.

I'll go back and edit the piece later. It isn't my usual style of late, and by that I mean for the last fifteen years I'd written more or less exclusively about people. So, in my mind this story was about the councillor and his corruption. I can't get online because I have no wifi and no mobile phone. I need to get the password of the pub next door's wifi, but that would entail a conversation with Katherine Power and I wasn't quite ready for that.

When I still had my own money I could splash out on products whenever I wanted, but now I was borrowing off Auntie I'd had to tighten my belt. There is no landline telephone either. They never had a phone here and my godmother went next door, to the quiet end of the bar, if she needed to make a call. It seems like a different life. I'm going to buy a pay-as-you-go phone from the shop just as soon as I ask Connor to lend me some money. I can't ask my Auntie for more cash. I tried to manipulate her into giving me money for a phone and she told me I can use her phone anytime I like and handed me a bag of food shopping from the Spar.

And because there's no landline, there's no internet. There's a downward spiral of administrative frustration. I can't get a phone line installed without an engineer inspecting the property and it costs 205 euros, paid upfront. I can't get an Irish bank account without a proof of address and they will not accept my godmother's will as proof that I live here. There's no branch of the bank here so I have to drive to Limerick City and they don't know Auntie there. Regardless, I couldn't open a new bank account without the correct documentation. I've decided to put Auntie's bank account details on the invoice to Kelly O'Hagan and that will pay her back for the money she has given me and she'll withdraw what's left in cash for me.

My credit card might possibly work, but I've suddenly become very wary about who might be able to look at my credit card statement and see where I'm making transactions. I will try and make do.

The steam from the boiling kettle melts the condensation on the window. Ryan Tubridy gasses on the radio. A truck pulls into the back yard that we share with the pub. It's a large area the size of a tennis court in rough cement and flanked by the dilapidated sheds that were once, a lifetime ago, a milking parlour. The beer delivery is a regular weekly occurrence that no longer merits comment from Rosie and me.

In the yard outside, a woman – not any woman, but the legendary Katherine Power – instructs the men who are delivering barrels of beer. I can hear her voice. She still has the soft Irish lilt that rasps like a rock star, but there is a new pronounced American twang.

I spy on Katherine Power while sipping my tea.

"I feel sad," Rosie says, eating her Weetabix.

"Why?" I ask, pulling away from the window and putting down my cup.

"I didn't want to tell you, but I miss my friends from my old school."

"I know." I put my arms around her. We cuddle to acknowledge her loss and then she moves on and turns back to eating her breakfast. Rosie likes Weetabix with fresh cold milk and plenty of honey. I try to get her to have hot milk but she won't stand for it and I'm such a useless mother that it is easier for me to serve it straight from the carton. She can easily eat three, which is impressive because I was brought up to believe only Royal Marines and giants could eat three Weetabix.

We use my godmother's crockery. Most of it is worn: patterns faded and rims chipped. Rosie's bowl is fine china, pale and cracked with a delicate yet faded blue feathered pattern. I had planned on buying everything new, but since I have no cash we are embracing these heirlooms and giving them a second life.

"What were you looking at out there?" she asks with her mouth full of cereal.

"Nothing," I say.

"You're sneaking around," she says, "spying on that lady."

"Am not!"

"Who is she?"

I flatten myself against the wall. I'm not ready to face Katherine Power yet. I need to smarten myself up and emotionally balance myself. I haven't slept properly in what feels like years. I have bags under my eyes. I have grey roots showing through. All my clothes are old, the material bobbling because I've been too preoccupied to shop, and now I have the time, I have no money to shop.

"She's no one I know," I say, "now give your teeth a brush, and don't get toothpaste on your uniform."

I can't believe that Katherine is here breathing the same air as me. I never thought, never even considered her in my plan when I ran. In the past I had looked for her online. I went through Facebook and Instagram and Google News but she never showed up anywhere. Someone like Katherine Power wouldn't need the empty recognition that social media affords us.

This isn't Rosie's first ever day at school. Her proper first day of school was at St Frederick's. I'd posted a picture on Facebook and all my friends had posted how cute they thought she was, making my heart swell.

There would be no pictures on the internet this time around. There would be no opportunity for strangers to view them, and comment, and make vicious threats against me and against her. It kills me because the one thing I wanted to do for her was keep her in the same school, give her that stability and community.

The school is a single storey red-brick building with a large playground. The rough floor is damp. A low fence surrounds it. It's so open compared with Rosie's school in London.

"Welcome, Rosie," says Father Aidan, drumming his fingers together as if he doesn't know what to do with his hands. "And welcome, Dolores," he says to me. His name is Father Aidan Lynch and when I met him to talk about Rosie joining the school he was a most unexpected finding. He is new, like me, filling the void of a long-standing local priest who had been in the parish for fifty years or even more. Father Aidan's accent is pure Dublin estate. He talks like a member of Boyzone or Westlife.

"Thank you."

Father Aidan has thick black hair expertly parted and combed but with an unruly tuft on his crown that he can't tame. There's a tiny sinew of rebellion running through the priest, that he fights against for control. His biggest fight is within himself, it radiates from him, it is fascinating.

"Are we all ready for school, Rosie?" He stoops to engage her. She'll be in charge of this school within days, running some kind of racket, and starring in the school play. "I've been expecting to see you for the last two Sundays."

I won't go to church. As much as Auntie tells me that I have to, I just can't bring myself to do it.

"I explained to your aunt that we'd be very happy to enrol Rosie for the remainder of the term and for the spring term but that we would like to see you at Mass regularly. It's as much for Rosie as for you. To feel part of the community."

Connor is outside the school gates smoking. His brown curls bounce and his smile lines wrinkle up ready for banter.

"We applied for a grant from the EU and look what we got." He lights another cigarette from the lit end of the previous one.

I turn to look to make sure the priest and the children can't see him, but he doesn't care.

"Oh, the playground," I say, looking at the impressive climbing frame in red and blue. "It's pretty cool. I was hoping you'd be here, actually, Connor."

"The council is good. Good people. They don't get enough credit."

"Connor, I want to ask you a favour, please, I lost my card and I'm having a few technical problems getting cash from my English account."

"Okay."

"I was wondering if you could loan me a bit of money just until I can get some transferred over?"

"Have you not got internet banking?"

"It's all locked down. I have to take my passport into the branch in Hampstead in person."

"Really?"

"I've been hacked or scammed or something."

"Have you cancelled the card?"

"I've done that."

"Well that's a pain in the arse. Sure, how much do you need?"

"I was thinking a grand?'

"A grand?"

"Five hundred quid then. I've no money, not even for food. I've a freelance job coming up and money in England but–"

"Say no more. I'll bring you the cash. I'll go to the bank later today."

"Thank you. Thank you, Connor."

"I have a favour in return."

"Anything."

"I want you to meet somebody. Keep an open mind, that's all I ask."

"Who?"

"Sean Gallagher, the councillor, wants to speak to you."

8

WIFI

Katherine Power looks the same; she has not aged in the past decade. Her hair is shorter, a trendy choppy crop, and her clothes are better. I can see the label, the cut of the jeans, the way they cling to her, and the drape of the slash-neck top looks expensive. I think she's more muscular, but then everyone I know is getting into fitness, except for me. She's got an athlete's physique. Something about her shines even brighter than before. Momentarily, I think I see a twinkle in her eye when she first realises that it's me. It gives her away but it quickly disappears again and she drops her eyes to the floor. She moves to the table in the window where one lone customer sits nursing his pint.

"Another one in there, Paddy?" Katherine asks, busying herself tidying his table. Her voice is a dark black treacle. I recognise Paddy as a local farmer with ruddy cheeks and a big awkward smile.

"Only the one at lunchtime, Katherine, you know that!" Paddy says, chuckling. "How are ya?" he asks, greeting me.

I haven't been inside this pub for more than a decade. My hands were trembling before I came inside, my stomach turning.

The times that we had here. I remember being bought glasses of Coke and packets of crisps as a child and then pints, lots of them, and dancing as a teenager. There used to be a pool table around the far side of the bar. It feels the same, only much smaller. The walls are the same orange colour. There are hurling sticks crossed above the bar and black-and-white framed pictures of local sporting clubs. I can see a young Connor in several of the photographs, and other cousins, and Pat Power. There's a picture of Katherine winning a cycling race. They loved cycling here before it became popular in England, they already had a real appreciation for it in the eighties and nineties. There's a large flat screen TV that wasn't here before. As soon as I notice it Katherine Power turns it off with the remote control.

"Can I help you, Doll?" she finally asks, asking me by name, more confident with a mahogany bar between the two of us. She does know it's me; she does know that I'm here. Paddy swills down the rest of his pint and gets up and leaves. I find myself alone in the now silent pub. I can feel the tension building.

"How are you, Katherine?"

"I'm fine, Doll, thank you. You moved in next door I hear."

"Yes, we're neighbours."

"Not for long. I'm just here to help Pat while he has his hip replaced."

"Oh." I hide my disappointment. "Is he all right?" Her brother, Pat, is a nice enough chap, but rough around the edges, and prone to bouts of depression and excessive drinking. He seems very young to be having a hip replaced.

"He's too young, right? He's only forty-eight. It's far too young but that's rugby for you. It's a three-month recovery. He couldn't run the pub, so here I am."

"Must be nice to be home." I'm still in my fantasy Ireland of perfection.

"I'll be glad to get back to New York."

"New York?" I repeat, naively. It's just that I love New York and Katherine and I, as teenagers, used to dream about going there together. We used to listen to U2 and all of the 'Irish in America' kind of music and she really did it, she went there and made it her home.

"So, how can I help you, Doll?" She is actually being quite unfriendly to me, but I must press ahead with my own agenda. I'm not here to rekindle our friendship, I'm here to survive. But I could do with a friend.

"Half a lager, please?" I don't want to get into day-drinking, but I figure that I should at least buy a drink before I ask to use the phone and have the wifi code. I haven't drunk a half a lager in years.

"Harp?"

"Yes please."

She bends to pick up a glass and then pulls the half pint that she pops onto a bar mat. I've got no money. It's very quiet. I have to stop myself from talking and filling the gaps. She was never this cold before. Around her neck and on her hands she wears shiny polished silver, or perhaps platinum, jewellery. There's a huge costume ring with a jade green stone on the middle finger of her right hand. She has no wedding ring. However, her wedding finger looks pinched, I think, as if she has once had.

"I've just realised that I've no cash on me." Katherine stops in her tracks, her face lights up and she laughs, I think, in disbelief and the sheer cheek of me. "Can I set up a tab?"

"You can pay by card. You know, this is Ireland, but we're the technological hub of Europe. Facebook has its headquarters here, and Amazon, and PayPal, and Mastercard, and Microsoft, and even Uber, so you know we take other forms of payment other than potatoes or cash." This is the Katherine that I remember.

"So," I say, straightening up, sipping the drink before she takes it from me. "I'm having an across the board, days on the phone to a call centre, frozen out of all my accounts type of situation."

"I see," she says.

"And as part of that situation there's no phone line next door. Do you think I could log in to your wifi until I get it sorted?"

Katherine reaches behind the till and picks up a small mounted sign with the wifi code written on it. I thank her and take the laptop out of my bag and fiddle around to find the correct place in settings to enter the code. It's difficult to concentrate. I feel her eyes on me. I want to look like I know what I'm doing.

"And one last thing?"

"What?"

"Can I use the phone?"

"Is it an Irish number?" she asks.

"Dublin."

"It's just there at the end of the bar. It's a regular phone, just pick it up and dial. Don't be calling England. I get an itemised bill."

I move to the end of the bar. I knew this telephone was here. I've already memorised Kelly O'Hagan's number.

"You don't even have a mobile phone?" Katherine asks. "An iPhone?"

"Not at the moment, no," I reply, dialling Kelly's number.

"Hello, Kelly speaking," Kelly says, answering the line above the familiar hum of the office. Will I ever cease to love the sounds of an office?

"Kelly, it's Doll."

"How are you, Doll?" she asks, but doesn't wait for me to answer. "I'm glad you called because I need to speak to you."

"This is my new number. Has it come up on the display?"

"Yep, it's a Limerick number?"

"Yes, you can call and ask for me here. I'm in a kind of co-working space," I look back over my shoulder at Katherine, who is chatting and pulling pints, "or leave a message with Katherine and she'll pass it on to me."

"Fine. Look, my editor loves the piece. Well done."

"Oh, that's great."

"But we need more. The toxicology report is damning but we just feel that there's more to it. Who's behind this? Exactly who's responsible for ordering illegal discharges? We'd rather wait for more evidence and run it as a major investigation, rather than just the tox report on its own as news. This is good news, Doll. More money. Possibly a big story."

"Okay, I get it."

"And one more thing. The dog."

"The dead dog?"

"The allegedly dead dog. Peter Crowley's dog really brings home the scale of the problem. It's a wonderful human story. Well, canine and human together, but the editor wants more on the dead dog. It won't run without the dog."

9

KIELTY

My aunt parts my hair and applies the ice-cold hair dye with a little blue plastic brush. It smells of spiced chlorine. It's strong but not unpalatable. I've dropped Rosie at school where she kicked up a fuss all journey about her hair going into her face. I tried to put clips in to hold the hair back, but it wasn't good enough for her. I offered her a hairband, but she said it wasn't the right colour for the school uniform and we argued. I told her she'd be late for school and get into trouble with the teachers.

Auntie used to be a hairdresser. She had a little salon before she started the never-ending career of being pregnant and having babies. I need to smarten up my act but it feels weird having my hair done by her. We're in very close proximity. She is in my zone. We're bonding. It's nice, I guess, if a little awkward. If she turns too quickly I get her soft squishy breast right in my face.

"The editor says we need more evidence."

"What more evidence could we possibly give? The water test shows everything. It was 395 euros for Jesus' sake!" She tugs my hair.

"I'm going to pay you that back just as soon as I get to the bank."

"What more evidence can we get? Can't you hack the councillor's phone?"

"No, Auntie!" I protest, pulling my head away. "No, I can't hack someone's phone. You can't do that. It's against the law!"

Auntie raises her eyebrows and makes a big O shape with her mouth. She thinks she has rattled me. "I thought you were all at it!" she says, firmly pushing my head back into position.

"Not me," I lie, as she applies more colour to my roots.

"Would you even know how to hack a phone, Doll? In fact, how did they do it?"

"It's much harder now, I think. You couldn't really, as an average person, do it now, with all the advances in security and face recognition and whatnot. It's much harder." Some people are still capable but I tried not to think about him.

"But what did they actually do?"

I think back to how I did it. "They used to do it on the older voicemail set-up. Anyone could call and tie up the line, and then they'd call up the same phone again and the caller would be automatically put through into their voicemail, and most people never bothered setting it up properly and kept the default pin of 0000. So they just put in 0000, or guessed the pin, and they heard all the messages and of course most of this was before texting, etc., so there would be lots of personal information being talked about."

"Is that why you've no mobile? In case you get hacked? How am I supposed to phone you if I need you? Who, in God's name, doesn't have a mobile phone in this day and age? And no phone line in the house either!"

"I'll get a phone." I've not a penny in cash to buy one. "When I send my invoice, I'm going to get them to pay it into your account so that you get it right away. It will really help me until I get an Irish bank account set up. Is that okay?"

"Legal, is it?"

"Yes, of course. I can have my fee paid anywhere. It's only for ease, really, until I get things properly set up."

"Hiding money or something, are you? For the divorce?"

"What?"

"I wasn't born yesterday, Doll," she says. "You probably don't want David pestering you all the time, but he *is* Rosie's dad."

"I seem to be temporarily frozen out of my bank accounts, that's all."

"Leave it on for thirty minutes. I'm going to speak to Peter Crowley about the dog. He swears it was ill from the water." Auntie pulls her hands out of her plastic gloves with a thwack, and picks up the telephone.

"I suppose I could interview him."

"No. It's evidence you need," Auntie says, taking off her plastic gloves and lighting a cigarette. "Sure, the dog has only just died. We'll dig it up. Take its blood. The vet is Peter's cousin. Don't come if you're too squeamish." She's as impressive as she is scary, all at the same time.

The dog formerly known as Kielty is grotesquely shrivelled. He's been wrapped in a shroud, a large head scarf belonging to the reclusive Mrs Crowley, which has kept off the bugs, the worms and the maggots. His long face looks drawn, spongy and mummified but he also looks like he could just be asleep. Peter Crowley had wanted Kielty's eyes covered in the ground. He did not know why. It just reminded him of burying his mother and he wanted Kielty to be wrapped in something familiar and comforting to him. The dog was only five years old.

Peter Crowley's farm runs down to the banks of the lough where he grazes two hundred head of cattle. Friesians to be precise. Milking cows who need to be tended to each morning from 5am through to 7am, and who then grazed for most of the day on his land and the two adjacent fields rented from my aunt.

Peter always had a dog. Just one, mind. His companion throughout the day but sleeping, like a proper farm dog, outside. There were no dog spa days for Kielty like the dogs in Crouch End, but he was happy and healthy with the run of an entire farm until he suddenly got sick.

Peter had been building, or rather renewing, a section of wall down near the outpipe entering the lough. He had spent three days down there with a team of two other farm labourers and of course with Kielty, who had run around and enjoyed himself for the entire time.

Attending one morning in early October when it was still unseasonably warm and bright, Peter had finished milking just after seven and made his way down to the loughside and there, from the remnants in the outflow pipe and by the scum floating on top of the water, he knew that something had been dispatched overnight from the outlet.

He despairs. He wishes now he had picked up that little dog and brought him home and locked him straight in the house, or in the barn, and kept him there. But of course he didn't, because this wasn't the first time and it was well known that liquids were occasionally dispatched from that outlet pipe, but he had never had any problems before.

The cows had never become sick, but as he now realises, a fully grown Holstein Friesian weighs around 700 kg in comparison to tiny little Kielty who weighed only seven kilograms. I start to cry. I can't help it. But Peter Crowley is bent over, too, weeping about this dog. He makes fists of his hands, angry tears rolling down his red cheeks until my aunt pulls him to his feet.

"Let Suzie do what she needs to do," says Auntie, and we stand there in the lashing rain averting our eyes while the vet finds the little blood left in Kielty and extracts it into a vial. The vet, Suzie

Crowley, is a heavily pregnant woman of my age. She wears a padded jacket that will not fasten anymore and so the bump protrudes like the domed tip of an iceberg. No one mentions the bump and I certainly do not.

I know better than to ask any woman if she is pregnant, even when it is blindingly obvious. Her size makes it awkward for her to lean over, but her fingers are fast and adept and she is expert at manipulating the poor dog's paw, the needle and the vial.

"I think we'll get just enough to test, hopefully."

"I should have done this before. I should have reported it," Peter says. "He was just a pup. He never hurt a soul."

I don't expect this from a farmer well used to euthanising cattle, used to blood and shit and toil. I do not expect his regret, his raw emotion and his anger.

"You're doing it now, Peter, and that's all that matters," Auntie says with pure tenderness.

As I drive away I'm replaying it over and over again in my mind. It's not just some abstract thing called corporate negligence, it's causing suffering for these people and their animals, and they're too frightened to speak up because the dairy employs hundreds of local people and without it none of the employees will have jobs. We are not saying that we want it gone. We want it cleaned up and safe. That's not too much to ask. I am a good person. I can do this. I want to help people. I think about the vet, about to give birth herself and yet here she is in her community working, doing what needs to be done. She's an inspiration. I want to do something good too.

"That vet's amazing," I say. I couldn't even touch a dead dog, never mind respectfully turn it over and take its blood.

"Suzie? She's the best in the county," Auntie says.

"And doing all of that while she's pregnant too."

"We don't talk about the pregnancy."

"Oh, why's that? Is everything okay?"

"She's not married."

"Come on. That's a bit outdated."

"Oh, we don't care, but they'd booked and paid for a big wedding before they realised, and now she's worried the priest won't marry them if she's pregnant."

"But he'll know. He'll clearly see; the bump is huge."

"Well, no one mentions it and the priest doesn't mention it, so that's that."

"So she's going to get married in church, heavily pregnant, and just pretend it isn't happening?"

"That's about it, yeah," Auntie says, and I love the simplicity of the elephant in the room. No one ever mentions it and so we can pretend that it's not happening. This seems normal to my aunt and it would have seemed normal to my mother too. I have done this with my mother. There have been so many awkward moments where the truth stared us both in the face and we just carried on talking about the dinner. In those moments the sickly spike of adrenaline, worrying about whether Mother might mention something embarrassing, something I had done, or wanted to do. She once read a letter sent by Katherine from the pub. I was twenty years old. She read my letter. She found out my secrets and we never discussed it, never argued, never acknowledged what we both knew. I can't be silent anymore. It drives me crazy and I never want Rosie to have to do this. I want honesty and for her to have confidence in me not to judge her.

It's just as I'm thinking about the future (which I try not to do) and making a vow to firstly always be open and honest with Rosie, and secondly to get a dog and call him Kielty, after this poor little dead dog, that I see the runner again. I see a man running, again. An intense burst of adrenaline sends me giddy.

He's wearing tight blue running trousers, and has a hood that's pulled up over his face so I can't see any of his features. But it's more than that, a man running in the pouring rain, in the middle of nowhere in west Limerick is odd in itself. It's more that the stride, the gait of this man, his silhouette, the way he pulls up his knees so unusually high and seems to effortlessly move at speed. He looks familiar. I know this stride. I know that wherever he is, and whatever he is doing, he runs 10k each and every day. He has one day off each week to eat and drink whatever he likes but every other day, no matter what he's doing, he runs 10k.

It is *definitely* the same runner I have seen around here before. I stop the car. Auntie stares at me, confused. I can't live like this. I might as well be dead as live in perpetual fear. I stop the car, get out and turn around to face him but he's gone. I look around frantically but there's no one there at all.

10

FOR SALE

Connor knocks at my front door. His knock is, I sense, unusual for him and formal in its speed and strength. He has the councillor with him and it's as if we both know that it is strange. I had agreed to this meeting only to secure a loan from Connor, but there's a nervous knot of excitement in my gut. Call it intuition. Call it the experience of years of people asking, 'Can I have a quick word with you?' I'm ready for whatever the councillor might want, and I hope that he has underestimated me.

I open the door. Connor looks shifty. He's not smoking, which is odd, quite frankly. He quickly shifts into a big beaming smile.

"Doll, this is Sean Gallagher."

I hold out my hand. "Please come in, Sean. The kettle is on."

They waddle into my front room. I've been looking into the local business scene, and so I know exactly who Sean Gallagher is. I can't believe my good fortune that I am speaking directly to the head of the local council so easily, that he has sought me out. Of course I've noted that he is also a minority shareholder of the dairy. And what of my Connor? He is seemingly a benign and friendly local estate agent, with the unexpected seasoning of being some kind of fixer for Sean Gallagher.

"Your mother was a fine woman, Doll. A proud woman," says Sean. He has a speech impediment so that he pronounces 'was' like 'wash'.

"Thank you," I say, momentarily disarmed. Sean is a round man and his hair is slicked back with Brylcreem. He wears his trousers high at the waist, and has sharp piggy eyes.

"I'll help you with the tea, Doll," says Connor, and in the back room he gives me an envelope with 500 euros in 50 euro notes. I'm so relieved to have cash in my hands I become euphoric. I will take Rosie to Supermac's as a treat. Maybe take Auntie to Adare Manor for a meal at the weekend. I thank him and hide the money in the bread bin.

"Connor, who is the runner around here? A man in a blue tracksuit?"

"A man?" asks Connor.

"Yes, I've seen him many times."

"I don't know. I don't know anyone who runs," he says.

"On the hills by the lough, and on the main road?"

"No one's crazy enough to run on the main road. Cycle, yes. I could name plenty of cyclists but I don't know a runner."

But there is someone running because I have seen them with my own eyes. To me, it looks like Andrew Marlow.

Back in the parlour Sean is perched on a chair, perpetually leaning forward as if he might fall. It gives him a precarious edge. It's disconcerting. It makes me feel ill at ease.

He sips his tea and places it on the side table.

"I know what you women are like, and it must feel just lovely to be back here, in what was your godmother's house. Connor tells me your mother taught your godmother to walk in this very room."

"Apparently so." My eyes and wits sharpen. He is cutting straight to the point, little preamble, no foreplay. He talks about my mother, and my godmother, but why?

"What is this about?" I ask.

"It's only natural that you would want to reconnect with your Irish roots. I saw all the photographs on the walls there of you growing up as I came in. It must feel very cosy to be back here, especially since your good mother's passing. A fine woman."

"Thank you," I say. Auntie would be freaking out listening to this!

Connor coughs. He's prompting Sean to move along to the point.

"Your cousin Donal, or was he your uncle?" asks Sean.

"He's our second cousin, but we called him Uncle Donal because of the age difference," says Connor.

"Poor Uncle Donal, taken from us so quickly after the death of your godmother. Only a few months separated their deaths. It was a shame you couldn't attend either of their funerals."

I blush with shame. He is making a point and continues. "It was a lovely funeral for your godmother, and so soon afterwards, for Donal. You see, Donal had a dream. Some called him a simple fellow but he had hopes and dreams like anyone else."

"I'm sure he did." I hadn't seen Donal for many years and even then I had hardly spent any time with him. He was an oddball. I wouldn't have wanted him around Rosie. As a young girl I knew to keep my distance.

"He wanted to move into town, into some new purpose-built flats, where he could have assistance and friendly company as he got older."

"Really?" I ask. "I thought this was his home and he enjoyed the nearness and company of the pub next door?"

Sean looks up at Connor and indicates for him to bring over a folder. Sean pulls the side table between us, handing Connor his empty cup to take to the kitchen, an act which he performs dutifully. Sean opens the papers in front of me. Title deeds. A sales ledger. Documents addressed to Donal.

"What am I looking at?" I ask. Although I need Sean to say it clearly for the record.

"Donal wished to sell this house. In fact, a sale was agreed. A generous price. Papers were about to be exchanged but then he died before the sale was completed. As he had no will, the probate reverted to his mother's will and specifically the clause that if the sole beneficiary, Donal, died before he could inherit the estate, it went to you."

"Sean, are you the buyer?"

Now he is seething. "I bet it was a great day when the lawyer turned up at your door."

I had inadvertently scuppered his plans. But what plans?

"It was a phone call actually, and it was bittersweet to be honest. I'd rather they were all still alive, my mother included, but here we are. Are you the buyer?"

"The buyer is the dairy and I am acting as a consultant," he says, scrawling a number onto a piece of paper in his spidery handwriting and turning it to me.

It's a huge price. Double what I would have imagined. 280,000 euros for a run-down, ramshackle two-bedroom cottage.

"It's a very generous offer. I have authority to extend this offer to you," Sean says.

"To me?"

"For a limited time."

"What's your plan? What do you want it for? It's not worth half what you've offered."

"Doll, it's an amazing offer, you could buy something else. Somewhere much better, for Rosie," Connor interrupts.

"What are you going to do with it?" I ask again.

"This is confidential, but the dairy has plans to create a water treatment works."

Bingo, I thought, I've hit the jackpot here!

"Flatten it?"

"Redevelop."

"What about the pub? You'd need to flatten that too."

"They want to sell. They were about to sell when Donal died. Katherine Power came back from America to do the paperwork. But we need both properties together. This is a limited time offer and we need the pub and this cottage together."

"But why here? The dairy already owns so much land."

"Potable water. You're on a spring. The original dairy and the original pub was situated here because of fresh drinking water. We need access to it."

"Why? Is there some problem with the water?"

"Waste water. It's to process waste water. The dairy has grown."

"And what happens to waste water at the moment?"

"Don't trouble yourself with that. Just know that you'll be making a tidy sum while contributing to jobs and welfare in the local area. It's a win-win. You can buy a nice house or take your inheritance back to London with you when you go."

"This is my home," I say, and he laughs.

"It's not really, is it? And you're holding up the Powers from getting on with their lives."

"Don't give me that emotional blackmail! I'm very happy here."

"Just don't drink the water," says Connor. "These are the two nearest properties to the dairy. You are also in the run-off, downhill. This is a more than fair offer and you should take it."

I stand up and look out the front windows, across the road, towards the lough, which is hidden by thick hedgerows.

"What exactly is in the water?"

Silence.

"As I say, we wish to build a water treatment works on this site that will benefit the community," says Sean.

"Benefit who? More like cover up illegal tipping and disposal."

"We are the biggest employer in the area."

"What would you say to people whose livestock have been hurt?"

"Poppycock! No one's been hurt!" Sean shouts.

"Then why the urgency? It sounds to me like you've dumped into the spring, or into the ground water itself?"

"Rubbish," he says.

"Where then?"

"You're very nosey for someone I'm trying to do a solid favour for."

"You are dumping toxic waste in the lough." I feel my confidence, my righteousness, surfacing, I feel sure of myself.

"Don't look a gift horse in the mouth, Doll."

"The only question is, why? But I guess the answer is money."

"How dare you! Connor, what is this? She's meant to be your cousin. She comes in, swanning around as if she owns the place."

"I do own the place. I'm just asking why you are polluting the land and lough?"

"What do you know, you're English. We're creating jobs for people here."

"Can I draw your attention to this water analysis from Lough Goren that shows significant levels of mycotoxins. In particular aflatoxin B1." I hold up a typed summary of the report findings.

"What have you done?" Sean asks, furious.

I take out another typed water report. "Let's park the mycotoxin contamination, and can I ask you about pesticides?"

"That's enough!"

"So, in your mind it's acceptable because you are making a profit and creating jobs. And that's fine, killing pets in the process, just so I'm clear?"

"Don't be a naive young lady. It's like taking a pish – sometimes a little bit lands on your shoes."

He means piss and he's just compared killing pets with taking a piss. I know instantly that this guy is finished. As long as my tape recorder has picked that up clearly, he is compromised. I want to hurry to get him out now. Get this over and done with, finished. I have what I need. I want to make sure that at least one of my recordings has worked. It's like taking a pish! Is he for real? What an arsehole. But I'm going in for the kill.

"Are you not concerned that people might be ill because of your actions?"

"That's enough."

11

A PLAN IS HATCHED AT
BALLYMAURA

Bruce Springsteen's 'Born to Run' calls us to action. The range gives off an affectionate heat. Mr Todd drinks milk from a large bowl, his little tongue keeping beat. Auntie wipes her hands on her apron and puts on her glasses. She turns down her radio so she can listen to a recording of Sean Gallagher's testimony. Auntie fondles the Olympus Dictaphone, admiring its sleek lines though it is already ancient technology. I press play and we listen, our heads bent together as if in prayer.

"Like taking a pish!" Auntie says, disgusted. "Ugly, disgusting, fat bastard." Her face is a picture. She dissolves into a coughing fit, she's that worked up.

"He can't even say 'piss', never mind piss in the right place. It's an awful metaphor."

"The bastard. To think he's going around shaking hands with everybody, and he thinks poisoning us is like taking a piss!" She shakes her head and throws her hands up in the air.

"I think this will do for the paper. The story is pretty incendiary now that we've got Peter Crowley's dog, the report, and this utter contempt for local people from Sean Gallagher."

"But first, Doll, think of yourself. Are you sure you don't just want to take the money and sell the house?"

"Absolutely not!"

"Good." She nods her head proudly. "Good. We've come so far." She's trying to cover up her back-peddling. I sense some last-minute nerves.

"But are you sure you want to go ahead, because Connor is deep into this?" I ask. "It will affect him, there's no doubt about that."

"He's only the estate agent. There'll be other deals. He has no association with the dairy other than acquiring property for them. I can't see how he'll be implicated."

"Sean Gallagher will be furious with him."

"He shouldn't be working with Sean Gallagher. Better to nip it in the bud now before he ends up in serious trouble. He'll recover," Auntie says, and touches her neck coyly. "Just so you know, I shot a rabbit and Rosie helped me skin it."

"What?"

"It's natural and I've been doing it my whole life." Rosie won't even pick up a worm, never mind skin a cute little rabbit. "I wanted to tell you before she told you and you got all fuddy-duddy about it.

"Wild rabbits are different from pets. If you have a pet rabbit in England then you might have a lop-eared or a Flemish Giant. Those are very different from wild rabbits. How lovely to be hunted, free and in the wild and taken in your prime. No getting old, no suffering, no deterioration, no cancer." She gives a big hawking cough, and puffs on her cigarette. "We saw the rabbit jump and buck before we shot it. It was completely free."

"You didn't let her touch the gun, did you?" I can't even be angry with her.

"No, not yet, but we'll come back to that in the spring if you're still here," she says.

It's midnight when I finish my article back at home. I can't remember the last time I stayed up so late on a story. I used to do it all the time before I had Rosie. I would stay in the office all hours; I'd even sleep there sometimes. You could sleep on the sofa in the editor's office. I'd done it so many times, waking fuzzy-mouthed and dehydrated from drinking wine while finishing the story.

I'd be woken by the sound of the cleaner's hoover, or sometimes an eager junior coming in early to get ahead of himself or to quickly do the task he'd failed to do the day before. The office was a vast open-plan space with row upon row of desks grouped into pods.

David had been on a different floor. I didn't really know him until we covered a big story together. It was about the illegitimate child of a Tory MP and David accompanied me to the interview and to serve legal papers. It was in Little Venice. I'd had a set of coups, big front-page stories that drew attention from my bosses.

Whenever he showed up on our floor people jokingly called him, behind his back, NDD. It meant Non-Disclosure David, a play on the non-disclosure agreements that he liberally bandied around, silencing those who needed silencing according to the newspaper's wishes and best interests. Sometimes it would kill a story, meaning if someone gave us information and we didn't use it, they couldn't offer it anywhere else, and the newspaper could leverage that against a bigger exclusive.

For instance, if you had someone come forward to say they had slept with a celebrity, you get them under an NDA. Then the newspaper would go to the celebrity and threaten to publish unless they gave an even bigger story, like an exclusive coming-out.

At that time the corporate bods at the newspaper were on a cost-saving exercise, so we took the Tube to our meeting as it was at the opposite side of London. David flirted with me all the way. He let his leg rub against mine as we juddered to and fro on the Bakerloo line to Warwick Avenue.

He was wearing a sharp navy suit. I was in jeans and a cheap pink woollen winter coat. I tried to be businesslike. He was surprisingly excitable.

"I don't get out of the office much," he said, staring at me intently. I figured he did this with all the women in our department.

We had a five-hour session with the mistress. It was full-on. The child was now five years old and starting school. She was a former aide, a political advisor from a posh private girls school. She wasn't what I expected at all. David couldn't understand why she wanted to go public. He cautioned her but she loved her former boss and was heartbroken when he finally put an end to the relationship.

"A woman scorned..." David said after the interview. "Come for a drink with me? Just one. I won't take no for an answer."

He persuaded me to join him in the Prince Alfred, a beautiful Victorian pub near Warwick Avenue Tube. I went for one drink, but I drank a lot in those days.

"I have to start writing this up," I said, trying to get away.

"I'll just say you were with me. That I had concerns about the legal implications of this story that I needed to talk through with you in some detail." He was in with the bigwigs. He was the shining, glittering boy, the man of the moment. His good looks were lost on me but after a bottle of wine he started looking rather more attractive. He curled his finger around a lock of my hair. He went to the bar and bought another bottle of wine. We laughed. We talked about the mistress. I interrogated him about his love life. He liked cricket, football and tennis. He had a season ticket at Chelsea, he played in a cricket team throughout the summer and went to the gym. He was so wholesome and boring. He had no edge at all.

When I told him that my mother was in hospital recovering

from a stroke, he held my hand. He shook his head in sadness when I told him I had no dad as he was already dead from an aggressive colon cancer. So there was just me and my mum, clinging on. More wine. More laughing. Him suddenly looking more attractive. Then suddenly we were kissing in the pub. Hands fumbling. Proper deep snogging. My hands holding on to the leather of his belt, pulling him to me. The barman called, 'Closing time! Come on, you two!' Then we were in a taxi on the way back to my empty flat in Crouch End. We were still kissing as I fished for the keys in my handbag.

He wanted to do it on the stairs, but I had a hard-wearing, scratchy carpet. We had sex on the sofa, and then later in my bed. The next morning, sober, we had sex again. I insisted that we used precautions that time. For me, it wasn't about finding a man, it was about being close to another human. Men seemed to want to spend time with me. I think they can smell vulnerability. They recognise when a woman is damaged. David certainly could.

I refused to travel to the office with him but he insisted on treating us to a taxi. By 8am we were in an editorial meeting with the team. He was in the same navy suit but underneath wore a pair of my knickers. Sometime during that eight hours we managed to make Rosie.

Rosie sleeps soundly upstairs. My face is cold to the touch though there's still a log smouldering in the fire. I could put on another log or I could go upstairs and get into Rosie's bed and snuggle up with her. I feel like I want to toast the article, to celebrate, to mark the occasion, because even if the subs edit it, I know it's a good story.

I read the article through twice, editing and making changes, and once I'm happy with it I email it to Kelly O'Hagan. The pub's wifi works great. When it pings to let me know it's been sent a wave of adrenaline surges through me. It is a *Times* investigation written by an anonymous 'staff reporter', so no one around here will ever know definitively that it was me. As long as Auntie and Peter Crowley don't go bragging about it, which they probably will. I don't care about that. It's more that I want to remain here quietly.

But the state of my email and bank accounts tell me that Andrew Marlow probably already knows where I am. I know this is how he works. He is destabilising me, making life difficult for me. It's exactly the way he operates.

I head upstairs and look out of Rosie's bedroom window into the darkness. There's light in the yard. In one of the outbuildings I can see Katherine cycling on an exercise bike in the shed. There are no walls to enclose these sheds. They were once milking barns but long since used only as storage for the pub.

Katherine has strung little fairy lights around one of the stalls. In the darkest black of an early winter's night in rural Ireland the little shed glows like the stable in the nativity. Stars as bright as plutonium line the sky.

She's standing up on the bike going at full pelt. She's got music on. I can hardly hear it, it's Depeche Mode. They were always her favourite.

I go back downstairs, put on my coat and go outside across the yard. She doesn't hear me because she's in her own world, pedalling to the beat of the music. How can she do it at this time of night? I'm nervous but compelled to speak to her at this precise moment. She can't run away, she's glued to the machine. She'll have to talk to me.

"What is this?" I gesture to the bike and music set-up. The music is low and she carries on pedalling but I know that she can't walk away. She's completely out of breath. She sits and takes her hands off the handle bars and puts them behind her head. She's wearing a grey sweatshirt and a hat. There's a heater in one corner and, although it defies logic, it is warm and toasty despite it being freezing.

"Want a go?" she asks, and I'm relieved to see her smile. Well, I say smile, but it's more of a coy, cheeky grin. She tends to smile more out of her eyes than her lips, and it's sometimes difficult to work out what she's thinking unless you really know her.

"Not at midnight!" I say. "I should be asleep!"

"But you're not."

"You haven't changed," I say, as she picks up a plastic water bottle and drinks from it. There's a buzz of electricity evident in the crisp, cold night air.

"What are you doing here? After all this time?" she asks, still pedalling.

"Do you always cycle in the middle of the night?" I ask.

"I've just closed up, plus it's safer than riding on the road in daylight. Do you always watch people out the window in the middle of the night?"

"Can you not stop?" I ask.

"I won't be able to walk tomorrow if I don't cool down!"

"Not quite as young as we were," I say, though to me we'll always be young, and the time we spent together twenty years ago seems like yesterday. I think of it all the time. I tried finding her online, but after all these years here we are. I look up to Rosie's bedroom. "I'd better go back inside. I'll let you get back to it. Goodnight."

"Goodnight," she says.

"You came home to sell the pub, didn't you? My showing up has ruined your plans?"

"Not mine. I'll go back to New York. Pat's maybe, for now. He wants to sell up and leave."

"I'm sorry," I say, turning to walk back into the house.

I'm sorry for what I didn't know I'd done and I'm sorry for what I am about to do.

12

THE POWERS

Buoyed by my exchange with Katherine and high from submitting the article, Auntie and I go to the pub, primarily for lunch but also to await a call from Kelly O'Hagan with changes or feedback. Auntie reads the finished article directly from my laptop. She presses her face close to the screen with her spectacles balancing on the end of her nose. She's most concerned about why we're not featuring in the piece with descriptions of ourselves. She doesn't care about notoriety anymore and wants to shove it to the priests, though for all our digging we could not uncover any wrongdoing by the Catholic Church.

The Powers are a long-established family in West Limerick but only two remain, Patrick (Pat) and his sister, Katherine, eight years apart in age. Their mother died when they were tiny. They were raised in the back rooms of the pub by their father, a kindly bruiser of a man who keeled over from alcoholism years ago, leaving them to inherit the pub when they were teenagers.

As if the community needed any encouragement to drink more beer, they saw it as charity to be in the pub to ensure Pat and Katherine had income and security. Pat stayed and everything remained the same for more than two decades. No wife, and no children. Katherine escaped to America. She got the glorious green card in the USA raffle and just like that, she was gone.

I glance across at Katherine but she never looks at me. I've secreted Auntie and myself conspiratorially in a corner. I want to look busy. Katherine must know about my career, about everything that I achieved. But she doesn't need to know that it's all finished. That I'm washed-up. Maybe I can reinvent myself here? I've spent hours watching her in the outhouse cycling on the static spin bike, the whirr of her legs at speed creating electricity, a few feral cats sleepily unperturbed by her display of strength.

Pat is a big man. He has made it downstairs, which has taken massive effort. He played rugby and has knackered his hip joints. His cheeks and nose have a ruddy complexion derived from country air and pints sluiced through his constitution with whiskey. He was fun once, but life has dragged him down. He doesn't bother to make small talk with me but I don't take it personally. They've installed one of those high-backed chairs that people have in elderly care homes.

Rosie and I have bought Pat a bottle of Lucozade, a copy of GQ magazine and a large bar of milk chocolate. I present it to him, excusing Rosie's absence as she's at school. There is a coyness in his delight that warms my heart. He's a man unused to treats and kindness.

"Thank you," he says, his eyes glassy, his voice catching. "And thank Rosie, will you?"

The pub is warm. It's glowing happily in orange and green. A fire roars. A bodhrán on the wall and an old-fashioned 1980s Pac-Man machine.

Katherine is an inch taller than me, and slim. She has blue eyes the colour of the streak of blue found on a jay bird's wing. Her skin is porcelain white. She's one of those Irish people that does not tan, only burns. She was always jealous that I could go so brown. Her hair is a couple of shades lighter than black.

What was her life like in America? Where has she been all this time? What has she been doing? To go there is to be free, to be a person with no limits, with no family to live up to, and nothing to prove to anyone except yourself. You could be free there. Free to be on your own, to be anything you imagined you could be. She always used to fantasise about going to New York when we were young. Who would I be if I had gone to New York with her?

"Katherine is a fantastic cyclist," Auntie tells me so that the whole pub can hear. "She could have cycled for Ireland." I don't like it when Auntie speaks like this because I understand her and I know that what she's really saying is that Katherine wasted her talent. But what could she do with no support to push her?

"Who's the guy that runs outside here and all the way up to the lough?"

"A runner? I don't know. No runners around here that I can think of," says Katherine. My aunt shakes her head.

"Well, it's not feckin' me!" says Pat from his hospital chair. "I'd be happy if I could run my own bath." Right at that moment Pat drops his glass and it smashes all over the floor. The telephone rings. I know it's for me.

Katherine answers the phone. "Power's Bar," she says. Her eyes land on me. She holds the receiver away from her face. "It's Kelly for you."

"Oh, okay." I move sheepishly, acting surprised when I've been waiting for hours for this call.

"Are you free to take the call, or shall I take a message?" Katherine looks at Pat and Paddy and they are laughing. "Shall we put it on her imaginary tab?"

"Why do you need New York, Katherine, when you can be Doll's secretary right here?" says Pat.

"And your nurse!" says Katherine.

"Hello," I say, taking the phone from Katherine's hand. I turn away from the crowd so they can't hear what Kelly is saying.

"Good news," she says. "My editor loves the piece. It's going in tomorrow's paper."

I take a very deep breath. My heart races. I have a pang of nerves. Have I done the right thing?

13

FRONT-PAGE SPLASH

I dream deeply. In my dream there's a man's feet descending a staircase in a house in Kent. I know the fragrant scent, the US army desert-style boots brutally assaulting the ancient red carpet. In the dream I panic at the computer screen. I've got seconds, no, milliseconds to complete my task, my heart is anxiously bursting out of my chest. There's a bang and I wake with a start.

Rosie is at the bedroom window, holding the curtain back.

"Mummy Doll? Why is Connor throwing stones at the window?" she asks, softly. I sit up abruptly. There's another hollow bang on the window followed by an angry rattling of the letter box.

"Come away, Rosie."

"But it's Connor, shouldn't we let him in?"

"Not right now," I whisper, opening the curtains. Outside, Connor's car is roughly parked, its wheels pointed at unnatural angles as if parked in a rush. Connor has his own key so there's not much we could do if he's insistent on getting in.

"He looks angry," Rosie says, as I open the window and lean

out. There's an oppressive heavy morning mist and it's making the sunrise unseasonably mild.

"What the fuck have you done?" shouts Connor. He's wearing unsightly grey jogging bottoms and battered old trainers. "You've really fucked me over, Doll!"

"Rosie's here!"

Katherine pulls up on her bicycle in a luminous yellow reflective racing top and cycling shorts.

"Are you all right, Connor? You're very agitated," she says.

"Your name is all over it! Ma's already told me that you'd arranged not to be mentioned, but your name is all over it, Doll, so you've fucked yourself as well. Everyone knows that it's you."

I turn to Rosie. "Go and brush your teeth, please." Rosie looks worried and I make a light-hearted face to show her that I'm not at all worried and that Connor is crazy.

"You don't know who you're messing with," he shouts.

"I'll come down," I say, checking on Rosie in the bathroom before descending the stairs.

I open the door. Connor slams the newspaper into my chest.

"I lent you five hundred quid, and this is how you repay me." I can see that on the passenger seat of his car there is a pile of newspapers. He must have read the piece online, or been telephoned by Sean Gallagher and then raced to the shops to buy up all the copies.

"Did you buy every copy in the Spar?" I ask, and he slams the car door shut with a loud bang. "Connor, I'm sorry, but this isn't about you. It's about corporate negligence."

Sometimes the most devastating news comes as a front-page story. Sometimes it arrives unassumingly as a simple, short text message and no one knows about it but you. That's how I learned that Andrew Marlow was coming out of prison, and with more knowledge about me than he went in with, ready to find me and make me pay my dues in the currency of his choosing. And that's why I ran away to Ireland.

"Shall we all go inside?" asks Katherine. "Talk about it there?"

Connor thuds into the hallway. Rosie comes down the stairs half dressed in her school uniform.

"Rosie, I washed your school jumper, here it is," I say, taking it off the hanger. Katherine takes it from me.

"Come, Rosie, do you want some Rice Krispies? You can show me where you keep them," says Katherine. She goes through the front room, the very place where I had recorded Sean Gallagher, and into the kitchen.

"Sean Gallagher's going to kill me!" says Connor.

"Sean Gallagher compared poisoning local animals and agriculture to pissing on his own shoes." I hold up the newspaper. "He's the one that deserves to be finished."

The front-page lead story is about export problems and border controls in Northern Ireland because of Brexit. But there it is, my story splashed further down on the front page, and I realise as I open the paper that the lead page three news story is my piece. It's been subbed and the headline edited which now reads:

Toxic Lough
Police alerted to illegal waste operation at Limerick beauty spot

By Times staff reporter and Dolores O'Rourke in Limerick

Not only does it say Dolores O'Rourke but it also gives my location. I specifically asked her not to credit me. I've been so stupid. But I need the money. I need the kudos, for me, too, the proof that I am still myself, and that I can do it! If Andrew Marlow is hacking my bank and email account he will already know where I am. We'll have to run further away. Maybe New York. Would that be far enough? Kelly O'Hagan should have made sure my name was nowhere near this. I need to phone her.

"Did you write the *Times* piece?" Katherine holds up her

phone, she's reading it in the kitchen while Rosie eats cereal. "It's all over the internet."

"Yes." I wince at my cousin.

Connor sparks up a cigarette. He uses an empty mug as an ashtray, sharpening the red burning tip on its rim.

"You can't smoke in here," I say, and he drops it into the remnants of my tea from the night before. "Did you know about the contamination?"

"Of course I didn't!"

"You're not mentioned anywhere in the article, Connor," Katherine says, pouring more cereal into Rosie's bowl. "Why are you so angry?"

"Because it looks like I am in cahoots with *her*." He flicks his eyes at me in disgust, wiping his mouth on the sleeve of his coat. He is unshaven and there are dark bags under his eyes.

"You're not mentioned either, Doll," Katherine says.

"Really? I am in the print version, look, here."

"Not online, it just says that it's written by a staff reporter."

"Can I look at your phone?" She passes it to me and I scan the piece and sure enough it just says Staff Reporter which is excellent because anyone reading this online won't know it's me. If, for instance, someone had alerts set up for my name it would be unlikely to trigger a search, or if someone was looking at this from England. I google my name and it doesn't come up.

"Are you going to be all right, Connor?" Katherine asks.

He lifts his watery eyes to her and nods. It's a thousand-yard stare, he's looking right through us, wondering what Sean Gallagher is going to do to him.

"I'm sorry, Connor," I say and hang my head low in deference, but in truth I don't really know if I am sorry. There are lots of reasons why I shouldn't have written the piece. Maybe I shouldn't have done it because I'm supposed to be keeping a low profile, but their wrongdoing is so blatant and easy to uncover that I couldn't not do something.

Connor leaves. I hear his car alarm ping, the door opens, and his engine starts.

I throw on some clothes and give Rosie's hair a quick brush. We're running late for school but I have to speak to Kelly. I ask Katherine if I can use the pub phone to ring the newspaper. As we enter the bar the telephone rings. It's a woman asking if she has reached the pub and so I pass the phone to Katherine and watch her, listening. She tells the woman that she should try Airbnb.

"That's someone wanting to book a room." Katherine looks astonished. No one has stayed in the pub as a bed and breakfast for years. There's no website, no advertising, and no real desire to increase sales and maximise profits.

I call Kelly at the newspaper. She's not at work yet and not answering her mobile. I leave a message.

"You've done a really good thing," says Katherine. "Rosie, you should be really proud of your mummy. She always wanted to make a difference."

I burn with embarrassment but simultaneously shine with the delight of being seen by her as who I really am, who I want to be and not the flawed person that I have become. I was so fresh and new and excited about the world when I hung around with Katherine. I had forgotten. Something about her makes me feel like that again now.

14

FATHER AIDAN

Father Aidan is running at me before I have a chance to escape the school grounds unnoticed.

"Dolores," he shouts. He's young and fast, he plays football with the lads on Wednesday nights. He gets in front of me, between me and the car, and I have no choice but to stop. "I'm shaken to my very core about the revelations printed in today's *Irish Times*!"

"Shocking, isn't it," I agree.

"Am I to believe what I've been told, that it is you, Dolores, that has uncovered this wrongdoing?"

I nod.

"The Bishop has telephoned. He will be at Mass on Sunday morning. He wants to see me deliver my sermon to the community; what should I say? It's expected that I support the parishioners."

"I did not uncover any wrongdoing on the part of the Catholic Church, Father, if that's what you're worried about," I say tentatively.

"I mean to reassure the parish. The police have not yet

85

investigated. What shall I say to people, and with the Bishop there watching me?"

"Reassure them that their health will be okay, and that the Environmental Protection Agency will ensure no further pollutants are ever issued. That they should not be worried. Perhaps speak to the police and make sure they look into everything."

"Would you consider taking a look at my sermon?"

"I have to make an urgent call, Father, but if you let me use your mobile then yes, I might have a few minutes to spare."

Kelly O'Hagan is genuinely apologetic.

"They fucked up, Doll. Your name shouldn't have been on there. Add another half day onto your invoice to make up for it. It's not so bad, is it? It's an important piece."

I turn the phone away so that the priest can't hear the swearing.

"This story is going to run. See if you can capture the responses of local people. We'll get you a few more days out of this and I will personally ensure that it's credited to a staff reporter. Send your invoice and I'll see that it's paid."

"The parish priest perhaps?" I suggest, looking across the playground at the young and nervous Father Aidan, completely out of his depth and comfort zone. Any moment I'm expecting him to rip off his dog collar and disappear across the Irish Sea to Manchester to marry a woman and start a new life.

I follow the priest back into the school, giving Rosie a sly wave and a wink while she watches, agog. What is *she* doing here? I'm sure she's thinking. In London I was a cool mum, but here I'm just different, a loose cannon, unlike the other families, and a liability. We cross the playground to the rectory. It's a pebbledashed building with large windows and faded curtains. In the past, several priests would have lived here but now there is only one and a passing stream of visiting priests from Africa and the Philippines.

Inside, a cleaner is on her knees dusting a coffee table by the window. She's a frenemy of Auntie's. Large-breasted Mrs Egan lives in the village and always seems to be wearing a house coat as if to imply she's always busy cleaning, cleaning, cleaning. Auntie can't stand the women who clean the church and look after the priest, washing a priest's pants. She insinuates there is something sexually deviant about them, and that they fantasise about sex with the priests.

"Dolores," Mrs Egan says, acknowledging me. "How's your aunt?"

"She's very well, thank you." She's probably regaling customers in the aisles of SuperValu with the extent of her involvement in the controversial exposé.

"A terrible business at the lough," she says, balancing herself up onto her feet.

"Let me help you, Mrs Egan," says Father Aidan, but she bats him away with her duster.

"How can we help you?" she asks, and the priest flusters a reply.

"Doll is going to help me with the finer points of something that I'm writing, thank you, Mrs Egan."

"Very well," she says, as if she owns the place. Over her shoulder and through the front netted window I see the RTE television vehicle drive by topped with a large satellite dish.

"Fuck," I say in the house of God.

15

THE HAIRDRESSER

If Auntie is to be on the television, and even though she isn't mentioned in the article by name, she's going to try her best to get on TV anyway, then she needs to look her best. She's having a rinse put through her hair; it's a honey colour and I'm not too sure about it but the hairdresser tells her that it looks great. There's a tremendous buzz around the town that's making me feel quite sick.

We drive up to the lough and there's the solitary television truck in position. It gleams against the verdant landscape like a beacon of truth. The reporter munches a sandwich and chats with the producer. People are beginning to gather, to mass here to examine the carnage but there's not much to see. There are photographers with long lenses.

As the sky begins to darken with the evening drawing in, there is a smattering of rain. We head back to the car. The car park at the lough empties out and it appears that is that. That was its fifteen minutes of fame and now it can return to its normal, quiet existence.

We draw up to the pub but struggle to find a parking place. I turn and go back up the lane to park at the back of our house, in the shared yard.

There's the beat of music coming from the pub. I want to use the wifi to submit notes to Kelly O'Hagan. We go in through the back entrance. Katherine is in the kitchen buttering slice after slice of white bread.

"I'm on my own," she says. "Pat tried to help but it's too much for him. I've sent him back upstairs." A customer calls her, and she takes off her apron, hurriedly placing it on the countertop and emerging back behind the bar.

"What can I get for you fellas?" she asks, and they order pints and vodka and tonics.

The bar is as busy as I have ever seen it. It's reminiscent of my youth, when the pub was in its heyday, and I used to come on holiday here every summer, and of that particular summer when I was eighteen and I hung around here a lot.

There are about fourteen people in total. I nervously scan faces for Andrew Marlow. A couple are regulars that I recognise – a farmer smiles at me. But the others are new faces that I've not seen before. More people come in through the front door.

"You'll have to help yourself," Katherine says to me. "Get your own drinks and put it on your tab."

As I turn around Auntie appears from the kitchen. She has taken off her coat and is wearing Katherine's apron, giving a big cough to clear her throat.

"Show me where everything is, Katherine," she says. "Doll can help you with the drinks. Rosie, come and watch the TV with me in the kitchen and I'll make you a snack. I wasn't expecting to be cooking with my new hair, but there you go."

"Really?" asks Katherine, but she doesn't wait for an answer. "I'll show you the pan for the chips."

Auntie pushes me behind the bar and I feel like an alien, completely out of my comfort zone when I tentatively enquire:

"What would you like to drink?" It's a man in his sixties and his wife. She goes and sits at a table by the window on the red velvet banquette. She gazes around. He's wearing a beige V-neck jumper and beige chinos that bulge and crease with the contents of his pockets.

"Busy tonight," he says, and I can tell he's fishing. He's clearly from a nearby town and has come to have a gawp at the goings on. I get it now. I understand why it's so busy. "Pint of Harp, please, and a vodka and tonic."

"Pint of Harp," I say, picking up a glass and examining the taps. There's nothing written on the back of them so I can't see what they are. I start guessing. Paddy, the farmer, points to the last one and winks.

I tilt the glass to the side and flick the tap on. I have done this before, many years ago. Katherine returns and sees me pulling the pint and laughs.

"He wants a pint of Harp and a vodka and tonic," I tell her. "There you go," I say to the man, putting his pint down in front of him, but he's already speaking to Paddy.

"Terrible business at the lough," he says, and I turn away. I don't want to be incriminated. It's fascinating to listen and observe. I wink at Paddy and he nods. He won't say that I wrote the piece. Katherine holds the glass while I put in a slice of lemon. The door opens again and more people arrive.

I want to speak to Katherine more but there's no time. I want to ask what she's been doing all these years. I want to ask her what New York is like to live in. I want to hear her laugh. But the new arrivals want their drinks and Paddy wants another pint. Rosie appears carrying a plate of sandwiches.

"Good girl," I say. She's loving working in the pub.

A few hours later Auntie reappears saying that enough is enough, and that I should run her home in the car. The crowd has dispersed and only some regulars remain.

16

THE NEWSPAPER EDITOR

Rosie sleeps in my bed, her legs lain heavily over me. It's lovely. Her lips pout when she's asleep. I've always thought, since she first passed the newborn stage, that she looks like a cat. She has perfectly shaped almond eyes with thick feathery eyelashes, a ruby red mouth and a button nose. Her hair is a shade or two lighter than mine.

She manoeuvres herself onto my side. She is boiling hot, kicking off the covers and breathing in sweet little whispers. I blow on her face to wake her and she wriggles her nose. Her eyes open and she smiles when she sees me. I look at my watch. It's after 10am. We've slept in.

"Are you hungry? Shall I make pancakes?" Pancakes are her favourite food. I make them thin. She smears them with a thick splodge of chocolate spread and rolls them up and eats them with her fingers.

There's a knock at the back door. It's Katherine. She smells freshly scrubbed from the shower, there's a light minty fragrance from her skin and hair. I usher her in.

"Am I late?" I ask, confused.

"Hi, Rosie," she says, looking from me to my daughter and back again. "Doll, there's a bloke in the pub looking for you."

The blood drains out of my body.

"Did you tell him I'm here?" I spit back. I lock the back door.

"He seems to know you're here. He said he asked after you in town and someone in the Spar said to try the pub."

Rosie stuffs more pancakes in her mouth, oblivious, her free hand sketching on a pad. I don't know what to do.

"Is he a bald guy? Tall? Blue tracksuit?" I'm thinking of Andrew Marlow.

"No, not bald. He's English. Posh. Kind of preppy looking." Strange. I relax only slightly.

"Did you ask for a name?"

"I'm not your secretary. It's a pub. He just walked in. Anyone can."

"Will you wait here with Rosie for a minute?" I ask. I take a hammer from the hallway. Men will always win in a fist fight with a woman but I've always thought a hammer is difficult to miss with, and in connection with a man's body, it will do some damage. I slip through the parlour and out the front door. My mouth is dry. The stone path outside is washed wet with rain. In the window of the pub I catch my reflection and see an older version of myself. Please God don't let it be *him*.

I take a deep breath. I've dealt with pressure my entire life. I've faced so much that I can even face him. I open the door of the pub. It's Julian Harper, my old editor from the newspaper. I sigh with relief. It's not long until the lunch regulars arrive but for now the bar is completely empty. He's sitting at a table in the window reading yesterday's *Irish Times*.

Women always thought him dashing. I never did. His floppy hair is in the first flushes of grey, affording him additional gravitas. He's wearing a blue shirt with a stiff collar and a navy jacket. In the breast pocket of the jacket a light blue and red handkerchief adds a splash of colour. I imagine him taking his time dressing himself while considering the dastardly deeds he's going to do that day.

He doesn't stand up. He folds the newspaper over and places it on the table, then pulls his face into a wide, smug smile. He hasn't been my boss for years yet I still prostrate myself to him.

"Doll." His smug smile widens.

"I did *not* expect to see *you* here, Julian."

"Aren't you going to offer me a drink?"

"Technically the pub's not open," I say. He taps his thumb on the table with a slow and intense beat. "But I'm sure I can stand you a drink."

"I'll have a pint of the black stuff then, please," he says. "It always tastes so much better in Ireland, it's the water, so they say, but you'd know all about water, I'm sure." I go behind the bar and select a pint glass. I don't look at him but I can feel his eyes on me. "You're looking rather trim, Doll. Very nice. Always thought you'd make an excellent barmaid."

"Thanks," I say, deadpan, pulling the pint.

"Good with people, aren't you? You've got a natural gift for gaining people's trust and getting them to tell you their secrets. I expect people here are telling you all sorts of confidential stuff. Are they?"

In the back room the dishwasher starts a noisy spin cycle. The tension runs as thick as the creamy head on the stout.

"It's on the house." I put the pint down carefully.

"It's probably your round anyway. All those drinks I used to sign-off on your expenses back in the day." He picks up the pint and sips from it. His sip is measured and ladylike, a small film of stout coats his upper lip. He licks it off. "Do you know how hard it was to find you?"

"No."

"Not very fucking hard at all," he shouts, holding up the

newspaper and waving it at me. I feel like he could hit me around the head with it. He's done that before. "Why, Doll?"

"I was trying to do something good."

"You want me to believe that you've got any sort of moral code?"

"I have and I've changed," I say. "I've always had ethics."

"You were always able to give any decision a good rationale, I'll give you that."

But I had changed. When I knew Julian Harper I was not myself, and now I am. I've gone back to being me, the real me, not the person that I briefly was when Julian knew me. I'm the person that Katherine remembers. The person that is Rosie's mum. The person I was when I was young.

"What do you want?" I ask, reluctantly sitting down.

"Uncle Andy," Julian says, the name that I never want to hear again.

Andrew Marlow is not my uncle, and he's not Julian Harper's uncle, yet the world knows him as Uncle Andy. How could eight years pass so quickly?

"What about him?" I ask.

"He's a free man. I assume that you know, and that's why you suddenly took off to Ireland."

"Yes, I know he's out," I say. I have counted every moment of Andrew Marlow's incarceration, watching time running out, becoming increasingly frightened the closer he got to the end of his sentence. The older Rosie got each year, the nearer we got to his release. "When I knew for sure he was coming out, I had to move quickly to protect myself and to protect my daughter."

"You're not taping this, are you?" asks Julian.

"Of course not." He'd arrived too spontaneously for me to pick up my recorder.

"There are things that only we know. You, me and Harry," he says.

"What do you want?"

"I've left the paper. I won't have the same resources at my disposal, but on the other hand I can speak freely now. You've got to think about yourself, Doll. Think what's best for you and not the paper." He takes another drink of his pint.

"For the last eight years, Julian, you've told me that we're in this together and that the paper will deal with this and that I'm to shut up."

"Well, I had to say that."

"I've done everything that you told me to do."

"Well now it's time to think for yourself. Come clean to the police at home."

"Are you for real?" I ask.

"Be protected. I've been keeping tabs on Andrew Marlow since he came out." I bristle with nerves. "He's under licence for twelve months following his release. He has to check in weekly with his probation officer. He can't travel. You follow?"

"Yes."

"I'm guessing a bright girl like you came to Ireland knowing that he wouldn't be allowed to leave the UK?"

"I'm almost forty, Julian. I'm no longer a girl."

"I'm telling you I have it on good authority that he had notified his probation officer that he intended to travel to Ireland." I shiver. "Without reason to object, it's been approved. He's coming. In fact he could already be here."

"When?" I ask, standing.

"He could be here now. He might never come, I don't know."

"If I went further away, he wouldn't be able to follow me, would he? He would breach his probation and be sent back to prison."

"You should have run to Spain or somewhere more difficult for him to find you. Nevertheless, you need to come back, Doll, come back to London where you can be looked after."

"I'm not going back to London."

"David will look after you. I'll make sure that you're safe. We will involve the police, properly."

"I'm not going back. I don't want to be looked after. I want to be free. I've been trapped by all of this bullshit for too long. I can't do it anymore," I say.

"Come back to London, go to the police and come clean about what you did. The truth will come out and he will be vindicated. I think that's the only chance for him to leave you alone."

"No fucking way," I say. "I could end up in prison."

"I saw your article and knew you had to be local because the lough is just there, right?"

"Yes."

"They removed your byline. It was credited to you at first and then it got changed to Staff Reporter. I got on a flight to Shannon from Heathrow, the last flight last night. It took less than an hour. I rented a car and checked in at a nice hotel in Limerick City. There's a Savoy Hotel in Limerick now, who'd have thought it? I asked after you in a shop in Bruff, and I was directed straight here. I sat outside for thirty minutes and then approached the very attractive woman who runs this pub, and she more or less confirmed that you lived next door. And there's a knackered old Saab with English number plates parked out the back, which I assume was what you came here in."

"Well done you."

"It's not rocket science. I've been calling you. I've been driving past your house in London but once that article came out it took me all of twelve hours. It was credited to you originally, your name quickly removed thereafter, but I had a Google alert. How long do you think it will take Andrew Marlow? Someone with his skills and desire for revenge?"

He's right, I know this. I know that I'm a sitting duck. I know that I should never have written this piece but I wanted the money and I wanted the approval of my aunt. I wanted to feel powerful, and useful.

"Is David in on this with you?" I finally ask, suspecting a ruse to get me back.

"No," he says. "I care about you, Doll. I know there's an awful lot of water under the bridge but I do care about you. It's not for me that I'm worried. He's not interested in me. I'll be fine and I don't know if you've seen the news but I'm off to America. I've scored a chat show in Los Angeles. I'm in the big leagues now. They love us opinionated Brits out there."

"A TV show in Los Angeles." A person could be free on the West Coast of America.

"People with criminal records are prohibited from travel to the States by the way. I'm here to say goodbye, and tell you to look after yourself. I split up with Debs, and I've got a new girlfriend. She's twenty-six. She's like a young Debs, except she likes having sex. She's coming with me to America. It's a dream come true."

"You're very lucky to have a fresh start in life."

"This is my last warning, Doll. Please be careful. He's out there and he wants his revenge. For your daughter's sake, come back, admit what you've done, take your punishment and put it behind you." I shake my head. "Get lawyered up. I know you've got a few quid put by. Get a good lawyer, go to the police and get this sorted out once and for all." Julian stands and walks out the pub.

I hear his feet crunch on the gravel outside. The empty thud of his hire car door closing, and the growl of the engine starting up. He's gone. I listen for him, off into the distance, until I can hear his car and his warning no more.

17

TAILED

I drive to the priest's house to have a last look at his 'rally the people' sermon. Rosie is with Katherine. I can't believe Julian made the effort to come out here and see me. It makes me feel ill. It makes it feel really dangerous, serious and real. It has just rained and so the sky is soft, fluffy and white with splashes of blue.

Father Aidan is alone. He is wearing a bright green Limerick GAA sports top and I admire the way he can remove his dog collar and be transformed completely into a different person. I long to change my top, my hair and be set free, but clothing will not change what's coming for me. He seats me at his laptop and I scroll through making a tiny change here and there.

"There!" I say. "It's done." I stand up to leave and we shake hands.

"If I can do anything for you, Doll, please just ask." I nod in thanks. "If you want me to hear your confession and absolve you from anything that is on your mind…"

"If only it was that easy, Father," I say, and he looks aghast.

The journey back is just over two miles of winding country lanes. I'm playing the Depeche Mode CD Katherine has given me. My eyes are ahead and I'm thinking about Julian Harper when I first see a black jeep in my rear-view mirror.

It's not a car that I recognise and, unlike living in London, you get to know people's vehicles when you live somewhere like this. It's not the rental car that Julian Harper was driving this morning. That was white. The car flickers in and out of my vision as we go round bends in the road, and each time it seems to get a little bit closer.

At first I slow down, I guess to reassure myself and allow it to overtake me should it want to. I'll just let it fly by me. But it doesn't. It speeds right up behind me until its image fills the rear-view mirror and as my heart picks up it gives me a firm bump from behind. My whole car lurches forward and I lose control for a moment and wrestle with the steering wheel to stay on the road.

I feel like my bones are being scraped by a metal brush. I can't think straight. Rosie, my Rosie. I've got to get back to her. I've got to get safe. I put my foot down, then break hard and take a firm left into a road going away from the pub in the opposite direction.

The jeep is on my tail. I'm driving these roads faster than ever in my life. Still it sticks to me like glue. I can't remember all of these lanes, all of their nonsensical bends and before I have a chance to react, the road is bending to the right at a ninety degree angle and I have to slam on the brakes and pull the steering wheel to the right and I nearly make it, I nearly do, but the back wheels are moving too fast and the rear slips round, smashing into a gatepost and dragging the whole car down into a ditch.

I have to get out. Fuck. I have to get out. I fumble with my seat belt unable to find the latch at this strange angle. The jeep passes me and then slows and turns, its engine roars. I'm free. I don't take my eyes off the jeep. It takes all my energy to hold the door open and climb up and out, and I jump down onto the earth.

The jeep drives slowly past me while I stand there. It could do anything to me now. He could open the window and shoot.

But instead it stops, like a feral beast assessing its prey. Smoke plumes from the exhaust. The engine rears up. The jeep speeds off.

Rosie, Rosie. I need to get back. I look at the sky. Which direction is the pub? I have twisted and turned and then, yes, across the fields, through the wood. I turn, clambering over the gatepost I have knocked over and run for my life. I run for Rosie's life. I'm panting, churning up mud, slipping and then scraping through the hedgerow at the other side. I won't stop. I run and I run and I run.

Back at home, at first I can't find them. They're not inside and I scream their names like a banshee. It's too late, he's got them! He's got Rosie! I leave and run to the pub. The front door is locked. I head around the back; the door is open.

Rosie is sitting in a booth in the pub folding knives and forks into red party serviettes, a delicate origami. They are for the expected crowds and she's piling them into a basket ready for the lunch serving. It's beautiful, and so innocent that I burst into tears. She looks up at me gently.

"What on earth, Mummy!" she says, staring at me.

"Good, you're back. Now you can get started on the–" Katherine begins, and stops. "Jesus, Doll. What's happened to you?"

"Lock the doors," I whisper.

18

A ROOM FOR THE NIGHT

Rosie dabs efficiently at my forehead, nurse-like, with a damp blue kitchen cloth. Something hurts inside my knee, a new click that wasn't there before. And in my neck there's a turgid gut-wrenching pull that starts between my shoulder blades and runs up into the back of my head. Katherine pulls a whole thorn from my forearm. She gently smears a tiny diamond of antiseptic cream into the cut on the bridge of my nose.

"Blackthorn, here," says Katherine. She has already telephoned the garage to tow my car back.

Rosie loses interest and excuses herself to go and play.

"The man this morning, it's not my business, but is everything okay?"

"Yes." I'm still caked in mud. Blood from my nose is splattered across my T-shirt.

"That man visits unexpectedly, and then you crash your car?" She opens a can of fizzy drink and hands it to me.

"I'm distracted. I could do with a stiff drink to be honest."

"Is it about the article?"

"It's a coincidence, that's all," I say, but I am unnerved, and frightened.

Rosie and I are working in the pub again tonight. Rosie chooses an outfit for me while I shower with the door open. I hardly dare close my eyes. I listen like a hawk, my cricked neck angling my ears to the direction of any sound downstairs.

Now I have no money, no phone, and no car. But I'm still here. I remember standing in front of the jeep, with my hands at my sides. I could be dead. He could have done anything to me. And if it was Andrew Marlow, why would he let me run away? Why would he drive away first? Because he wanted to scare me. He wanted to put the fear of God into me, and it has.

I have the number plate etched onto my brain. I have to discount one possibility first, then I have to take action. I can't do nothing, and make sitting ducks of us all. The waiting, the constant waiting for a knock at the door is driving me mad.

The waiting is over. Andrew Marlow can't be ignored. I have to do something.

Behind the bar I pull pints. Rosie is tucked safely in the kitchen with a vast array of games on Katherine's phone, homework and miscellaneous waitressing tasks for which Katherine is going to pay her twenty euros.

I reach over to the landline telephone, which Katherine now calls 'Doll's office'. I call Connor to ask him to come in and speak with me. Of course, he doesn't answer because he hates me but I leave a message inferring that everything can be made good if he comes to see me, and sure enough before an hour passes he arrives, still bedraggled, at the pub.

"What do you want now?" he asks, irritated.

It's after six o'clock on a Saturday and people are starting to come in for the evening or pop in after the football. Two people have 'checked-in' as if it's a hotel when in reality one is staying in the spare room, and one is staying in Katherine's bedroom. Such is the power of my news story: the pub is becoming a hub for the media, reporters, environment agency personnel, activists and nosey parkers from neighbouring villages. They all have the same agenda. They chat in a superficial, friendly manner and once established, begin to home in with questions about the lough. No one puts two and two together.

"I was run off the road today, Connor," I say, keeping my voice down, drawing him to the end of the bar so that no one can hear us. "By someone in a black Mercedes jeep with blacked-out windows."

There's a long pause.

"Are you okay? You've got a cut on your nose."

"I wasn't seriously hurt, no thanks to the prick who tried to kill me."

"You should tell the police, Doll."

"I will, but I'm giving you the opportunity to tell me if you know anything about it."

"Ah, fuck off."

"Not you personally, but Sean Gallagher's lot."

"It wasn't Sean Gallagher, or me, or anyone from around here. So you think about who else you've fucked off, because I'd say the list is pretty long."

"I need your help. I have a licence number. If you can find the person who did this and deal with them then I'll sell the house tomorrow. No questions asked. I will move into Auntie's, and I'll sign whatever papers you need me to sign and sell the house immediately."

"I can't trace a number plate, I'm an estate agent," he says.

"If we can find him, then we can deal with him," I repeat, because I need them. It's as if we're ten years old and discussing the ambush of an older cousin. Connor will always play the part I want him to.

"There's no 'we'."

"You can make it up to Sean. You can put it all right. I'm sure Sean Gallagher has many resources. Speak to him. Tell him that if he tracks this vehicle and sorts out my problem, then I'll sell the house to him. That's a promise."

19

POWER'S BAR

The following night the pub is buzzing. It's like an advert for Tourism Ireland. The bodhran is off the wall and squeezed onto the corner banquette is a four-piece Irish band. There's a rich, earthy smell of turf burning. Katherine smells of delicious expensive perfume that I can't place but will never forget.

The band starts off slow and then speeds up and up through the song, making everyone jig their feet. It feels like the walls are coming down. Peter Crowley, described by Auntie as a 'fine singer', has already been up to deliver the 'Wild Rover'. He stands tall and closes his eyes when he holds long notes.

There's a huge roaring fire, which Katherine pokes and prods and throws occasional knobbled logs onto. Pat sits in his high-backed chair. Auntie conducts a central packed table with the Crowleys and Rosie, who taps her feet and claps. She has an array of games to play, of course, and plenty of Coke and crisps, but her transition to pub-child is complete.

Also at the table, although her bump is now so big that she's pushed at least thirty centimetres away from it, is Suzie, the vet, and a jolly red-cheeked man who Auntie introduces as the doctor from Charleville. He is Suzie's intended husband and expectant father of the baby who no one comments upon, at least in public, until after the impending nuptials. I note that she's drinking orange juice and rubbing and arching her back.

"You're a brave woman, Doll," says the doctor. "Taking on Sean Gallagher and the dairy. Make sure you watch your back. Take care of yourself, promise?"

The pub is packed from wall to wall. As well as the two scientists staying above the pub, I discover there are numerous agency personnel and journalists. The agency people look the same in unofficial uniforms of beige cord chinos and soft green jumpers. At one table sit three from the Environment Agency, and two from the European Environment Agency. And there's also another chap from the Environmental Protection Agency. The Europeans are from Switzerland and elude a calmness and glamour that makes them stand out. I wonder which nationality is most likely to mention Suzie's baby bump.

From my vantage point behind the bar, I ask questions. I store their answers in my mind but for more specific scientific notes I keep a pad handy.

We're pulling the Guinness in advance to give it time to settle. Katherine and I work in synchronicity. The man that owns the local Spar store takes a moment to grab my hand and thrust a fifty euro note into it.

"We haven't had business like this ever. Thank you, Dolores."

I wouldn't normally take the money but seeing as I'm completely broke, I thank him joyfully and pocket it.

There's a staff writer from the *Irish Times* here and she rather bitchily tells me that I am flavour of the month. I give her a free drink and wink. Elsewhere there's the crew from RTE and RTE radio. The local Limerick station, Live95, isn't here because they'll drive over tomorrow. The media are still here because there's to be a presentation at the lough outlining agency findings and setting out the route forward. There will be an investigation.

There's no one from the dairy in the pub. Auntie enquires about Ryan Tubridy with every employee from RTE. She also asks the journalist from the *Times* if she has met Bono.

I should be enjoying tonight but I'm too rattled by the car accident to socialise properly. Kelly O'Hagan has offered me regular work as a freelancer. It could be very exciting. She wants me to go to Dublin for a meeting but there's no way I can go because I won't leave Rosie here without me, especially after today.

Father Aidan arrives flushed with pride from his rousing sermon. He delivered it very well. Everyone wants to buy him a drink. He has eight pints queued up on the bar. He leans in toward me.

"I can't thank you enough, Doll," he says. "If there's ever anything, really anything, I can do to help you then just ask." I am so touched that he would bother to thank me.

Other customers are from the town and neighbouring towns, here to follow the goings-on. Katherine is in her element, busy, social, and there's a twinkle in her eye. I always thought she was so natural and athletic and so different to me. She didn't read books, she listened to music and cycled. She played all sports and excelled at them. She could have done something, anything she wanted if she'd had the right kind of support, which of course she didn't. But watching her work I see that there is such a skill in being the host, in enabling people to enjoy themselves, that it is a natural talent.

We are both almost twenty years older, it's as if we have been in a time machine. I saw her once fleetingly on the last trip I made to Ireland with my mother. I saw her one more time in London but only briefly from a distance, so that I can barely remember it. She was upset that time, because it was my mother's funeral. It was unexpected that she was there. I should have made more effort to thank her for coming. But I was focused on other things then.

Sometimes when I am with Katherine I flush with embarrassment, I'm suddenly the giddy kid again that I was when I was sixteen. She always had a coolness about her that made me act silly. I always thought she wouldn't want to hang around with me, someone a year younger, and someone so mollycoddled by Mother. My mother and I were so intensely close, we argued a lot, and we didn't see eye to eye but we were always together.

As a teenager I lacked the rawness of Katherine. And I lacked her *fuck it* attitude and ballsiness. If we were at home in London then Mother would, I think, disapprove of our friendship. But it was okay here in Ireland, as it didn't interfere with my school work and the big plans that Mum had for my education. Katherine was kind of one of those kids from the wrong side of the tracks.

Connor walks into the pub. He spies his mother sitting with the Crowleys. There's a hush but it's in spirit only so the music doesn't stop. He's wearing a long coat that swishes, and underneath a shirt and tie which is distinctive and odd. He is clean-shaven and the look of utter despair that has cloaked him since the article came out has vanished.

He doesn't need to tell me that he's spoken to Sean Gallagher because everything about him tells me that he has, and he has regained his confidence as a result. Connor's look screams, *'I'm back in the gang.'*

"Pint?" I ask, and he nods.

"Ma's enjoying herself." He stands tall surveying the scene and then raising his voice, says, "It looks better in here with you two behind the bar. You're much prettier than that ugly fella there!"

"You're no oil painting!" shouts Pat from his throne. I fill Connor's glass.

"There's a presentation tomorrow about the route forward, there'll be an investigation and there'll be fines and penalties for the dairy," I say.

"I have never seen it this busy in here," Connor says, as Katherine squeezes behind me to take a bottle of tonic water from the fridge. She rests her hand on my waist, takes the bottle and moves away to serve.

"I have news from Sean. You're on." Connor sips his drink, leans in and is suddenly extremely coy. I lean in too so that no one else can hear us. "They traced the car to an address in Ennis."

"That's quick," I say, already regretting this line of enquiry.

"It's just a computer search. A click of a button."

"Ennis, County Clare? We need a name." I don't want to say it because I try to avoid thinking about him. I try to avoid naming him. "We do need a name."

"Andrew Marlow."

Uncle Andy was the nickname I had given him in the newspapers, his sinister alter ego that I had created. The name Uncle Andy crawled all over me, it made me feel physically sick, still now after all this time. When I gave him that name I didn't realise what I was creating. It was a big front-page story that ran and ran for weeks, and in other ways that story came to define my life. Would I be here right now if it were not for Uncle Andy? I don't think I would be. But looking around at how happy Rosie is, at my aunt, and at Katherine zipping around the bar with me, I wonder if it was all meant to be and that perhaps it might work out after all.

"You're going on Tuesday. You'll be collected from a farm up near Bunratty Castle. Arrange childcare for Rosie."

"Me?" I hadn't imagined that I would be going. I freeze. I balk at the idea of it. "I never meant that I would go."

"How will they know that it's the right fella? You have to identify him."

"I'll give you a photo, a description."

"No. Sean insists that you are there, otherwise it's not happening. He's told me to tell you that."

I have no choice.

"So I have to drive up to Bunratty?" I doubt my car will be fixed by then. I'll have to borrow a car from somewhere.

"Drive up there. I'll give you directions and you'll get into another vehicle to drive up to Ennis."

This is crazy, but I have to take action or else sit here waiting for his next attack, each one getting more and more dangerous. Connor nods, it feels silly pretending to be covert with him. He's taking this seriously; he gives me a nod and then stands back and tries to join his mother at the table. Something irritates me, how do I know it wasn't Sean Gallagher himself that ran me off the road?

The band bangs out a beat. The crowd sways and taps their feet. Peter Crowley stands up, shouts over the music and says to Connor: "You killed my dog."

"I did not. The dog had cancer. It's not my fault the dog had cancer, Jesus Christ." Connor smirks.

"There was no cancer. You do this to your own community. To your own mother," says Peter Crowley and the band plays more furiously.

"I haven't done anything!" Connor protests.

"How do you sleep at night?" Peter Crowley sits down, shaking his head.

The band plays harder and louder. Connor's eyes tighten, screwing up in rage.

"Who the fuck do you think you're talking to?" Connor says, blowing his top and banging his hand on the table. It bangs down in time to the beat of the music.

Peter Crowley's son stands, moves around the back of the

chairs swiftly and then rears up and pushes his chest against Connor's. "I've had enough of you," he says through gritted teeth.

"Now, boys!" Auntie says, not rising.

This is part of a long-standing grudge, years of competition between the two men since they were kids. Rosie watches agog. Auntie puts her arm around her. The band plays on.

"Get your hands off me!" says Connor, pushing Peter Crowley's son, who instantaneously pushes back and sends Connor tumbling into the next table, hitting Father Aidan who cannonballs across the floor. The music erupts into an energetic fiddle piece. Someone even whoops.

The two men tussle: wrestling, banging into tables, and people hold up their drinks to avoid spillage. Father Aidan is helped to his feet. He wipes himself down, beer splashed onto his front. Katherine bounds over to the fighters.

"Out!" she shouts, pushing them as a unit towards the door, which is held open for her by another patron. They are pressed tight together, spitting whispered threats. They protest yet move easily, stepping towards the exit, reconciled to their eviction, and bang into the frame of the battered wooden door. A smoker outside asks what's going on. Katherine closes the doors behind them and rolls her eyes.

"Let's hear it for Katherine!" shouts the band's leader, and the entire pub erupts into applause. Katherine holds up her hands like a champion, but it is my eyes that she looks into.

"Are you okay?" I mouth to Rosie, she nods her head vigorously in a state of ecstatic excitement. I see myself in her. I see myself here as a child, loving it, and in awe of this wonderful community. I've been dreaming of this place my whole life.

20

THE BROWN ENVELOPE

My new routine is now fixed. It begins with breakfast in the kitchen. Rosie has cereal. I tried porridge, but she won't eat it. Now that I have time to be a proper mum and make more nutritious food, I've found I can't afford it, so cereal it is.

Today, we have Pat's really old banger, a Nissan with four gears and soft grey seats that you might disappear down into and never be seen again. I have promised Katherine that I won't crash the car, or end up in a ditch, but to be honest, that rather depends on who I encounter on my journey.

I plan to use main roads at slow speeds only. Uncle Andy won't be expecting me in this car. Katherine hasn't told Pat that I'm borrowing it and there was a ruffling of curtains above the pub in the room that is Pat's bedroom. Pat's room is at the back. Katherine's room is next to mine. Can you believe that? I put my hand up against the wall and imagined her on the other side doing the same thing! So childish.

Most days I take Rosie to school and then circle back via my aunt's. She'll have a hot pot of tea on the go and it is one of my life's rare comforts to come in through her back door.

This morning when I dropped Rosie off, I saw several parents that were in the pub last night and we nodded at each other to acknowledge the shared experience of bad heads. I rarely drink now so there is no hangover for me. I have to have my full faculties about me all the time these days. I can't risk something happening when I am not fully in control. The thought of being drunk under these circumstances is terrifying.

Auntie and I park up to collect Katherine before we travel the short distance to the lough for the findings of the environment agency. I park at the back and I'm not about to go in but then we decide we need to use the toilet before the meeting. We enter by the back door and as I walk to the stairs, I notice a brown envelope on the front mat. There is no stamp, no return address.

I put it on the counter in the kitchen. I don't want to open it. The package stares at me ominously. I'm not expecting anything. Very few people know that I'm here.

"What is it?" Auntie slowly ascends the stairs. I have a sudden fear that it might explode, so I run with it to the open back door and put it out on the bins. "What on earth are you doing?"

"I don't like the look of it!" I say.

"Why ever not?"

"I don't know."

"What's the matter with it?" Auntie comes back down into the kitchen, concerned.

"Gut feeling."

"Are you expecting something?" she asks.

"Absolutely not." Katherine arrives at the back and gives a little knock.

"Is this yours?" she asks, holding up the envelope.

"Give it to me," I say and take it and rip it open. I go into the front room. "Can I have some privacy?"

"What is she like, Katherine? Have you heard the latest about the priest? Apparently he has the hots for Dolores."

"Oh, really?" asks Katherine slowly rolling the 'r'. I don't want Katherine thinking that. It's so ridiculous.

"Don't be so silly," I shout as I open the envelope and take out large photographs of me and Rosie. There's a note addressed to *Claire Halliday*, so I know right away who has taken them. It's the fake name that I gave Andrew Marlow all those years ago. I shudder. They are six by four inches in size, a standard size. The flimsiness of the paper and greyscale of the image feels as though they have been developed in a home studio. There is no date stamp on them, no printer's watermark. They have been taken by a camera with a long lens.

There are ten images in total. There is a picture of me getting out of my car, the crashed car, the Saab. There's a photo of me and Rosie in her school playground. I can tell by the light that it's morning. I can tell the particular day from the plait in Rosie's hair. There is a close-up of Rosie eating chips at Supermac's in Limerick City. There's one of Rosie eating in the kitchen, taken from an odd angle. It's inside the house. Perhaps from a vantage point at the front, through a window. Horrific.

My stomach turns. I need to get to Rosie. I need to get to her now. I go into the kitchen and grab the car keys.

"I've got to go." I run out of the kitchen and into the yard and into Pat's car. It's a blur. I need to get to Rosie. He could be there. He could take her. Katherine gets into the passenger seat. I'm already reversing and she has to jump to get in. Auntie has come out the back door and looks fearful, deranged.

"Wait! What's happened? Tell me, Doll." Katherine puts her hand on my leg. "I can help you."

I wouldn't even know where to start with this story. How could I explain how we've got to this position? It seems so ridiculous, so outlandish that someone would be coming for me after all this time.

I hand her the envelope. She opens it. The engine is still on and it hums. The radio purrs in the background. Auntie knocks on the window and I jump out of my skin. She pulls open the back door and climbs in with Mr Todd in her arms.

"I hope you've got your keys because I pulled the door to."

"Who took these?" Katherine asks.

It seems too complicated to spell it out in its entirety right at this moment. I'm not ruling out telling Katherine, but I can't bring myself to say it out loud. I just have to make sure Rosie's safe.

"I have to get to Rosie."

"Drive," says Katherine, and I put my foot down and wheelspin out of the yard. I turn left on the main road heading for the school. I stay in a low gear accelerating over the engine's high-pitched scream.

"What am I looking at?" Auntie puts on her reading glasses.

"They've just been put through the door," says Katherine. "Someone's threatening her. Over the story, I guess. Some bastard connected to the dairy."

I hammer my foot down to the floor. I don't disagree. I let them think that it's to do with the dairy, but this goes way, way back. I brake suddenly and Mr Todd flies off the seat.

"Slow down now, Jesus, or we'll all be killed," says Auntie. "Katherine, call the gardaí and get them to meet us at the school."

"No!" I scream instinctively.

"Yes, Katherine, please do. This is out of your hands now, Doll. We're not going to allow any harm to you." My eyes are burning with tears. I've got to get to Rosie. I should never have come here. I'm putting everyone at risk.

I leave the engine running. I race into the school. It's not like London, they don't have security here, they don't need it, until now. Katherine follows. I hear our feet pounding across the tiles and into the corridor like an out of body experience. I see kids' coats hung messily on pegs, a pair of trainers strewn across the floor, a scarf lays motionless on the cold red tiles. I hear the hum of children working, and a woman's voice.

I grab desperately at the door handle and emerge breathless into the classroom. I swing my head back and forth urgently assessing the threat. But there is none there. The children turn their heads to look at me. They are sitting at their desks looking at the blackboard where the teacher is explaining a large diagram of the solar system.

Rosie is in shock. Realising that it's me, she bursts into a big smile and waves. I wave back and pull a weird smile. Katherine steams into the back of me.

"Mrs O'Rourke, is everything okay?" asks the teacher, holding up a marker pen. It's not a blackboard, of course, it's a whiteboard.

"Yes, I'm sorry, I–"

"My fault," says Katherine. "I thought there was a meeting here this morning, but we realise now that it's at the lough."

"The meeting is at the lough, it's nothing to do with us. We're in the middle of our science lesson!"

"Apologies. We're sorry for disturbing you. Have a great day, everyone," Katherine says awkwardly, stepping back in the corridor.

"I'll pick you up later," I say to Rosie and she nods, bewildered, and turns back at the teacher, putting the top of her pen into her mouth. I share her embarrassment. She is fine, oblivious.

"It hasn't changed. I haven't been back here for twenty years." Of course, this is where Katherine went to school. "This was my peg," she says, curling a finger around the metal hook.

"Where has the time gone?" I ask, realising that I am starting to cry with relief or panic, I don't know which. Katherine wraps her arms around me and I put my head into her neck and it's so soft. For the first time in months I feel safe.

"She's fine, she's absolutely fine," Katherine whispers into my ear and I pull away out of her arms. I can't look at her because I'm shot through with embarrassment, and if she sees my eyes then she will know how I am feeling. "I can come with you to Dublin if you like, next week? I can look after Rosie while you're in your big meeting."

"That's too much," I say. "What about the pub?"

"I'll close it for one night. I haven't been to Dublin for years."

Outside, Auntie is huddled in the playground with Father Aidan and a garda. Father Aidan is holding the envelope; I can tell that they have all looked at the photographs.

"Let me tell you, Doll, that we will not allow this kind of threatening behaviour in this parish," says Father Aidan.

"We're going to ask you to make a formal statement at the station, if that's okay," says the garda.

"Sure."

"And we're going to do a regular drive-by of the house for the time being until things start to calm down again. Once this press conference is done today, things will start returning to normal. You'll see."

They think the photographs are related to the story of the lough and the dairy. They don't have a clue who has really sent them, who has taken them and developed them himself, but I know it is Andrew Marlow.

"We're sure that nothing will happen," says Father Aidan. He has the distinct redness of eye that characterises a hangover. He is unshaven and smells of stale beer.

"It's a threat, that's all, to scare you," says the garda.

"To shut you up, to shut us up!" Auntie says.

"But we're going to lock the school, once everyone is in," says Father Aidan. "And we are going to lock the playground gates. We will ensure there are eyes on Rosie the entire time for the next week or so until this blows over. Let me reassure you that she is completely safe here in our care."

"Thank you. I think I'll take her home with me now if that's okay?" They don't know what they are dealing with.

"They will never silence us," says Auntie.

"We are one community, united under God, Doll, and when they try to attack one of us, they take on the entire parish." Father Aidan smiles and places a hand on my shoulder. It's another chance for him to impress the parish.

"Thank you," I say. But they have it all wrong. I have come here to hide, and I've brought trouble with me. I thought I could run from him, but he has caught up with me already. I must make sure none of these good people are harmed. Perhaps I should move on again?

2 1

THE DRIVE TO ENNIS

It's a filthy night. It is freezing cold with driving rain that slams down diagonally like a quiver of tiny frozen arrows. I don't want to leave Rosie but I must take my chance to deal with Andrew Marlow. I will never have the opportunity to confront him with an army of men again, so I leave Rosie with Auntie at her house on the strict provision that Connor stays there with both of them all night.

It's already dark. Auntie washes Rosie's hair, bending her forward over the kitchen sink, slowly rinsing out the shampoo using a glass jug. She guides Rosie to straighten up and wraps her head in an anaemic pale blue towel. Auntie's arthritic fingers have kinks at the knuckles, reminding me of trees planted on windy hills that keel to one side unnaturally.

"We'll be fine," Auntie says.

"Don't take too much off, will you?" I ask. The slowness, the delicacy of Auntie trimming my child's hair is at odds with the hard masculine world into which I'm going. I wish I could stay. I've told Auntie that I have a meeting with a local reporter about our story. It's an easy lie to tell, Auntie is desperate for our fifteen minutes of fame to run and run.

I hold Rosie for a moment longer than usual until she wriggles and says, "You can let go now."

I kiss her head and leave by the kitchen door.

Bunratty Castle. The stuff of childhood dreams. How we loved to come here in the holidays for a day out. I drive about one hundred metres past the castle and then I take a left turn, which I almost miss, onto a single-track road. I must be mad. It's like a horror film and I'm going deeper and deeper in. After half a mile I turn into the sprawling yard of the farm where I've arranged to meet Sean Gallagher.

Even though it's cold, sweat prickles on my forehead. What am I doing? Several large modern barns glisten in the wet moonlight. Domes of plastic-covered soilage cower in the rain, at the feet of an immense rocket-like silo.

There are four parked vehicles. They are black four by fours, not unlike the one that ran me off the road. Could it have been them? Have I inadvertently walked into something much bigger than I anticipated? Maybe there's more to the dairy story? More to the lough. I park Pat's bright yellow Nissan and someone approaches me underneath an umbrella. He knocks at my window. It is Sean Gallagher himself.

I take a deep breath. I have no choice. A man like Uncle Andy can only really be handled by the likes of Sean Gallagher. They speak a mutual language, and share a cultural appreciation of intimidation. I open the door and step out into the yard.

"Well, you picked the right night for it!" Sean rocks forward on his toes.

"Sean," I say, "no hard feelings, I have a job to do."

A second man approaches. No umbrella this time, just a long black raincoat that covers him entirely. I glimpse his face but I don't recognise him.

"Raise your arms." The man beckons me to stand forward. He runs his hands along both sides, top and bottom of each arm, around my breasts, my back, my stomach. "Spread your legs." I comply and take a step to the side standing in an 'A frame'. He runs his hands up the inside of my legs. Believe it or not it's not the first time I have been searched in such a manner. His fingers are careful around my vagina, I'll give him that. He shows at least some respect.

"You have no listening devices, no recording devices?"

"No, of course not."

"That'll do," Sean says. "She wouldn't be so stupid as to do it again. Follow me." He leads me to the middle of the yard. I've dressed for wet weather but I can already feel my feet getting damp. It's going to be a long night. The noise of rain above, on metal roofs, creates a blanketing background sound. Sean speaks quietly. "Now you will sell me the house, Dolores. That is our agreement."

"Yes."

"The car is at the house right now. Parked in the garage."

"What if he's not there?"

"There's someone on the property."

"But if he gets away, what then, will you find him?"

"We'll keep you safe. You and your daughter. When he appears we'll make sure he can't chase you anymore."

"Okay." I ask for more information about exactly how or what they are going to do with him afterwards, and what if it goes wrong. I mean, I don't want them to kill him, do I? Or maybe I do.

"It's better that you don't know, for many reasons including your own safety."

"Okay."

"It's me who should not *trusht* you. You've caused me so many problems."

"I'm sorry."

"It's important that you keep quiet about this. You can't spill the beans all the time."

"Of course I will."

"The boys will take you with them, so you can identify him and so that you are–"

"Your insurance policy so that I can't talk about it without compromising myself. I get it."

"Indeed, Doll. You love to share the news." Sean takes a phone from his pocket. "And I have my own little recording just in case. I'm glad we understand each other."

I'm marched across the yard and into the back of a Land Rover. I travel with three men. The driver is big. He wears a beanie hat and reminds me of a rhinoceros. He is without a neck and his head bridges straight into his arched back. His eyes flick back to look at me as if he wants to speak but has been told not to.

The man next to me is tall, slim and moustached. He smiles as I get in and then looks forward, never once glancing over at me. The car smells of polish. It has recently been cleaned. The radio mumbles quietly. The rain cocoons us. A few hundred metres behind us, so as not to be an obvious convoy, is another vehicle and behind that another. What am I doing? What have I done? Is it too late to change my mind? Is it bad enough to warrant this? And what if they are too heavy handed and they kill him? Is it too late to call it off?

Rain puddles in the road. What sort of person have I become? I've tried to live a quiet life. But Andrew Marlow won't let me live a normal life. His appetite for revenge will never be satisfied.

Julian Harper wants me to go back to London and talk to the police. Julian is an entitled weasel of a man and although his advice is not motivated by the love of me, it will be strong common-sense advice all the same.

But if I go to the police at home in London there's a very good chance I will be sent to prison. My mother and father are dead. I have no siblings. I'm all alone. If I go inside, Rosie will be taken from me and given to David. I can't be sure I would ever get her back, not fully, not full custody. I can't do that. I can't risk losing her.

Julian told me to get lawyered up and face the music. But that's not what he said nine years ago. I had been in his office when all this began. His star has risen in the last decade but back then he was simply the News Editor. His office was an old-fashioned box room cloaked in white plastic venetian blinds that caught on the string, leaving gaps through which you could see into the large, bustling open-plan office where I sat at my desk.

Julian was always fighting with those blinds. He wanted them open to keep an eye on everyone doing their work, but when he wanted to talk privately about a story he wanted them closed. He would call a reporter into his office and then close the blinds. Often they would snag and he would scream and shout and call for his assistant to come in and fix them. In a sense his shouting was really about instilling fear and a sense of chaos into his workforce.

In the years following the Uncle Andy story, as he became a regular pundit on the late-night television circuit, making smart comments about the week's big news stories, he mellowed. His reputation became more important and he couldn't be perceived as a bully. He set his office up as a meeting room and sat at a desk on the main floor with everyone else. He did an interview in *MediaWeek* about how he was a business innovator for sitting out amongst the team that he managed. He became a proponent of 'open door policy' and when competitor news operators were in trouble for illegal practices, bullying and phone hacking, Julian spoke about this 'open door policy'. He rewrote history, telling people that he'd always insisted on sitting amongst the team to ensure that rules were correctly followed. He was on the ten o'clock news once talking about the responsibilities of modern newspaper management. In the new digital media landscape Julian became the face of modern leadership. He lied and then vlogged his way to the top.

I had made mistakes before, but none like this, and I shouldn't have been asked to do it. I could have said no, but that seemed impossible at the time. One random day, like any other, Julian called me into his office and as he did so the entire floor went quiet. I had, for some time, been 'out of sorts', to put it mildly. After my mother's stroke I was rudderless. I went suddenly from a career girl, arguably one of the best reporters of my generation, to someone who had come completely off the rails.

Initially, I sat by my mother's bedside for days. She'd had a stroke while shopping at Westfield on a normal rainy Wednesday in February. St Mary's hospital was tall and antiseptic. Each time I got in the lift it seemed like I shared it with a porter and someone nearer my age, someone yellow, someone with broken legs. With my mother's illness I felt like I was ageing too. I was changing. I could see it happening. I was becoming cynical, my once solid belief in the infinite possibilities of the future had dried up. My solid and practical mother was broken.

She was in Accident and Emergency, and then moved to the Intensive Care Unit where I wasn't allowed to see her for two days, and then they let me in. The surgeons inserted some sort of coil into her brain to stem the bleed. It worked. For those two days I sat in the foyer downstairs. I ate chocolate bars and drank coffee. They told me to go home, so I did and slept for twelve hours straight and then I went back to the hospital. Mother's friends telephoned me incessantly.

The nurses didn't ask me where my husband was but they gave me a look that told me they felt sorry for me. I had kind friends who jumped to help me. Auntie came over from Ireland but stayed with my cousin and so I went back there. But it felt like a temporary warmth, like I was welcome when Auntie was there but not when she wasn't.

My greatest fear was staring me in the face. If my mother didn't make it, I was going to be all by myself. The thought was petrifying. Of course I couldn't even picture that, never mind talk about it. I entered a kind of constant state of panic. Since then I've been told that my body was running on cortisol and adrenaline. With my job I was used to pressure anyway. I was constantly running to targets. There was never-ending stress to hit deadlines, to be the first to break stories, to come up with new ideas. The job was changing with the internet. All the old daily, weekly and monthly slots to plan were thrown out the window and it was a new race to break stories online before anybody else. Corporations were just figuring out how to effectively use Twitter and which stories should be held for print and which stories should go up there and then.

I had the constant sensation of being on amphetamines. After three days Mother was moved to a ward and when she woke up and saw me she smiled, and it was the happiest moment of my life. Her eyes were so kind. I'd never really thought about her eyes before but she never spoke again and so they took on new meaning. It was a while before I realised she was never coming home.

We didn't live together. I had a flat in Crouch End and she lived in the house where I grew up in Willesden. Her house was empty and so I moved back in. At first it was to feed the cat, Barney, and then it was to sleep in her bed. Is that weird? To sleep in your mother's bed? I couldn't use a cup, a spoon, or a dinner plate, they were all imbued with such emotion that I would weep while I ate and drank. I made plans in my mind of how I might care for her when she returned home.

But mine wasn't a normal job where you get signed off for something like this. I think Julian felt that I should just carry on so that's what I did. He gave me leeway to manage my own time, to work late, or start early or even work from home. But the set-up of a news room is not conducive to someone who can't be there all the time.

I think Julian would have been happier if she had died. It would have been a tidier process to follow but of course, life is never tidy. I had led a charmed life with my kind and gregarious mother. We used to meet in the West End to go and see a show at least once a month. She used to come and meet me for lunch spontaneously. I would go for my tea and stay over once a week. We'd often see each other on weekends.

The doctors decided that she needed intense rehabilitation and so she went to the acute stroke unit at Northwick Park hospital. It was a pain to get to the furthest side of Wembley but I tried to go every day. Time began to stretch. She wasn't getting better. No speech, just muffled words, and incontinence. I never told a soul about that, such is the shame that my mother would have felt. Still, I would bring her home. I would manage somehow. There were conversations about carers and care packages and the assistance that I could access.

At work I spent most of the day googling 'subarachnoid haemorrhage'. It seemed there was no miracle, no instantaneous fix and no 'out there' doctor that we could pay with our life savings to fix her. Slow and steady but intensive rehabilitation was the order of the day.

And time passed. Weeks passed and then it was eight weeks and then a whole summer was gone. Long bright evenings spent by her side with the window open for air. Her legs were thin and the skin was dripping from them. The soles of her feet were flushed pink and soft as a baby's foot once again.

She was thinner and I was strung out. I was drinking. I was doing cocaine. I wanted to block the whole thing out. Looking back, if I'd had a partner at the time then perhaps they would have spoken sense to me, made me calm down. But I just had a sense of anxiety that the longer it was going on the more mad I was becoming.

When Auntie telephoned, she asked about Mother. When anyone saw me they asked about my mother, and not about me. How was I coping? I wasn't coping. I wasn't coping at all. If I met friends all I did was moan and cry. No one could counsel me or make me feel better. I used to stare blankly at my reflection in the glass of the Bakerloo line train as it shuddered toward Wembley. This couldn't be happening.

I was working. I was drinking. I didn't want to be alone. I was so very lonely. I would have sex with men just so I would have someone to wake up beside. I had one-night stands – lots of them. It was embarrassing to come into work and be in the same room as someone that I had fucked the night before. My phone beeped late at night, flush with booty calls. I think some men love damaged girls; can sense their desperation and use it.

One night, drunk, I telephoned Power's Bar in Limerick. I remembered the number. It's amazing how those teenage phone numbers are tattooed into our brains. I felt like I wanted to talk to Katherine, that she would understand me, and that she would care. Pat answered, there was a beautiful noise in the background and I longed to be there so much that it felt like a popped spring in my chest. Katherine wasn't there, of course, she was in New York.

Around this time much of the conversation with clinicians turned to Christmas and whether she would be able to come home. I was insistent. I was obsessed with it. They were talking about residential nursing facilities, but I was determined to have her back at home. I felt like they were patronising me, but they were right, as I could hardly look after the cat. Still, I had a financial assessment with the council, I met an Occupational Therapist at the house in Willesden. I paid to have a wet room installed downstairs and the living room would be my mother's bedroom. A hospital bed was delivered by social services, and a hoist. A care package was applied for. I invited Auntie for Christmas. I would cook and invite my mother's friends. But they wouldn't let me bring her out. I should have demanded it. I spent Christmas Day at Northwick Park hospital. It was okay. We made the best of it. I got into bed with her. I kissed her face. She smiled.

After we've had our first Christmas like this and go on to whatever is next, at some time around this point a young girl goes missing in Kent: Amy Smith, aged only fourteen.

22

AMY SMITH

The Amy Smith disappearance is a massive story and Julian puts a team of seven people on it. Every newspaper places the story on the front page. It's on the television and radio. She was walking home from her friend's house at half past seven in the evening and disappeared. There was CCTV and it's clear that someone had taken her.

Both Julian and my corporate superiors are by this time waning in their support of me. At the start there was a charity run for the Stroke Foundation. I was given time off and flexible working. At first, they did everything they could but the longer it went on, the more they wanted me to get back to normal and focus on my work.

Julian had begun instructing me to go straight home from the office and not be drinking in the pub with my co-workers. I missed a few important meetings. I wasn't nurturing contacts and PRs and press officers so I wasn't being offered stories. As I say, it was an all-consuming fast-paced daily job. At one stage Julian was going to speak to someone in the newly created online SEO department where I might face less pressure but I didn't want to move.

When Amy Smith went missing, we were behind the curve. Other newspapers seemed to be getting information before us. They had opinions from the police. They had Amy's teachers. We had nothing. Our corporate overlords were furious and embarrassed. From time to time Julian employed the services of various private investigators and one I worked with a lot was simply known as Harry. Honestly, I don't even know if that was his real name. We had a fling for about a month but I never went to his place – always mine. We never saw each other on weekends – only weeknight evenings. I didn't have feelings for him, or for anyone during that period. I was numb to the bone – I had to be to make it out of bed every morning.

I know it's wrong but Harry and I had a technique for listening to phone messages. Phone hacking, as it has become known. From time to time it was requested by the powers that be and if we couldn't get information then we'd go straight to the source, namely people's answerphones. There were others doing it too. A lot of journalists, more senior than me, were doing this. It was an open secret. And because professionals that I looked up to and admired were at it I thought that it was part of our job. I never believed it was a good thing but I understood it was an integral part of our style of news gathering at that time. I guess it was like smoking. Everyone smoked in the 1960s before we knew how bad it was for us.

You forget but in the noughties no one took security remotely seriously. As I had tried to explain to Auntie, when you got a mobile phone you should change the default setting password but no one ever did back then. So the password was either 0000 or sometimes 1234 or 4321. If it wasn't one of those Harry had a sequence of likely numbers that he would try.

One of us would phone up a target and get them on the phone and keep them talking. While they were talking Harry would call them and get an engaged tone, and at this point the phone would ask if you wanted to go through to the message box. When you went through to voicemail you could type the four-digit pin to get into the messages of that phone. Sounds ludicrous, I know, but it was that easy. Should the phone companies take responsibility for creating such lax security? Yes, I think they probably should.

It was wrong. I know it was wrong. But from time to time it was wholly sanctioned by Julian, in fact ordered by him, and who knows who else above him, because it went all the way to the top. They thought they had a God-given right to hack people's telephones. When suspicion started to fall, Julian would call a halt on it. I'd be told disdainfully over a glass of wine at lunchtime that there were to be no more covert operations. Everything should be above board. Harry would disappear for a couple of months.

All it would take to get dirty tricks sanctioned once more was a few missed stories. By missed stories I mean exclusives that we didn't get but our competitors did. They were doing it too. And whoever was doing it was getting the best stories.

If a tabloid newspaper didn't use this technique during a certain period in the noughties then they would not be credible. We all knew it. We didn't like it but for the most part it was celebrities and royal clingers-on. These were people who actively courted publicity so in journalistic circles we considered them fair game.

There were many big stories as a result. It wasn't just me doing it, it became par for the course. When I look back at it now, I know that it was wrong and I wish to God I had never done it. But at the time it was just part of the job.

So when Amy Smith disappeared and we had nothing – no leads and no sources for the story – it was sanctioned by Julian Harper, and by those above him, to do whatever it took to get new angles and new information. Our rival newspaper seemed to be in contact with the family, the school and the police and was turning up its own leads all the time.

Julian was in his office with the blinds closed. My colleague Kelly O'Hagan, now a news editor in Dublin and essentially my boss, was just a reporter. She leaned in conspiratorially. "He's going fucking mad in there," she said.

"Is someone with him? I didn't see anyone go in," I ask.

"Harry's in there with him."

This could only mean one thing: a return to covert tactics of information gathering. The blinds twitched. Julian's eyes winced through the gap. The office hummed like a productive beehive, pinging from time to time with the pip of the telephone ringing. Julian's door was flung open and the room went relatively silent. Julian stepped out in shirt sleeves and a tie.

"Doll," he said, "have you got a minute?"

Of course there was no saying, 'no' to Julian. I stood up from my desk, Kelly winked at me. The eyes of the office were upon me. They were pleased it was me and not them, yet jealous too. Everyone knew that my mother was ill and that I was only just clinging on to my thread of reality. In pictures of me from that time I was stick thin and pale. My eyes had a haunted look. When friends complained of minor bumps in their lives I told them about my situation with an emotionless glare. It was cruel but I never meant for it to be. I realise now that all suffering is relative. We can't really feel empathy for something until we feel it ourselves.

When we see people squirming under the pressure of pain that we have already been through we look down on them like an omnipotent god and smile through the sadness. They think we're saying that everything will be all right, but actually what we are really saying is that they're metamorphasising into someone else. Once they get through the change and become a sadder, harder and more emotionally knowledgeable person, they might just be able to get through it. But bye bye, baby! Goodbye to the person they used to be.

I walked into Julian's office. He had a beaten-up wooden desk.

"I thought we'd get Harry on it again to see what we can turn over on Amy Smith."

"Good idea." I nodded like a pantomime horse. I needed that job. At that point in my life, and at so many other times in my life, I needed that job. It gave me self-belief. I never disputed the importance of a story. I never went against my editor. I always did what had to be done, I always rose to the challenge of anything that was asked of me. Even then when I cried every day, when I couldn't cry any more because I became rigid and frozen, I always turned in for work.

"Amy Smith has a mobile phone," Harry said. Julian pouted, his eyes glaring from me to Harry and back again. I must have instinctively pulled a look of disgust. I was usually poker-faced at work but the thought of looking into a missing girl's answerphone… Amy Smith wasn't fair game like some desperate celebrity, she was a young, innocent girl who the police were supposed to be scrambling to find.

"Really?" I asked.

Julian flipped. "Harry, get going, mate. Bring your car round to the front and Doll will meet you there."

Harry got up and nodded. He picked up a black computer bag that he trailed around with him everywhere. He wore utility trousers with lots of pockets, the type you might expect to see on an electrician.

"You are on very shaky ground, Doll," Julian said. "Now, I don't want to add to your burden but you are going to have to start putting work first."

"I do," I said, but I understood clearly what he meant, whether it was right or not, whether it was bullying or an HR issue. He was right. But how the fuck did people work when all this shit was going on in their lives? I suppose this was why some people didn't work, or couldn't work.

"You always used to put your writing first. I'm doing you a

favour because I like you. Most people would just manage you out. You wouldn't know a thing about it until you were out on your arse, scratching your head and wondering how the fuck you haven't got a job anymore."

"Oh!" I was suddenly aware of how bad the situation had become.

"It's time to put out, or fuck off," said Julian.

I was sure you weren't supposed to talk to your employees in this way but this was Julian's style. And I'd had much worse from other news editors.

"I really love this job, Julian." Pathetic looking back, but I needed it, I loved it, and I still do.

"Well fucking show it then!"

"I will, but this is totally illegal."

"Don't fucking talk back to me. Just get on with what you're supposed to be doing. Stop drinking so much, and stop shagging people. Coming to work drunk, drinking on the job, and having sex with colleagues are all sackable offences, and there's plenty of evidence for all three. Give me something to show the people upstairs that you've still got what it takes to do this job. It's your last chance." It felt like something else that I loved was at risk of being taken away from me. I couldn't risk losing my job. Not just for the money but for self-esteem. I was on my own. My friends were making themselves less available, I know that I was difficult and depressed. I felt like I was unloved and loved only by a mother who could no longer show me.

"I will." I didn't know whether to speak or to shut up.

"Right. Go with Harry. He knows what to do. Follow his lead. Bring me something new on Amy Smith."

"Thank you," I said, gratefully.

Remembering this now makes me feel so uneasy and disbelieving. I was actually so grateful to be working there. We were told that not just anyone could do this job and especially at our newspaper. We were the best of the best. We were lucky to be there, at the forefront of breaking news. There were plenty of people waiting in line for our jobs. If we couldn't cut it then there were plenty of others eager for the chance.

If we couldn't cut it in news then we had to admit it and look for something else. I could have moved to what I would have considered a step down by taking a job in magazines, or if I were really finished and just wanted to rack up some cash I could double my pay with a job in public relations.

I walked out of Julian's office and stopped at my desk. I shut down my computer. I slipped my jacket from the back of my chair, filled my handbag with my laptop and charging cord. I slid my mobile phone into my back pocket. All eyes were on me. They didn't know if I was clearing my desk or going home.

"You are coming back, aren't you?" asked Kelly in a whisper.

I stood up tall. "I'll be back later, or in the morning," I said loudly for all to hear. The gentle clatter of the office started up around me. I thought how much I would miss this place if I never came back.

23

THINGS THAT I REGRET

Most private investigators were ex-police, but not Harry, he had done a course. A six-week intensive course entitled 'Private Investigation Level 1'. In a former life he'd been a rugby player, like Pat Power from the pub, all hopes and dreams of professional sport dashed in a single incident in a single match, or in Pat's case in the boozy session that followed. Harry sustained a catastrophic injury to his knee and walked with a limp that prematurely aged him. He had to retire early from the game and often sneered at the toffee-nosed snobs that he had played with. He had shovels for hands and the tiny burner mobile phones that he had hundreds of looked like children's dominoes in his fingers.

Harry drove a Ford Galaxy, an unassuming and spacious vehicle in navy blue. When he pulled back a cunningly positioned tarpaulin in the boot it was full of laptops and charging cables, routers, batteries and wires. I didn't know what most of it was for but I told him that he should watch out. If the car was ever stolen, and the police discovered what had been illegally recorded on those hard drives, he could end up in prison.

His car smelled of coffee, and strawberry from the air

freshener that hung from the rear-view mirror. The smell made my eyeballs sting. It seemed fitting that such a strong unnatural odour was present, perhaps to hide the stench of filth that Harry emitted in his work. Nothing could wash it away; nothing could rid his hands of that dirt. Why didn't I walk away? Being part of this world is what I regret. I wanted to expose wrongdoing, and I wanted to help people. I wanted to pull back the blanket of corruption and expose those who were hypocrites, but in doing so I had become one myself.

There was a whoosh and a sniff. Harry coughed and pinched the bridge of his nose as he did a line of cocaine off the back of a CD case and then passed it to me.

I took it from him and snorted the coke through a twenty-pound note. I hated myself, still do now, thinking back to this moment. The baking soda and dull sulphur scent gave way to an instant hit. I was alert, interested, everything had slightly more definition, and I was more curious. Harry didn't seem such a dick anymore; he was arguably more interesting. He smiled. He was better looking too. He shepherded the minute leftovers off the case with his fingers and rubbed it into his gums. The CD was *Affirmation* by Beverley Knight.

"Let's get started."

"We shouldn't be doing this. It's wrong," I said.

"I'll just do it myself. Don't sweat it, everyone's at it. It's your funeral. You can get out of this car and walk back to London at any time." He goaded me. We'd driven south east through a part of London I didn't really know, out towards Kent, and had parked up in an industrial estate outside Gillingham. It was a cool day with blue skies and thick grey clouds. Seagulls squawked at the promise of nearby sea. A warehouse building rusted in front of us, collapsing in on itself as if dreaming of better days.

"What am I doing here?"

"Drama queen," said Harry. "We ain't hurting nobody. I haven't taken that girl. You haven't taken that girl. We're not the villains. We won't jeopardise the police investigation. No one knows we're doing this. We want to raise awareness, follow the leads, we're trying to help, right? Anyway, I'm doing this, not you. And you get the story, a possible front page and you don't get sacked. You should be thanking me, and thanking Julian for giving you another chance. Sorry about your mum and all that, you know I am, but you can't go on in this state forever." Harry holds his hands up in mock innocence.

I felt like I had no choice. My job was on the line. "Are we doing this or what?"

"Make the call."

I held up the phone and pressed the green button. Harry had already typed Amy Smith's number into the handset and, of course, we both knew that she wasn't going to answer. I was expecting an engaged sound, instead it said the phone couldn't be reached. I started leaving a message for Amy Smith so that the mailbox would connect to me. I just said what I always said when I was trying to reassure an interviewee: that if she was in trouble or didn't want to go home then we could help her. I know now how awful that sounded, and still sounds now. There wasn't room to leave another message in the mailbox but Harry was quick. He was already connecting to it.

At the same moment Harry had dialled in, and as the phone line was primarily connected to my call, he was automatically shunted into the mailbox. I saw him tap in the passcode 0000. The phone companies should have made it harder. That's a lame excuse, I know, but it should have been harder for people like Harry and me.

In his other hand Harry had a recording device. It was rudimentary, but he just held it next to the phone while it was on speaker and recorded all of the messages.

"Make sure you–" I started to say and he stopped me, and stopped the recording.

"No speaking. You don't want your voice on this recording." He made a squiggly sounding fifteen-second deletion of my voice and recorded over the top. If he had not done that, I would have already been in prison or on remand. I would have been in serious trouble and part of the initial prosecution, because that recording was later uncovered as evidence in Harry's and the newspaper's trial. I spent a year sweating about that recording. But Harry never mentioned a word about me and I will always be grateful to him for that, and ashamed in equal measure. He got paid a good fee for keeping quiet, not that he was ever able to enjoy it.

The mailbox was full so Harry wanted to delete some messages to make room for new ones. He wondered who else of interest might call and what leads it might turn up. He could then hack in again at a later date. He assured me that Amy had never deleted any messages so the ones he got rid of were old and completely irrelevant.

Afterwards we played back Harry's recordings. One stood out. The first time that I heard Uncle Andy's voice I just knew there was something wrong about him. His voice made my skin goosebump. The message said; *"It's Uncle Andy. I was sorry to have missed you. I would really like to catch up. Give me a ring back."*

"Who's Uncle Andy?" Harry asked. I remembered his furrowed brow, that look on his face, like it was so simple, that we had stumbled on something that everyone else had missed.

Later that night, by the time I had visited the hospital, I was already well down from my earlier high. I watched my mother wasting slowly away, thinner, as if she was being eaten from the inside out. I didn't think it was hard at the time. I couldn't believe it was happening to me, and to her. She had been so gregarious and so full of life. I know now that I was hurting myself to cope, that I was clinging on to something that was familiar. Many nights on the way back from being with her I bought a bottle of cheap wine and drank the whole thing in an hour or so watching the Amy Smith disappearance story on the news.

24

ST ENDA'S, ENNIS

The thin man with the moustache turns to me and tells me that we have arrived in the town of Ennis. I snap back to the present. Men in dark jackets are ready to deliver a message with their fists. The smell of aftershave and leather fills me with dread. It is already in my mind that the number plates are probably cloned but what I have set in motion with Connor and Sean Gallagher has moved so quickly that I can't stop it.

"Stay in the car, don't come out, don't move until one of us comes back."

I nod. The glass in the rear is blacked-out so everything looks even darker. I can hardly make out the bungalow with its white-washed walls beaten grey with the rain. The men get out, rummage in the boot, then cross the road carrying long items covered in black material. Coming up the road I make out the shapes of the others approaching to join them. My stomach is flipping over and over. I feel sick. There's no noise, no traffic, just the hard pelt of raindrops on the sun roof.

I wait with only my own tepid memories for comfort. I try to think about Rosie, and this makes me smile, and then I feel guilty about the danger I am putting us in.

The windscreen wipers spring into automatic action and I jump because I'm so het up. I am breathing heavily, panting as if in labour. The door swings open and the thin man gets in next to me. He pulls up his balaclava.

"A vehicle is in the garage with those plates." He swings his head so that his eyes are only inches from mine. "Have you seen him before in person?"

"Yes."

"Face to face?"

"Of course."

"What does this fella, Uncle Andy, look like? What sort of age is he?"

"He's thirty-three years old, pretty muscular and fit." I haven't seen him in years, just a photograph from his appeal, so he could have changed. The tall man looks perturbed, rattled.

"You better come with me." He opens my door and I escape out into the rain. He runs with me, his sinewed arm slipped inside the warm crook of mine. We're out of step and out of sync, but I must move to his beat. I realise that I was locked inside the car. We are two ghosts slipping between the shadows of this country town. I don't even know this man's name. I am worked up, trembling, adrenaline is surging through my body. I feel so scared. What will I say to Uncle Andy? It's unbearable to think about all these years later. I only ever met him once. What I remember about him is his height, his assured physicality. He would not ever worry about someone overpowering him. I stop walking.

"No you don't, it's too late now." He pulls me through the open gate and into the back garden. I see a gnome with a little red hat being kicked over and smashed into a puddle under his boot. I'm starting to see what is happening here. It's not right. Have I been very stupid?

He pushes me inside, into a kitchen that is old-fashioned: a simple standalone cooker and a cupboard and a table with a turned-over teacup. A knife with jam and butter has slid off the plate onto the Formica tabletop. The thin man pushes me through and into the hallway. There are photographs in frames and I knock one off the wall, it's of a girl in her school uniform, and the tall man treads on it as I am trying to reach down to pick it up. The glass smashes across the child's face in the picture. He pushes me into the sitting room where an old man with white hair is tied to a chair.

His nose is bleeding in one single stream down over his white moustache, into his mouth and into the white stubble of his beard.

"Is this him?" A balaclava'd man turns the old chap's head towards me. He stutters and shakes. There is a tear in his eye.

"No!" They release the man's head and it wobbles back to the centre and he looks petrified. "It's not him!" I realise there is a light on me and one of them is filming me with his mobile phone. The whole thing is being filmed. The thin man pushes me back out and down the corridor. I hear voices.

"Have you had Andrew Marlow here?"

"Who?" the old man shudders.

"Andrew Marlow? An Englishman. Andrew Marlow."

"I've never heard of him," he says.

"When we leave, you sit there and you count to one thousand. You hear me?"

"Count to one thousand," the old man echoes.

"You feckin' tell no one about us. You open your mouth and you'll feckin' see us again another time."

"I won't tell a soul."

What horrors have I inflicted on totally innocent people? I am the kiss of death. The thin man pushes me out into the garden and through a door into the garage. I'm still being filmed. The car sits there with the number plate on show. This car is an Austin Metro, and at least twenty years old.

"Is this the car?"

"No, it's not the car."

"Your fella has cloned the plates. Let's get out of here." He pushes me in front of him again and in seconds I am out onto the road. It's still raining. He opens the door and shoves me inside.

The driver starts the car. The other guy slams the boot closed and jumps into the passenger seat. We pull away. They take off their balaclavas. I see the shapes of the other men disappearing down the road as quickly as we arrived. We must have been there no longer than five minutes.

"What a shambles," says the thin man.

"Fuck, fuck, fuck!" I scream as I bang my fist against the back of the driver's seat. This poor old man in Ennis having tea and jam. I have sent these men to terrify the wrong man. What have I started? What have I set in motion?

TWO DAYS IN DUBLIN

Two days later Rosie, Katherine and I drive to Charleville, a small town a short distance away, but over the border in County Cork, to catch the Dublin train. We have a train seat with a table and the sun streams through the window. It feels like we're escaping and the shroud of anxiety and shame that I've been wearing since well before Ennis begins to lift as soon as the train starts moving. The journey crosses most of the country in a diagonal line going north and takes almost four hours. It is so lovely to see more of Ireland. We are three runaways heading into the city.

Rosie has a packet of dog Top Trumps. She deals the cards. I move our water bottles to the side. Katherine is competitive with Rosie. They both love to play and it amazes me that Katherine spends so much time with her playing games. She's got so much more patience than me.

"Above average height," calls Rosie, and she wins the hand because she's got the Great Dane and that's the biggest dog of all. I still let her win like I did when she was small. I haven't ever stopped even if, I suppose, I should be playing her hard to teach her a lesson about losing, or to make her a better player. I just want her to be happy. Katherine often beats her and makes a big thing about it smiling, cheering and laughing. Rosie takes it well, and it makes her more determined.

After cards we play I Spy. We eat sandwiches. The carriage smells of digestive biscuits. Katherine offers Rosie her mobile phone to play a game on. I don't object. The poor kid hardly gets any screen time, and I realise I have started to say that every time she plays on a device. Katherine's going to meet with friends for dinner later and visit some old haunts. She says she hasn't been to Dublin for years and her friends are actually all from New York and have moved back home to Dublin like Kelly O'Hagan.

I told Kelly that I would need my invoice paying before I came to Dublin to talk about more writing, and it worked. The money arrived in Auntie's account. The relief of having cold hard cash in my hands has inspired me to think about buying all sorts of things. I fantasise about a keyboard for Rosie and toys and the best Christmas ever. But I know I should be careful.

I wasn't going to come. I hit the doldrums after Ennis. Uncle Andy is still out there, although I'm not really sure now whether it is him or Sean Gallagher following me and intimidating me. It could all be Sean trying to get this house sale through so that they can get on with building their waterworks for the dairy. But it could be Uncle Andy. I don't know which. But my bank accounts being frozen, being locked out of every email, every online account being altered and changed started before any of this with Sean. But did it start before I knew I had inherited the house? Sean might have known I would inherit the house before I even did.

I had expected Sean Gallagher to contact me but he hasn't. I expect that he is waiting it out and checking if that poor old boy in Ennis is going to keep quiet or make a fuss by reporting the incident to the police.

I have spent the last three days frantically scanning the news online for any stories about masked men in Ennis, but there is nothing. Not a single crime has been reported in Ennis in the last week, but I know different. Who was that poor man?

At the lough, too, there is quiet. The environment agency people all checked out and left. There will be fines and a report in time but it has passed and blown over. All that remains are some leaflets about water safety collated in a dispenser on the bar. They have erected signs around the village encouraging people to telephone an anonymous hotline if they suspect wrongdoing. Another reason for Sean Gallagher and his cronies to hate me.

At least they can never pollute the land again. We did a good thing. I should really feel proud of what I've done but the shadows loom large over me. I look out over lush green fields patched by hedgerows, the poisonous yew trees still green as every other tree loses its leaves. Is Uncle Andy really out there or not? Or is it just my guilt? I suppose selling the house and allowing them to knock it down and build their treatment works is going to further help people. I'm running out of reasons not to sell. The ground on which I stand is getting more and more shaky.

"Do you think about your mum a lot?" Katherine asks. Rosie's eyes lift up off the screen momentarily and then flash back again straight away. She hears everything and mulls it over and stores it for future use.

"Yes." She's always with me, and my father too. "I think about them all the time. I might go a while and then something reminds me, a smell, being here, my aunt, or Rosie." I start to well up straight away, feel the ache in my throat, the sting of tears wanting to come. I wipe my eyes to keep them away. I'm not used to talking about my parents anymore.

"I'm sorry."

I remember the one thing that really drew me to Katherine

when I was sixteen was that she had no parents, and meeting her so soon after losing my dad was like meeting a long-lost twin. She didn't have to talk about her grief; it was etched into her face. It was in the tone of her every word. It was the full stop in every conversation.

"What about you?"

"Yes, me too, but it's so long ago that it's detached from my real life now. It's just a feeling of sadness. I'm back living in their house; I still use my mum's plates and cups. It's still as she left it."

I nod. I wait a moment to respond, I want to acknowledge what she has told me; it rings so true for me. "It still feels raw about Mum, like she's still here, or like I didn't grieve properly at the time. I was pregnant, you know, when she died."

"I know. I came to the funeral."

"I remember." I do remember but there was so much happening and I was the centre of everyone's grief. People shaking my hand and holding me, they transmuted all of their feelings for Mum onto me that day, and in those weeks. I realise that when you are synonymous with the person who died everyone tries to cling on to you because it keeps that person alive, but you are not them, and slowly they fall away. I felt so self-conscious walking through the church with everyone looking at me. I saw Katherine there, in the background, she was there for me and me alone, that I knew. How far had she travelled? Was she back from America anyway, was it just coincidental timing?

"Were you back from the US anyway?"

"No, I flew back from New York when I heard that she died. Pat called to tell me. I thought you might need a shoulder to cry on," says Katherine.

"Oh." I'm taken aback. I wished I had known.

"But you were with David."

Silence rings through the carriage. A sly look at me from Rosie. The hypnotic somnambulant sound of the train moving across the country. Yes, I was with David. I had a choice to make and I made it.

Can you imagine the stark reality of being all alone in this world, the only person that you really and truly love dying slowly in front of you. And then, very suddenly in tandem to such pain, you are presented with this tiny thing, inside you, a doctor congratulates you, a baby is growing. Your baby. A little you. A little Mother. A chance of new life, someone to love and someone to love you. Not a fleeting, we meet, we separate, we remember, or a friend – I'm talking about a mother's love for her child and the love that a child has for her mother, unquestioned, just absorbed by osmosis until one day it isn't there anymore and the child can never ever be the same.

There in my belly was my hope and my future. Forget work. Forget Julian. Forget the newspaper. I was growing my family inside of me. Nothing would stop this. It was fate. At my mother's deathbed I showed her a small and grainy black-and-white image of her granddaughter. You could clearly see the outline of her face, a little nose, the plump outline of her lips. I thought I saw my mother smile, but the real reason I know she knew is that she died that night. Of all the nights, she died *that* night. After holding on for so long, she was safe in the knowledge that I would be okay. She knew that Rosie was on the way for me and she allowed herself to finally leave me.

When the nurses told me it was happening, I telephoned David and he came straight over and was there holding my mother's hand when she finally passed away. After her body quietened and went cold, we placed her hands together and shut her eyes. The nurse brought tea in a white teapot with matching cups and some ginger nut biscuits (weirdly, Mother's favourite) on a plate, and David and I drank tea and ate biscuits. I told him about her and what she was like before all of this. I steeled myself to ring and tell Auntie, and David told me to finish my tea first and talked about whether to wait until the morning or ring now at 3am and we decided that she would want to know straight away, in the middle of the night. I left my mother's bedside with my new family: David and the baby growing in my womb. I melded my grief into becoming a mother myself, both things were one and the same, neither existing on their own, the whole thing altogether. I left for my new life, and I had hope, in spite of all that pain, I had hope.

We arrive in Dublin, Heuston train station. The light is thinning now, stretching out across the platform. There's a huge Christmas tree with beautiful white bright baubles. It's the first that I have seen this year. Katherine steps out, followed by Rosie and as she sets her small foot down onto the coarse cement platform, she says, "My first step in the capital city of Ireland!" We both smile proudly at this wonderful little kid.

"What shall we do first?" The answer is that we walk, we walk and we absorb the city. Katherine has booked a hotel in the centre of Temple Bar, the buzziest, most touristy part of Dublin, indicating that we are all three mere tourists here. Katherine tells Rosie she left Ireland for New York City when she was only twenty years old and so she never really visited Dublin, she was either too young to come, or had already moved to America. Rosie wants to know what America is like. She has seen it in the hundreds of films and television programmes she has watched in her short lifetime.

"What is America really like? Is it like this?" She walks along the River Liffey hand in hand with Katherine from the station to the hotel. There's a low-slung sky of clouds in grey of every shade. The Liffey is still and reflects the buses and buildings at its flanks. There's a succulent ring of green moss at the high tide mark. "I thought Ireland was all countryside!"

"You've been to Limerick City, right?" Katherine asks. Rosie nods. "So Dublin is even bigger."

"She's from London, though, innit," I joke with Katherine, "so, she's not easily impressed."

"Well, every big internet company is here, from Facebook, Microsoft, Netflix. You watch Netflix, don't you?"

"Of course I do!" Rosie says.

"They all have their head offices for the whole of Europe right here in Dublin."

"Very low corporation tax," I say.

"What's corporation tax?" asks Rosie.

"Really boring," says Katherine.

"It's a small percentage of a company's profits that they pay to the government for schools and hospitals and other useful things like street lights and the police," I explain.

"Oh, I did not know that!" says Rosie, processing tons of data. "Katherine, do you pay tax?"

"I try not to," she says.

"Katherine!" I turn full socialist. "We all need to pay tax to make sure everything keeps running properly. And we're happy to pay for it."

"What about your tab? Do you think you could pay your tab before you pay your tax?"

"What's a tab?" Rosie pipes up.

"Where you have an account with a shop," I say.

"Or a pub…"

"To pay for things when you can't afford to," I say. My tax bill is the very last worry on my mind.

We get to the hotel where Katherine has booked two rooms next door to each other. Rosie and I have a little balcony on which there are two metal chairs and a table. It faces out onto the busy thoroughfare of Temple Bar below. Katherine apologises, suggesting that we should have chosen somewhere quieter, but Rosie loves it. The wrought-iron railings have been artistically sculpted into an abstract pattern. Below, the street is alive. There's the sound of drums carving out a pulse. A bass guitar echoes deeply in time to flashing fairy lights that I glimpse in the window of a bar. There's so many voices, the hum of conversation, a bark of laughter, even in the middle of the afternoon. There is a Spanish accent, tourists chat while a motorbike speeds by. The street is lit by signs, welcoming orange lights in pub windows, and a huge screen showing sport. How are we ever going to sleep?

I notice the time. I've been worried all day that I would be late and now I need to get going. It's already after 3pm so I have to dash to get across town to my meeting with Kelly. I leave Katherine and Rosie in the hotel. They tell me they are going to have a look around and maybe even have a game of pool. I call a taxi from reception and reapply my lipstick. I'm dressing in the smartest clothes that I have. I arrange to meet them back in the room at 6.30pm so that Katherine can go off and meet the friends she's arranged to see, and Rosie and I will have dinner. When I get in the taxi I realise it's a five-minute walk but the taxi driver takes me anyway, charges me eight euros, which I think is very reasonable, and I'm early for my meeting.

I duck into a post office and select a Dublin postcard, a photograph of the river, and I buy a cheap biro and a stamp. I remember the address of the man in Ennis. I feel awful for him. I can't bear to think of him worrying about what happened, thinking that they might come back. I want to disguise my identity, but I want to reassure him. I want to send him money but I don't have any to send. I can't write with my left hand, so I think, sod it, and write him a note:

Dear sir, I must apologise and let you know that you were the subject of a terrible case of mistaken identity. You are under no threat to your well-being. Please forgive me. *I send you my warmest regards for your health and safety.*

I linger in front of the green post box knowing this is a silly thing for me to do, and yet the right thing for me to do. I don't sign it. I post it. Done.

2 6

THE JOURNALISTS

The newspaper office is your standard glass modern media office with a huge classic clock outside. I ask for Kelly, fill in a form and get a badge, and then there she is emerging from the lift in a beautiful green knit dress, beaming, giggling in fact.

"Who'd have thought it? Us in Dublin!" Kelly is a fearless journalist. I've seen her stand up for herself and get balled out on numerous occasions. She is extremely bright. You never have to explain something twice to her, she's always a few steps ahead. She reads between the lines, like whatever we are being told, she asks, "What is the real story here?" She is completely unassuming. It's her superpower. She enables people to let their guard down and then she strikes. She was taught by the best, and the best was me.

Kelly's default setting is friendliness. I trust her, of course I trust her. I trust her as much as the next person who worked under Julian. We embrace like long-lost family members. I even feel a sentimental tear in my eye. We hug and part, still holding each other as if to say, *We've been through a lot together, you and I.* I feel like I want to say that, but I don't. There might be more for us to go through together yet.

She takes me up in the lift to the third floor and when we emerge there is a jolly sort of vibe. It's late in the day but the news hour has passed. People are more relaxed and looking to plan for the following day. She introduces me to some staffers, some of who I admire having read their work. Then we move to a meeting room where I'm ushered in to sit at a large boardroom table.

"I usually finish at 4.30, but Kieran is picking up the boys." She met her fiancé in London at The Swan in Stockwell. He worked in construction and used to come out boozing with us back in the old days.

"How's Kieran?"

"He's grand. He's got his own building firm now. He's doing really well. He's great with the boys. But you are not here to talk about Kieran! Let me buzz Mr O.B." Mr O.B. is Terence O'Brien, the editor of the newspaper. Kelly picks up a receiver and puts in a call to Terence's secretary and is told that he is on his way. "He won't have long but he really wants to meet you."

He walks in. He must be nearly seven feet tall and as thin as a rake.

"Welcome, welcome, welcome." I recognise his voice from radio and television, where he is regularly interviewed about the big stories. In a way he's an Irish Julian.

"It's lovely to meet you, sir." I shake his hand. Hard to know whether to call him sir, Terence or Mr O.B.

"Likewise, my dear. Now, I don't have long, and I apologise for that. I am being summoned for dinner by the Taoiseach."

Kelly smiles and gets up and takes a cold bottle of water from the fridge.

"You need to go!" I say.

"I do indeed. When powerful men have their fancies we must jump and see what it is all about, mustn't we? So, to cut to the chase, Doll, we really loved the story that you gave us, so thank you."

"No, thank *you* for the opportunity."

"Well done, Doll," Kelly agrees.

"I hope you like what we did with it, and I hope you feel that we made a big enough splash. We wanted to push back to you that we needed more for the story, and by God, Doll, you brought us more. It was a very impressive investigation. Congratulations."

"You are too kind, Terence."

"And we want you to write more, which is over to you, madam." He signals to Kelly. "Kelly knows better than me what we are looking for so I'll bid you my adieu. Next time we will go to dinner, so let's make sure that is in my diary." We stand up and shake hands again and he is gone.

"And that's it?" I ask Kelly, but Terence pops his head back around the door.

"One last thing. Why don't you want to write under your own name?"

"It was a local story and I didn't want to drop my aunt in it."

"This is rural Ireland we're talking about, everyone knows everyone's business, so what's the real reason?"

I pause. I'm not telling him the real reason, that I'm in hiding.

"I'm getting a divorce," I say. "I don't want to look like I'm working."

He pauses to evaluate my response and then looks at Kelly and they nod.

"I really prefer reporters to write under a name. It gives us clarity and transparency. We're a little different to the UK in that regard. So will you think about it? Perhaps a pen name? Something consistent."

"I'll take that on board."

"Have a good evening now." He walks out of the meeting room. There he goes, another 'guvnor', another man to lord power over me. Is it my ego sitting here in this meeting or my soul? What am I even doing here? Why not just stop? Kelly bends down into the fridge and brings out a bottle of wine.

"Pinot? Just a little glass?"

"Just one then." I really want to get back to Rosie. What if someone followed us? Someone could be watching Katherine. No, I'm being stupid, paranoid, everything is going to be fine.

"It might feel like a waste of time to have just five minutes with Mr O.B., but he likes to see the whites of people's eyes."

"You've done so well, Kelly. You should be proud of yourself."

"I learnt from the best, Doll."

"Do you ever hear from anyone else?"

"God, no. I got out just in time. I dread to think what I might have been caught up in had I stayed any longer. What about you?"

"David, obviously. I did see Julian recently."

"That bastard! Great editor but such a bastard!" Kelly tops up my glass. "It's hard to believe he got through all of it unscathed. The way that he threw that fella under the bus, the investigator, what was his name?"

"Harry."

"That's right, Harry. He went to prison; he took all of the blame. But he got paid a fortune for it."

"Three hundred grand, supposedly."

"But what happened to him inside? Something happened to him, didn't it?"

"He was assaulted in prison."

"That's right, wasn't it something to do with Amy Smith's uncle, Andrew Marlow, or Uncle Andy as he was known, right?"

"Apparently so," I say, but I know all about it. I know every tiny detail, it's imprinted on my brain.

"That shouldn't be allowed, why on earth was he held in the same facility?"

"Different crimes. Harry was charged for phone hacking offences, technically nothing to do with Uncle Andy."

"Then why did Uncle Andy attack Harry?"

"Because he worked for the same newspaper that had ruined his life."

"I wonder what Harry told him?"

I want to change the subject. I know that she's fishing about my involvement, she wants to know how I got away scot-free.

"He was only held on remand at Wormwood Scrubs for two weeks and then he was supposed to be moved to Suffolk."

"But he's been in nursing care ever since, right?"

This is what my nightmares are made of. Harry said he'd never tell anyone about my involvement but under duress, his life under threat, I know that he gave me up. At some point in HMP Wormwood Scrubs over the course of two weeks, Harry admitted to Uncle Andy what we had done. He told him who the real Claire Halliday was; who I was.

"Uncle Andy gave me the creeps. I don't care if he didn't murder his niece, he's the type of man who is going to murder someone, and the attack on Harry proves it," Kelly goes on.

"I better get back." I stand up in panic, knocking back the rest of the glass of wine. All this talk of Uncle Andy makes me jumpy.

"You did the world a favour getting him locked up, Doll. It was only a matter of time before he did somebody damage."

I try to hail a taxi but it is rush hour, so I run the mile or so back to the hotel. It's raining and I have no umbrella, and no raincoat. I haven't run in ages. I'm out of shape so I puff and pant, get a sheen of sweat on my forehead. I know the way, kind of, but not really. I don't know the centre of Dublin, I've rarely been here. Only a few times to see Connor when he was at university but it was a blur of pints and parties. I follow my nose and make my way back, but increasingly I am paranoid that Uncle Andy is here and that while I've been with Kelly he's got to Rosie. He's either got into the hotel room, or grabbed her while they walked through reception. Or worse he has lured her from Temple Bar. He's bundled her into the back of a van.

By the time I turn into the busy street where our hotel is I am drenched. Rosie. Rosie! I bang straight into a man's back outside a pub.

"Sorry, love!" he says and I speed past him. "Don't worry I didn't spill a drop!" I glance at him and he's holding up a glass.

I run into the hotel lobby looking around me. I should have got a phone, a pay-as-you-go Irish number. I'm so stupid, so selfish. I'm ruining Rosie's life. I run to the reception desk.

"Can I help you?" asks the lady behind the counter.

"Have you seen the woman in room 420? A woman and a little girl?" I blurt out, as the receptionist shakes her head.

"I've just started actually, so I could phone up to her room?"

I'm already rifling through my handbag for the keycard and heading for the lift. I get inside. It's tight, claustrophobic and unduly small for a hotel of this size. I tug at the neck of my jacket, look up at the harsh strip lights in the ceiling. Why is it taking so long?

At the hotel room I hit the keycard on the door. It barks a red light at me and won't open. He's hacked the hotel system. He's locked me out of the room. He's taken them and changed the locks. I do it again. It turns green and the door opens. There's a fierce wind streaming through the window, blowing the curtains wildly. What's that outside on the balcony? Two figures. I fight my way through the drapery.

"Mummy Doll!" shouts Rosie.

"Hi!" I'm out of breath, and deranged. I open my arms for a cuddle. She runs into my embrace and I hold her and I start to cry.

"What's the matter?" She wipes my tears with her fingers.

"I'm just so happy to see you."

"Did you see our bubbles?" asks Katherine, blowing a big one with a plastic stick and tube of liquid. I realise they've been blowing bubbles over the balcony and out into the street so that I might see them. They are floating down and popping over the road.

"We've seen an amazing American burger place across the road and we're going to go there tonight!" shouts Rosie. "It does milkshakes!"

"I think Katherine is going out with her friends tonight, Rosie, but that's okay, we can go."

"I changed my plans," says Katherine. "I'm not meeting my friends anymore. Can I come with you two, if that's okay?"

"Yes! Please, Mummy? Can she?"

"Of course she can," I say, my cheeks flushing.

Later, after we eat and go for a stroll and the drama of my swirling mind has calmed and let my worries float away a little, Rosie goes to bed. I double lock the door and Katherine and I sit side by side on the balcony. I leave a gap in the curtains so I can see Rosie sleeping. She takes a little while to settle, calling out to me and I go to see if she's okay, and I kiss her and tell her to go back to sleep.

Katherine brings out a blanket and a bottle of red wine that she got from an off licence down the street. We hear the music from a bar below. We absorb the energy of people partying. We are wrapped up snugly together. I can feel her body next to mine. I wait for moments where her skin brushes against mine.

"What's it like living in New York?"

I'm thinking it's like this only more, so much more: more sirens, more energy, and more buzz. Danger lurks around every corner. Excitement bubbles up underneath New York's streets. I wish she could show me. What I really wish is that we could go back. Go back to being eighteen years old and I would run away to New York with you, Katherine. We would listen to The Cranberries and U2 until our ears bled drums and guitars. I want to run across frantic streets with you, five cars deep, taking your hand and weaving, bobbing, and landing breathlessly together on a New York sidewalk. I want you to show me, Katherine, show me the Statue of Liberty. Show me the twin towers, because in my dreams they are still there.

Show me it all and at the end of the day buy me strong drinks in a cheap bar where I'll laugh so much I have to spit out my liquor. Boys will try to chat me up, and you too of course, because of your blue eyes and small waist and because you are so beautiful, and sometimes I will dance with them, but my eyes will never leave yours. Nor your eyes mine. And later, after all this, we'll steal away and you'll take me back to your digs, a small room in a shared house with a view of a brick wall and flimsy metal fire escape, and we'll slam the door closed behind us, and with one candle to light our way, melt together under the blankets, your touch on my skin as welcome as the sun's rays on a cold day.

"Are you in trouble?" Katherine asks, her face illuminated by a neon sign across the road. She is so close I can see the pixelation in her irises; I can see inside the fabric of her.

"Yes." I can't lie to her.

"Is it to do with your husband? Or your work?"

"Both."

"Is it someone you've upset in the past by writing a story?"

"Yes."

"Tell me," she says. "You can trust me."

I do tell her. I tell her everything.

27

THE HIGHS AND LOWS OF A
CAREER IN JOURNALISM

I wake with Rosie twisted around me; her legs are pinning me to the bed. She is growing longer all the time. Her soft olive skin is perfect. A beautiful, determined child. A gift that I don't deserve. She's too big to be sleeping in my bed every night but she has plenty of time to sleep alone. I love it, I love cuddling her, I think mums these days are meant to feel guilty about that. Maybe I need her love just as much, or even more than she needs mine. I lift her legs off me and sit up straight in bed. I said too much last night to Katherine. I can't trust her. I might get her into trouble too.

There's a jaunty knock at the door. I hope it's Katherine. I know it is but I still worry that it's someone else. She might have left me here. She might have called the police. But the style, the feel of the knock, is Katherine all over. I ask who is at the door and she announces herself to reassure me.

"It's me, Katherine." I move the chair that I've wedged up against the handle and open the door. How do we greet each other now? Now that there are no secrets. Now that she knows what I have done.

"I couldn't sleep, thinking about everything." She hands me a coffee in a beige paper cup. It's hot. "I went down and sat by the river."

"This is not your problem. It's my problem. I don't want to involve you. I've said too much."

Rosie turns over in the bed and whispers, "Mummy Doll," and lets out a long fart. Katherine starts laughing and I do too.

"Mummy, why are you laughing?" Rosie says, waking.

"I'm not, darling, I'm just letting Katherine in."

"Good morning, Rosie."

Rosie sits up and I flick on the television with the remote control.

"Shall we make more bubbles?" Katherine sits on the end of the bed and takes the remote control to flick through the channels.

"I thought we could go to the museum?" I say.

"Is it like the Natural History Museum?"

"I think so."

"I go there at home, a lot. I love it. So if it's like that then I will really like it."

I wipe a sheen of white dust from a plum and hand it to Rosie and open a packet of chocolate brioches. I give one to Rosie, and then as an afterthought I offer one to Katherine.

"I'm not really hungry."

I raise my eyebrows at her and she changes her mind and takes one. She bites into its soft and buttery flesh. I take Rosie's water bottle into the bathroom to fill it with fresh cold water because she'll need a drink with the brioche. She doesn't like it if the water's 'not fresh' and screws up her face in disgust.

"Don't get chocolate chips in the bed," I say, because it happens a lot and they're a pain to get out in the wash. I can hear that Katherine flicks onto the news. It's British news, the BBC news channel. I can hear the presenter talking and it feels triggering. It's like home and it makes me feel very far away from home hearing it here. I can hear what he is saying and I swear that I hear him say the name, Julian Harper. It stops me cold.

"Doll," Katherine calls to me. "Doll!"

"One sec.'" I twist the lid back onto the bottle and dry it with a towel. Katherine is at the bathroom door.

"Doll, isn't the guy that came to the bar called Julian Harper? Your old boss?"

"Why?"

"He killed himself. It's on the news."

"Turn it off, I don't want Rosie seeing that."

"Sorry."

"Turn it off!" I scream.

I go quietly onto the balcony while Katherine and Rosie watch cartoons. Katherine watches me, she's rigid with fear and apprehension, frozen with the realisation that I'm up to my neck in shit. I've taken her mobile and I plug in her earphones and listen to the news. Reading between the lines this is what I gather: Julian Harper has killed himself in woodland near his house on the Wentworth Estate. *His body has been recovered from woodland* is popular media shorthand for, *has hanged himself.* Except of course, Julian would never kill himself.

The Wentworth Estate has cameras, security and all manner of exclusive benefits for residents. Nevertheless, anything is possible for someone like Uncle Andy, he was so tech savvy even ten years ago. In my last conversation with Julian only a week ago he told me he had a new girlfriend and a new job in America. He had everything going for him. This was the best time of his life when, finally, he would get the fame he believed he deserved. There is no way he would kill himself. Uncle Andy has got to him.

Katherine comes outside and places her hand on my shoulder. I just wish we could be somewhere safe in another world, where we could talk and be together and not have to worry about this. Her hand feels so amazingly perfect on my shoulder. I feel bad for liking it so much. I must have a screw loose for thinking about Katherine's hand with everything that's going on. I feel guilty. I should tell her to go away and leave me alone. It isn't right for us to be so close. I should save her, but I desperately want her on my side.

"You're going to go to the police," she says.

"He would never kill himself."

"Let's take Rosie to the museum, show her a nice time, then we'll get the train back and we'll go to the police tomorrow morning and tell them what you told me."

"You think so?"

"I know so. You can't sit around waiting. For Rosie's sake. These are Irish Gardaí so you're not going to get extradited to the UK. No one's going to give a shit. I don't even know if what you did was a crime. Immoral, yes, but a crime?"

The museum is wonderful and Rosie loves the huge dinosaurs. She runs a comparison algorithm with the Natural History Museum in London, which she considers to be her museum. By 2.30pm we're on the long train home. I pretend to be content and happy. I was expecting to feel more fearful but I'm beginning to feel hate now for Uncle Andy and the way he is playing cat and mouse with me. I am sure he is coming after me. We play a few rounds of dog Top Trumps. I let Rosie win, Katherine beats Rosie, and then we fall quiet. Rosie draws a picture of her time in Dublin, and then a detailed portrait of Katherine's face. Katherine stares at me and flicks her eyes away, and I wonder if she's thinking that perhaps she doesn't know me as well as she thinks she does after all. I hope I haven't blown it. But either way I am in no position to start something so ridiculous, so new. I'm married, well, separated, and so is she. We're just runaways looking for distraction, aren't we?

Here's what I told her on the balcony in the hotel. This is the real version and not the slightly sanitised version that I gave to Katherine, where I diluted my decisions so as to not appear as callous, as competitive and as immoral. Because, for whatever reasons, at one point in my life I was like that.

I told Katherine about the time immediately after we had discovered Uncle Andy. It was the day after the car park in Kent, and Harry and I had returned to the office to discuss our findings with Julian. I was hungover as usual. Mother was stable so that was one good thing and I clung to it, kept turning it over in my mind. Perhaps she would start to improve after all? If she improved and could move back home, I could settle down at work, and start exercising and being healthier and then I could turn my life around.

But in Julian's dark office, with the blinds drawn shut and the whispered voices, the pressure was very much still on. Harry had performed his bit in collating the information and the butterflies in my gut told me that something was off with Uncle Andrew. A cursory check had informed me that he was Amy's uncle through marriage via her stepmother. He was slightly removed from the core family. Amy Smith's parents were divorced and her father had a new wife, and Andrew Marlow was the stepbrother of the stepmother. So there was no blood connection and very little connection during day-to-day life. I was at the start of my investigations and at that point did not know how he featured in the family and if they were close. The only evidence was that he telephoned Amy one month before her disappearance asking to meet up. I had become extremely obsessed with his message, playing it over and over and over on my headphones.

'It's Uncle Andy. I was sorry to have missed you. I would really like to catch up. Give me a ring back.'

It made my skin crawl. I transcribed the message looking for the undertone, looking for the nugget that I was missing. His voice was flat, slightly nasal and monotone with a generic south east of England accent. There was no rise and fall, no natural music to his flow, no high notes to accentuate friendliness, to curry favour.

"The police must have looked at him?" said Julian, striding around his office then tinkering with the cord from the blinds. "Harry, find out if the police have looked at him."

"They have, and he was out of the country. Came back from Spain three days after she went missing."

"Right, well that's pretty much him in the clear then," said Julian. "Unless he's made up an elaborate alibi to remove himself from suspicion." He perked up and sat down on the edge of his desk, a sign of his excitement.

"The police will have thoroughly checked that out," Harry said.

"There's something not right about that message," I said. "I can't put my finger on it."

"We accessed his record and he was accused of indecent exposure when he was sixteen. No charges were made," said Harry.

"Could be nothing. Could be something," said Julian.

Andrew Marlow would have been twenty-seven years old at the time of Amy's disappearance. I would come to know that

Uncle Andy was extremely immature emotionally and that he empathised with people much younger than himself. He saw himself as a teenager.

"Harry, tell him the rest," I said.

"He's got a breaking and entering for which he was cautioned at age seventeen. He was trouble for sure in his teens and he then joined the army."

"I didn't think you could join the army if you had a caution," I said.

"Yes, they love it. The rehabilitation of offenders is what they do best," said Julian.

"So he's done, what, eight years in the army and left around three months ago and hasn't been employed since."

"Personal life?" asked Julian.

"His mother died two years ago. His father is alive. The link to Amy Smith is through the father's second marriage. Marlow's living alone in his mother's house in Chatham, Kent."

"Employment?"

"Qualification in coding, he's done an evening course in college. He's a computer geek and did communications training in the army, so more computers and tech, and no job at the moment. And he's a fitness fanatic."

"What I think is interesting is understanding Amy's relationship with him, after all he did phone her. Did she ever meet up with him? What did they do together? What did they talk about? What sort of people might Andrew Marlow have brought her into contact with? Was he grooming her?" I ask.

"Well, I think we're going to need some more information, don't you?"

I was pleased with this response because it meant we had brought Julian the lead that he so desperately wanted. It was going to reflect well on me. "Good job. Let's keep this to ourselves, let's do whatever it takes to find out a bit more about Andrew Marlow." *Whatever it takes* meant by covert means.

I didn't go and see my mother that night. I went out with Kelly and the team to an event in Leicester Square. We got VIP entry to the after-party and we saw Tom Cruise and that's one reason why I'll never forget that night. But the main reason I can't forget that night is because it was when the evening paper, not ours, the *Evening Standard*, went with a story that Amy Smith was still alive. According to an unspecified source, it looked as though Amy had been accessing her voicemail box and deleting old messages on her telephone, giving hope to her family and to the police that she was alive.

Andrew Marlow was unhackable. He was one of the tiny minority of people who had changed the pin number on his voicemail box. There are ten thousand combinations of a four number code. Even at that time Harry and I speculated that he was a clever boy. He was part of a very small number of people who realised that their security was under threat.

His mother's house was on a nice tree-lined street on Seacroft Road. She had a large semi-detached post-war house with a drive and a twisting acer tree in the front garden. It looked really unusual and beautiful. At the end of the road was a pub called the Red Lion that Harry believed Andrew Marlow frequented. He'd scanned the Red Lion's website and found a photograph of a New Year's Eve party the year before, and a photograph of a familiar-looking man who he believed was Andrew Marlow. Harry thought this was his local. On the drive was an old Land Rover. The bonnet and right front wing had been resprayed a dirty khaki green, clearly a do-it-yourself job. There were two aerials, one huge and sticking up from the rear middle.

"Looks like CB radio," Harry said. "Luckily for us I've got one." He rummaged in the back of his Ford Galaxy and then set up the system.

"How can we tell when he's online?"

"On CB, you mean? Well, it's all about the antenna set-up, so from here we're about sixty metres away, and my antenna is relatively small, so it's only going to pick up local signals. If we pick up someone talking then it's most likely to be him or perhaps his local mates, or network of local CB radio enthusiasts."

"Really? How long is that going to take? Are we going to have to wait around?"

"Plus, we know what his voice sounds like. You go into Chatham and make yourself look pretty while I sort this out."

I stormed off down the road. It was a fifteen-minute stroll into Chatham town centre. I went to Boots and bought make-up, blue eyeshadow and pink lipstick, stuff I'd never wear in real life. In River Island I bought a pink slogan top, saying 'Choose Life', a rip-off of Wham!'s famous line, with a slash neck that showed off one shoulder and the strap of my bra. I bought a new bra too, as the one I had wasn't fit for purpose. I wondered whether to buy new knickers but I didn't as a safety precaution. I was not going to let things go that far. I bought tight jeans. I kept all the receipts for my expenses. My story would be that I had come down from London to go on a date and the bloke didn't show up and I was all on my own. I spun it around my head a few times. What was good was that it cut straight to the chase and made me vulnerable and desperate. Anyone would take pity on me. It alleviated any need for local knowledge that might trip me up. Of course, he might not fancy me. If he was into teenage girls, I would be like an old grandma to him. I got some cheap perfume, Tommy Girl. At least I would smell like a teen.

I went for a McDonald's. When in Chatham, after all. I got a Big Mac Meal takeout for Harry, it would be cold by the time I got back to the car but it's the thought that counts, after all. When I arrived back, Harry was listening to CB radio with large half-moon headphones.

"This is too easy," he said, biting into his Big Mac, lettuce and sauce falling from his mouth.

"What's happened?"

"I've heard him talking to his mates. They'll be in the Red Lion tonight at six."

28

THE RED LION

They played The Jam in the saloon bar. I sat alone at a dark wooden table that rocked. The tabletop was marked with pint rings, a remnant from whoever had sat there before. A cold breeze kissed my neck and I sensed it was my dead father, or even my mother's spirit from North West London telling me to stop this madness and come home.

But I still felt I was doing the right thing. If this guy was involved then I wanted to find the evidence that would implicate him, and this was the only way.

Suddenly Andrew Marlow appeared. The first time I saw him he stood quietly, very still, not moving. I was expecting over-the-top, over-familiar greetings with the bar staff, but it was not like that at all. He barely spoke. The barman pointed to a lager and Andrew Marlow whispered 'yes please' and that was that.

He was well over six feet tall. Completely bald, a fine blond stubble glowed like a halo around his head. I guess you'd call it a buzz cut. He was lean but muscular. As he lifted his arm, I could see his muscles engage at the back. He wore black cargo pants with pockets, like army trousers only black, and a black T-shirt.

It was pretty cold that night but he had no coat. He wore desert boots.

You know that saying, *I wouldn't like to run into you on a dark night?* Well, it was made for Andrew Marlow. He was good-looking with a great physique but somehow wrong. There was an air of menace about him.

Harry came in as agreed and bought a pint at the far end of the bar and then sat at a table alone, reading the sports pages of our newspaper. When I saw them together, Andrew Marlow and Harry, Andrew looked much taller and more in shape. I wasn't entirely sure what kind of help Harry would be if it kicked off.

It was seven thirty already. So much for Harry's intel of six o'clock, but I still couldn't quite believe we were all in the same room together. What it boiled down to was that to keep my job I had to come back with a story. That's all. Somehow, from this bizarre set of events, I had to create front-page news.

I readied myself. I left my true self – the young me, the good me, the dutiful daughter – behind. I became this thing, this resourceful woman who wasn't fazed by anything. There was nothing that I couldn't do. There was no one that I wouldn't approach. I was confident, I had backing, I was making the news, I was on the inside of public life. It felt like I was inside the secret. I was special.

I stood up and went to the bar. I stood right next to Andrew Marlow. Honestly, I could smell him. It was a musky, manly smell. It was like I was falling under his spell. Why was he alone? Why was no one speaking to him? If he was a regular, where was the playful matey banter that went on in these kinds of places? I looked over and caught his eye. He looked behind himself, thinking that I must be looking at someone else.

"Are you on your own?" he asked. Honestly, that was the first thing he said and shivers ran up and down my spine. His voice was nasally, with a slow drawn-out speech pattern. Everything in my nature shouted, *run!* But I didn't skip a beat.

"I feel so silly," I said. "I was meant to be on a date but he hasn't shown up."

"You've been stood up. What time was he meant to meet you?"

I looked at my watch. "An hour ago. Oh, well."

Then there was a gap, half a minute of silence where it felt like that would be it, that we might not strike up a conversation at all.

"I'll buy you a drink instead then. To make it up to you."

I feigned a giggle. It's not very me, but anyone can flirt. "Okay then, why not!"

"What's your name?" he asked.

"Claire," I lied.

"That's a nice name."

"What's yours?"

"Andy. I've been stood up too. I was meant to meet my mates at six but they've not shown up."

I can't recall the whole conversation. It's a conversation that not many people outside of me, Harry, Julian and Andrew Marlow ever know took place. I'm not an actress. I don't believe that I'm a liar either. I was nervous as we talked and I think it came across to him as vulnerability. I was showing or acting out the most childish, and insecure parts of me. I knew Harry was nearby, watching me. I was a mirror. When Andrew Marlow asked me what I liked, I said the things that he said he liked: *Star Trek*, computers, exercise, aliens, conspiracies. Harry had found these listed on Andrew's Facebook profile. His eyes widened in disbelief at meeting someone who had more or less the same interests as him. I told him I was a nurse at Northwick Park in Wembley working on the stroke ward. This was the nearest to a bit of truth. I knew their schedules so well that I thought I would never be found out. There was more than enough to talk about.

He bought me a drink. His fingers were flat, squashed

fingertips with rounded fingernails bitten down to the quick. His mouth was red, with full lips for a man, they looked bee stung. His hair was not receding, it was shaved off completely out of choice, and I always find this a funny choice for young men when they'll spend most of their older lives miserably bald. Why not grow your hair? It makes me feel that it's tied up with aggression and control. From the outside he looked, dare I say it, attractive with his muscular arms and groomed appearance. When he sipped his beer a drop gathered on his bottom lip and he licked it with his tongue.

"I run 10k a day, every day, whatever the weather and wherever I am. I only drink once a week, but I always run. I love it. It gives me time to think, time to plan."

I watched how much I was drinking. I had to stay sober. Until he arrived, I drank Coke with a plan to say that it was rum and Coke. But I changed my mind when he bought me a drink and I asked for a lager shandy and it played into his view of me as young and vulnerable.

"Do you want to sit down?" He shot to the other side of the bar to get a stool for me to sit on. It was a heavy dark wood stool with battered red velvet upholstery. Andrew Marlow carried it in one hand.

"Thank you." I acted impressed and flattered at being cared for. "Don't you want to sit?"

"I like to stand." His T-shirt had been ironed. His arms were hairless, his knuckles, every surface of his displayed skin, was completely hairless.

"I'd love to have a CB radio," I said. "I bet the technology would be too tricky for me though."

"It would be a great way for us to stay in touch. If you want to stay in touch with me?"

I nodded, I won't say it was flirtatiously because there was a great deal of naivety and innocence in my performance so there was no overt flirting, if you like. But there was an intense eye connection. We spoke every sentence into each other's eyes.

"I could show you?" he said. "I only live up the road."

I mulled this over as if I was giving it true thought and weighing up the potential dangers of going back to the house of a strange man I'd only just met. I paused, not wanting to seem too keen and he seemed to read my mind, or what I pretended was going on in my mind.

"That's silly. I only just met you. Why would you come back with me? You don't know who I am, or anything about me. I could be dangerous." He stared into my eyes as he said this and it was the first time I saw the underside of his well-groomed appearance. There was a danger in what he said to me. He was telling me that he was dangerous. But the nuance was that it was kind of sexy. Something stirred in me for a second, not in the real me, but in the vulnerable nurse. Good, sweet and innocent girls like bad boys. Isn't that what society says? His question hung there for a moment. The atmosphere had changed. The pub had filled and I was aware of the noise of the bar, the drinks, the music, and people chatting raucously.

I glanced behind me and saw Harry had gone. I panicked a little and remembered the plan. He was going to be outside in the car. He would have eyes on me at all times.

"Okay," I said, like a little mouse being invited out of its hole by a big hungry tomcat.

"Come on then." He slid the empty glasses to the other side of the bar and helped me off my stool. It was the first time he put his hands on me. I'm not small by any means but I could feel the breadth of his hand span, the firmness of his touch around me. I did think, *what the fuck am I doing?* I had a moment of breathlessness, my limbs tingling, my stomach turning. I was walking into danger. I was going against every instinct in my body to run away. What the hell was I doing there?

Andrew Marlow's road was pretty with little gardens well tended by retirees, tidy fences and rose bushes. Andrew was incongruous on this street. He must have been the youngest inhabitant by a few years. The street had not yet been colonised by young families with prams. There was no risk of this part of Chatham becoming a hot commuter belt destination for young professionals working in the City. The pub served as a marker between Andrew's suburban post-war street and an altogether more desolate concrete estate with youths surveying from BMXs. I noticed an abandoned car with its windscreen missing and police tape around it at that end of the street.

Andrew walked me along the street. It is difficult to say that he walked me or even how he did that, but in my more vulnerable presentation he guided me with his hand on my elbow. He was in charge of where we were going and at what speed. It felt fast. I felt like he didn't want people to see.

"You're very pretty." It was odd and out of the blue, on our walk from the pub to the house. I couldn't see Harry but I was praying that he was where he should be. That he hadn't had a heart attack from all the cocaine he did and was lying slumped in the toilets of the Red Lion. The night was definitely getting more weird.

Andrew's keys jangled as he took them out of his pocket. They were attached to his trousers by a thick metal chain. He dropped them. Perhaps he was nervous? They didn't fall to the floor, they just hung there from his trousers before he grabbed them up again.

The hallway was old, like my English grandmother's house. A swirly red carpet ran up the stairs. A rack of coat hooks housed his army jackets. I had the overwhelming urge to steal one of them but then I spotted, in between his things, an old-fashioned red coat. And then another, a rain mac in pale blue.

"Can I use your loo?" Now that I was inside I needed a breather, I needed a second to catch my breath and calm down, to prepare myself for what I must do next while I was in his house.

"It's at the top of the stairs." He watched me from the bottom. "Don't touch anything, will you?"

This was fucking freaky. He'd gone full weirdo in that one sentence and it told me everything that I needed to know about him. I had been right. He was Chatham's answer to Norman Bates.

"Of course I won't." I paused, and then locked myself in the bathroom.

I panicked. I looked around the bathroom at his mother's things. I imagined him out there waiting for me on the landing.

After composing myself, I headed back downstairs and he rushed me to the back room, where I, posing as Claire Halliday, pretended to be interested in computers. Harry's friend came to the door. The clock ticked and I installed the malware, nervously, hands sweating, as if my life depended on it. I managed to escape through the front door, making my excuses but not without his tongue entering my mouth. I ran, my feet tripping over each other in their haste until eventually I vomited in the street.

Harry's car pulled up. I wanted to cry, caught between exhilaration and terror.

"Doll, you've done it!" He was high on excitement. He slapped me on the knee three times in delight.

"I am never doing that again." I threw my head back and breathed.

"Did I see you being sick just now?"

It was warm in the car; I felt cocooned and safe. The relief made me weak.

"Yeah, I was sick. Nerves." My nerves were from fear of Andrew, and fear of myself, and what my life was going to be like once my mother died. I was the weird one. I was going to be the oddball living alone. I was already leading a deviant lifestyle.

Would people, did people already, judge me as harshly as I judged Andrew Marlow? Who gave me the licence to judge anyone else?

"Did he give you anything to drink?" asked Harry.

"No," I said, and Harry nodded, ruling out poisoning. He handed me a tissue.

"And that's weird, right?" I continued, wiping my mouth. "It's odd not to offer a guest a drink, like it's the first thing you'd do."

"Personally, I think giving you a spiked drink and then raping you while you were unconscious would be much ruder, but I'm old-fashioned like that, so let's count our blessings," said Harry.

"Do you think he's weird, Harry?" I asked, and Harry made a mumbling sound like a guinea pig.

"I couldn't tell from where I was. Let's see what's on his computer," he said.

But I knew that Andrew Marlow was abnormal. I was sure of it. If he wasn't involved with Amy Smith then there would be someone else. He was dangerous. What made me hate him the most is that he was lonely and grieving just like me. It was an awful, ugly mirror that I had held up to myself, and I had seen my future, and where I was headed. I saw Andrew stuck in time in his dead mother's house and I hated myself. That was my life. That was all that I had. I had nothing. If and when my mother died, I would have lived a wasted life. I pushed my head against the window and cried. I thought it was over, but this was just the start.

29

THE GARDAÍ

When Rosie, Katherine and I return home to Limerick we are cold and tired. Nevertheless, Katherine has phoned ahead to the guards and made an appointment for us to come into the gardaí station. It's the last appointment of the day and the garda has stayed back to see us.

"I'd offer you tea, but it's a bit late in the day." The garda is a young man in his late twenties, remarkably lithe and muscular. His wavy hair has been locked into place with gel. He looks at his watch again. There's something of Father Aidan about him. There's a loud rumble from his stomach. "Excuse me. I'm starving."

"I'm sorry it's so late."

Katherine and Rosie sit in the waiting room sifting through tourist literature.

"Sure, it's fine, but let's get on with it. What's the problem?"

"I'm going to sound paranoid, but I'm being watched, and I'm being threatened, stalked."

"I've seen the photographs through your door, I'm not surprised that you're concerned."

"As well as that, my mobile phone was bombarded with messages, my bank accounts hacked, my credit card, my email, my Google account, everything online has been hacked and is inaccessible to me."

"When did you arrive in Ireland, Doll?"

"The 31st October."

"And this happened since the article? Or before? The article was late November?"

"Both."

"So, isn't this about the newspaper article?" he asks, and I shake my head. "You pissed off a few people with that report, but I think most people in the community are really thankful to you for bringing this to public attention. I certainly am. But the timing? When exactly did this all start?"

"I suppose it started before I came to Ireland," I say, reluctantly.

"You'll understand that there's not a lot that I can do about online fraud carried out in London. I can report it and do the paperwork so you have a crime reference number but there's not a lot I can do," he says, but I desperately need his help, or someone's help right now.

"Listen, just like the story about the lough, some years ago I wrote a story in London that angered an individual who has been in prison. He's been released and I think he's coming after me."

"Who was sent to prison? The person you believe is now stalking you?"

"Yes."

"You have a name?"

"Andrew Marlow."

"You think he's in Ireland? Have you seen him?"

"Yes and no. I do think he's here, and I think I've seen him but I can't be sure."

"And you've notified the police in London?"

"No."

"You need to notify the police in London. I can contact them. They will want to gather evidence from your phone, computer and any other witnesses. Depending on the what they find, they might be able to get a restraining order, and in Ireland the equivalent is a safety order."

My phone was in the Irish Sea. My old computer was in London. What evidence would they actually have other than my say-so about what I thought I had seen?

"I'm going to give you some forms to fill in and I'll drop by your property tomorrow and have a look at your security."

"Thank you."

"What with everything at the lough, and now this, you're keeping me busy, Doll."

"I'm keeping you from your dinner."

How many bad decisions have I made in my life? I was bright-eyed and keen to live up to my mother's pride in me, her only child. I rode eagerly into a career beyond my mother's wildest expectations. But I wasn't prepared for what I had to do. I was not schooled in entitlement and the right to say no like people like Julian. Deep inside, I didn't feel that I was good enough to be there.

I was brainy, yes, and good at my job, but I never had the casual arrogance to defy those I perceived as my betters. In many ways a 'yes' person, an optimist, and I still am! I was inquisitive and I was challenging but really I believed I was there because of a few lucky doors hanging open, allowing me to slip through. I had been tenacious my entire life, and I thought it was this vow to *never give up* that had got me to where I was. It wasn't until I fell from grace that I realised how high I had once flown.

30

PATRICK POWER

Pat hobbles around behind the bar. His energy is masculine, dirty and rugged, an ex high-profile rugby player with a taste for beer and a good time. He never married. He had a serious girlfriend for years and years. Everyone knew her and loved her. She was tiny and slim with tight curls that hung around her face. Then suddenly the relationship ended. I didn't know Pat well enough to know what happened; he didn't feature in my updates from Ireland. My aunt never mentioned him. Pat's waistline grew. His beard grew, he became other, different, the kind of person that needs to be looked after.

My worry is that now he is starting to get better, will he need his sister to look after him anymore? And if he doesn't, will she leave and return to New York, to whatever job and whatever people are waiting for her there? She checks on him frequently, telling him not to do too much.

It has been like a holiday at times, and Katherine's my new holiday friend that I've just met. At other times it has been a nightmare. I'm running on cortisol and adrenaline. If I was back in my yummy mummy life in North London there would be life coaches who could confirm this for me.

Auntie is at my house next door. She'll be looking at Rosie's artwork and when that is done they will pull out the jigsaw from underneath the sofa. It's a *Star Trek*-themed jigsaw featuring characters from *New Generation*, which appeals to neither of them, but was procured from Connor during the time of no money. It is lovely, and I am so happy that Rosie gets to have that time with my aunt, but what I'm fantasising about is my own real mother in there doing that with her, and my heart aches.

"Have you written it?" Katherine asks, and what she's referring to is my first commission from the Irish paper, an obituary of the infamous British newspaper editor and television pundit, Julian Harper. A much longer piece in UK news reduced to a mere three hundred words here in Ireland. I mention his long-term wife, his children but not his girlfriend. When Kelly phoned we were still travelling back on the train. I was still in shock at Julian's death. Katherine was still in shock at the revelatory story I had confided in her about my time with Andrew Marlow.

I didn't tell her how alike Andrew Marlow and I were at that time. That if I was a man, I might have been him. I didn't tell her it was like looking in the most grotesque mirror and that it was the best thing that ever happened to me because when the chance came to completely transform my life, I jumped at it. Perhaps I wouldn't have if I hadn't spent that time with Andrew Marlow. My dad's death and my mother's stroke – these were turning points in my life, but those hours spent with Andrew Marlow one evening in Chatham changed me, myself, who I am.

"What happened to the girl? Amy Smith?" Katherine asks.

"Andrew Marlow's niece? Her body was found the following month, and then a year later someone on remand for another crime made a full confession."

"So it was never Andrew Marlow. He had nothing to do with it?"

"No." I'm still thinking that Katherine might see me as being evil and beyond redemption. But she knew the young me. She knew me before I could have ever even dared to be so deceptive, so sassy, so in control and daring. She knows the real me.

"So he's just a bit of a loser? Like Pat? It would be easy enough for someone to come and accuse Pat of some shit, and people would probably believe it. You could rifle through his things and find weird stuff, I'm sure."

"Of course not like Pat. Pat's just Pat."

"Only because you know him."

Pat probably is a bit of a weirdo and if something bad were to happen in his vicinity I am sure the police would look at him. Journalists certainly would.

"I can't write anymore."

"How long is an obituary? What's the correct length of a description of someone's life?"

"I don't know, I've never written one before. It's not my department."

Katherine sits down across the table from me. "How exactly would you describe your department, Doll?"

"Mainly, I sat at my desk from nine to five writing stories. It's not what you're thinking it was like. "

"Well it sounded pretty high-octane, full-on to me."

"Within six months of going to Andrew Marlow's house I was finished in journalism. They got rid of me."

"Maybe Julian did kill himself, you never know what's going on in someone else's mind, do you?"

"You're talking about me?"

"You're not like that anymore. You've said that a hundred times. Isn't it the biggest killer of men, though? Suicide? Maybe he couldn't live with himself after all the bad shit he'd done."

"Julian didn't have it in him."

"How do you know?" she asks.

"Now that your brother is on the mend are you going to go back to America?" I say, changing the subject.

"Are you going back to England?" she asks, and I shrug my shoulders. "I have to go back to New York to sort things, but I don't know whether I'll stay there."

I don't have anything left to hide. I don't want to keep secrets from her. I want her to trust me and so I begin to tell her what happened next to Julian, Andrew Marlow, Harry and I.

"I want you to know that I'm not a bad person."

Two days after I went to Andrew Marlow's house, Julian requested that I attend a meeting. The weather was getting better and there was a smell of spring in the air. Usually, my favourite time of year.

I knew that things were moving up a gear because once I arrived in the office I was taken upstairs to the top floor by Julian. This was the executive floor and I had never been up there before. It's where the bigwigs sat and where the owner and his family had a suite of occasional offices for when they were in the country.

I was ushered into the main conference room. A newspaper boardroom was still pretty boring but it was the most sophisticated room in the building. It had its own coffee machine, which at the time was special.

In walked a tall man with dark brown hair, he was rather dashing and very dapper. His suit was expensive, and his shoes too. He looked at me like I was a naughty child brought before the headmaster. This was the first time I met David, my husband and Rosie's dad.

David shuffled a stack of papers and told me to sit down. He explained that the company, and he was very careful to use the word *company*, as opposed to *newspaper*, had been contacted by the police in relation to Amy Smith's voicemail messages, and those of several well-known figures. I should sign the documents to protect myself from unwarranted police intrusion into my work and private life. I would be protected. It was a non-disclosure agreement, and knowing them, it was tight. I was being paid off for my ongoing silence.

It meant I could never disclose information in relation to covert news-gathering, nor could I ever refer to any individuals employed by the company to carry out such work. I read on. There were pages and pages of similar clauses and jargon.

"We are doing this to protect you. You will be bound by the document not to be able to talk about any of the work that you have done here, whether that is reporting or covert surveillance, and as a result you will be protecting yourself."

I listened to David explaining the reasons why, but I zoned out. I wondered why on earth I was there? What was I doing with my life to be in this situation? All I wanted to do was write stories. I couldn't say no. I couldn't object. I was being ordered to sign it and at the time it felt like I was being both silenced and protected, if that makes sense. I knew I was losing my rights but my future silence, I knew, would protect me from any repercussions.

When I signed it Julian patted me on the back like a good girl and we left the building in a black Mercedes bound for Harry's office: a tiny unit smelling of stale digestive biscuits on an industrial estate off the Old Kent Road. Julian was wearing a new aftershave, his pale skin prickled red in the cool air like a freshly plucked turkey.

Harry's unit made up part of the top floor of a steel distribution warehouse.

"Watch your step," said Julian, pocketing his mobile and bounding up the outer staircase like a public school boy on his way to the tuck shop. He rapped his knuckles on the front door. It was locked. Harry opened a slit to look out, his bloodshot eyes were like piss holes. He looked like he was coming out of a nightclub into the daylight. He opened the door wider and I saw that he was in the same clothes as two days before, the trousers creased and baggy.

"You could've had a shower, mate," said Julian.

"No time." Harry locked the door behind us. Inside, I stood on an empty pizza box. A half empty cafetière loomed dangerously atop some computer equipment. Harry pulled up two desk chairs and returned to what must have been his position for the last two days.

"Well?" Julian tapped his fingers.

"So much porn I've had to have a wank." He really was disgusting.

"For God's sake, Harry," I said.

"What kind of porn?" Julian asked.

"Unexpectedly run-of-the-mill. Cuckold, my friend with my wife type stuff. Nothing suggestive online, however, there are some photographs."

"Of?"

"Naked teenage girls," said Harry. "Want to see?"

"Bingo!" exclaimed Julian. "Show us a couple?"

The girls were teenagers, kneeling provocatively, revealing their small breasts, looking uncomfortable.

"I recognise the wallpaper in the background," I said. "That's his house."

"Well that would be a Category C offence in the production of indecent images," said Julian. "Any evidence that he sent them on?"

"Yes, I've seen one sent by email, brazen, not even secured," said Harry.

"So that's production *and* distribution," said Julian.

"He could be looking at a two- to three-year custodial sentence for that alone," said Harry. "And he's got some other weird stuff on his computer. War photographs. There's some horrible pictures: decapitations, beatings, really awful content."

"What else?"

On the screen the cursor moved in real time but Harry wasn't touching the mouse.

"That's him. He's doing an advanced coding course online right now with the Open University. Other than that he searches guns, bomb recipes, hunting knives, you name it. I'm going to be having nightmares for some time to come."

Andrew's coding expertise would become his key into so much disruption, giving him the tools to understand the back end of the internet.

"Work?" asked Julian.

"He's applying for jobs in IT, but I can see that he can hack into code. He knows what he's doing, more than me, there's hours of it, lines of code."

"Well done," said Julian, "this is powerful stuff."

"I've copied the entire drive. There's a lot of shit on here but we could redact photos, obviously shield the identities of these poor girls, and publish them in part before handing them over to police."

"We'll say we found a hard drive in the bins, and on examination of it we found the pictures."

"Do you think he's a murderer, Harry?" Julian asked.

"Could be. He could have got her to his house and something went wrong. Who knows, but whatever happened he is a weirdo, so I won't lose a minute's sleep about dobbing him in."

"He gives me the creeps," I said, the hair on the back of my neck standing up.

"One more thing. He keeps searching for a woman's name. Over and over again."

I knew what the name was going to be before Harry said it.

"Claire Halliday. A nurse called Claire Halliday at Northwick Park hospital. He's been searching for her all the time. It's an intensive search too, beyond the electoral roll. He's running the search at a deeper level, like I would. He knows what he's doing."

My blood ran cold.

Two days later a large and furious policeman cut a run through the centre of our office. His brows and forehead were like a huge rugged cliff, his top lip curled into a snarl. Smaller police officers followed, but when the door was slammed shut in Julian's office it was only the big policeman's voice we could hear.

The lift pinged, its doors opened and David emerged with a team of overly coiffured junior lawyers. I remember that David was wearing a bright blue tie as he walked through the office. I remember praying that I wasn't called in with the police. David knocked on Julian's office door and then opened it without waiting for an answer. There was shouting at first and many raised voices, and then just the firm drawl of David talking and talking.

The police eventually emerged from the office. It was late in the evening but there was a good number of people still around. We all, that's at least fifty journalists, bowed our heads and looked down at our desks, lest we made eye contact with anyone. Of course not everyone was as nervous as me, none of the other journalists were involved in the way I was. They had their own skeletons, I'm sure, but this story was all mine.

David escorted the police officers out of the building, ensuring they spoke to no one else. The gall of David! It was quite surprising.

The insolence of the corporation bossing the police around was breathtaking. This is what I was a part of. I was at the centre of arguably the most important event taking place in my country at that time. The large policeman swept by my desk. I was waiting for him to bang his hand on it and tell me that he knew what I had done. I could smell him, cigarettes and peppermint. In his hand, a plastic bag containing a yellow and black USB stick. The stick that I had supposedly found in Andrew Marlow's rubbish containing various files and a number of concerning explicit photographs of unidentified teenage girls.

The story was already written for the next day's newspaper, already being printed, and with an online version embargoed until nine o'clock in the evening. A carefully arranged set of briefings ensured that no one else could leak the story before it was printed. Briefings had been carefully arranged with the ten o'clock news bulletins on both main channels and *Newsnight*. Julian emerged from his office and sat in one of the reporter's swivel chairs near me.

"How did it go?" I asked, and Julian nodded and held a finger up to his lips for silence. He wanted to receive official notification from security that the police had left the building. Julian's feet betrayed his nervousness, tapping on the office carpet, bringing up large amounts of static energy. Then there was a swift rumble of activity. A security guard in a black bomber jacket with high visibility tailoring whispered into Julian's ear and Julian beamed like the devil.

"Well done, Doll, what a story!" It was one of the few occasions when Julian Harper hugged me; the scrawny crenellations of his ribs, juxtaposed with his fleshy belly pressed against my bust. I thanked him but I wasn't happy. I wasn't entirely sure. I was vacant. My mother was dying and Amy Smith was missing and I wasn't at all sure if what we had done was right, even if Andrew Marlow had anything to do with it.

"You've taken a weirdo off the streets. Whatever happens, hold on to that," Julian told me.

"Okay," I mumbled, but something didn't sit right even then.

"And your nickname for him, *Uncle Andy*, really is perceptive, Doll. It will chime with people. You're a clever girl."

Uncle Andy, the stepmother's stepbrother. The psychopath hiding in the family closet. I hated myself. I felt ashamed. I didn't see my mother that night. She never knew my part in the biggest story that I ever worked on. I was glad that she didn't know anything about it.

When the police arrested Andrew Marlow that night, purely by chance, he was parked outside Northwick Park hospital in Wembley. Later, in court documents that are a matter of public record now, he told police that he was waiting for his girlfriend. When confronted with the USB stick, he denied all knowledge. But when he was shown the photographs he said he thought the girls were older, essentially an admission of knowledge of the photographs. He challenged the police to provide the correct ages of the girls. Some time later he changed his story and alleged that he was sent the photographs by someone else and they were not his. But the surroundings were clearly his home and after a search of his house even more photographs of girls were found.

Andrew Marlow's face was on every front page for weeks, months and even years afterwards. His name and pseudonym, *Uncle Andy*, became part of British history. Overnight he went from total obscurity to become Britain's biggest bogeyman. His notoriety made famous around the world.

After his arrest there was no evidence to detain him in relation to Amy Smith. After three days he was released on bail pending court proceedings for Category C charges in relation to production and distribution of indecent images. Somebody had daubed *Paedo* on the front window of his house. Police later sent someone to remove it. There is footage of him being doorstepped by paparazzi and journalists outside his mother's manicured house. It's still available online. There was no one to help him or advise him or assist in making a statement. He was given a junior solicitor.

When a reporter blocked his entry through his own front gate, Uncle Andy picked him up and threw him across the lawn. The reporter pressed charges of assault that resulted in another arrest, this time televised from the house in Chatham. People in the Red Lion, where I had first met him, were interviewed. All of them said that he was a 'loner', and that he was 'strange'. They were all horrified to have such a monster living in such close vicinity.

The photographs were deemed to be a Category C possession of indecent imagery of children, and he was tried and sentenced to eighteen months in prison. Category C means no penetration. I've thought over and over again about whether those photographs were acceptable or not, and they weren't. And sometimes I even wondered whether Harry had put those photos there for us to discover. But of course, Uncle Andy had admitted it. The wallpaper was in his house.

Julian was interviewed on every TV channel. The story was a massive success and it gave Julian the opportunity to flex his powers on television, being spotted by bookers and invited to talk about what we could learn from Uncle Andy about sexual predators and other big stories.

But Amy Smith was not abducted and killed by her uncle. Twelve months later a convicted murderer, in prison on charges related to other crimes, admitted killing Amy Smith and provided details of where her body was. Uncle Andy played no part in the abduction and murder of his stepniece.

31

____

WORMWOOD SCRUBS

I work in the pub cleaning glasses. I don't need the money anymore but I like to be near Katherine while Rosie is at school. I write on my computer and make calls on the phone at the end of the bar. The radio hums. Katherine hums. She makes coffee in a special machine that she brought with her from America and the smell is sublime.

My mind works like a cycle of despair and hope. It's a broadcast of worry about Rosie. I believe that I'm ruining her life and that Andrew Marlow may hurt her. I think she should be seeing her father and her friends. What about her education? The one thing I always wanted for her was to keep her in the same school, surrounded by community. I see Andrew Marlow finding me, murdering me, murdering Rosie and even worse things than that. I have to stop myself. When I'm not with Katherine, I think about her. Mostly, I fantasise about being young again with Katherine and running away to New York, and then I feel guilty about Rosie and it merges into some sort of reality fantasy where Rosie and I both go to New York with Katherine.

All Katherine wants to do is talk about Andrew Marlow. My

mind is so parched that I can't think straight about what I've told her and what I've omitted from my story.

"You framed an innocent man." She shakes her head, despairing. "Don't you feel bad?"

"I do feel bad." But I actually don't because he's a crazy psychopath and it's all too hard to explain. "I wish I'd never done it."

"So, you agree that you framed him?"

"No, I agree that I wish I'd never done it. But there was something wrong with him. He had disgusting images. He would have hurt somebody sooner or later. He already has hurt somebody."

"Who? Who exactly has he hurt? Is this your murder / suicide staging that is completely unsubstantiated by any facts?"

"No, it's not."

"What then?" She throws a tea towel onto the bar and folds her arms.

"He hurt Harry."

By the time Andrew Marlow was sentenced and sent to Wormwood Scrubs, a year had already passed. After we uncovered his search for my alter ego, Claire Halliday, Julian deemed it too dangerous for me to be involved. My mother's condition worsened and I was receiving daily calls from the nurses. She had a mini stroke and when I went to see her, I could tell she was not herself. It was the flatness of the back of her hair that told me she couldn't raise her arm. She had a habit of putting her hand through her hair. She had short, full hair, like Princess Diana, and she took pride in it. I could tell she was so much worse. So Julian sent me on a job to cover a kiss-and-tell in Warwick Avenue and the rest is history. David came with me as legal, we went to the pub afterwards, and Rosie was made that night.

My demise was swift. It took less than six months for them to manage me out, coinciding with my maternity leave. I knew when they gave me a bunch of flowers and a baby gift box filled with soft towels and teddies that I wouldn't be coming back. I wasn't sure what I'd need when I had a baby. I was clueless with no one to show me what to do. My mother had just died. I was grieving and looking forward to seeing my baby at the same time. I knew too much. I needed a break. I was potentially damaging to Julian's career as an emotionally vulnerable pregnant woman who could do or say anything.

Led by a left-wing broadsheet newspaper, a group of celebrities were gathering momentum for a police investigation into phone hacking. It was pure speculation at first. They believed some newspapers had been illegally listening to voicemail messages.

My newspaper had a total shutdown on hacking. David wouldn't even speak about it at home. I think they were paranoid that someone might do to them what they had been doing to others. The pressure grew all that year. In the end I was made redundant but David activated a clause in the contract to get me paid off. For the record, it was fifteen grand. But it ensured that I was never allowed to speak about what I had worked on at the newspaper, until now, and even now I shouldn't be speaking about it.

I think they believed that because I was tied to David I could be managed and kept quiet. From David's point of view, he did not want me anywhere near the police while they began their investigations.

We never discussed it at home. The only time David gave me any information was on frosty walks on Hampstead Heath where he was sure his words couldn't be intercepted. My walks became slower, my hips widening, preparing for labour.

When Rosie was born she had such bright red lips that there was only one name for her. It was David's idea. Her middle name was my mother's. For a moment everything seemed perfect The bright red crack of morning sky when I pushed with all my might and Rosie came into the world. The smell of Rosie's head. The gentle tug of that little mouth on my breast. The warmth of the car as David drove us slowly home from the hospital.

At the time of the birth, Andrew Marlow was a few months into his eighteen-month stretch. Meanwhile the hacking movement and subsequent investigation moved along at speed. It became clear it would not go away and that it was too broad and encompassed and involved too many diverse personalities to be stopped. David made a deal with Harry to use him as a sacrificial lamb. Payments were very cleverly laid out to be untraceable. That is to say they were set up through foreign bank accounts. Harry agreed to come clean to the police and accept blame and take whatever sentence. The agreement was that he would maintain he did covert surveillance under his own steam without the knowledge of Julian Harper or anyone at the newspaper. And that he worked alone.

Let me be clear that Harry took the blame for hacking phones, and not for the honey-trap that we did on Andrew Marlow. No one knew about that, and it never came out.

That would have been fine except one bleak January morning Harry was sent down on remand to Wormwood Scrubs. It meant Harry was inside with Andrew Marlow. It was only supposed to be for two weeks, until Harry was transferred to a low-security open prison. When Harry arrived he was high profile. He was on every news channel. He was implicated in some very big stories. Andrew Marlow must have suspected. He knew that the discovered hard drive had been planted. He figured out straight away that Harry was working at the time our newspaper broke the story about him, and he wanted to know what Harry knew about it.

I will never know the full extent of their conversations. Harry was attacked in prison and sustained a severe head injury from which he will never fully recover. He has a brain injury and he cannot speak. He lives in a residential nursing home in Kent. Andrew Marlow was convicted of grievous bodily harm while in prison and his sentence was extended.

Months later I remember Rosie toddling to the front door of our house in London. Children's television blared in the background. I was cooking lunch. We were late to meet a friend in the park. It was summer. The windows and doors were open. I was thinking that maybe it was the right time to get a dog. The postman pushed something through the letter box, and Rosie loved to pick up the mail.

"What have you got there, Rosie?" She gave the letter to me. She headed back towards the television. It was addressed to *Nurse Claire Halliday* with my address and a note that simply said, *why?*

32

MR TODD

Our hands are alike. When Auntie fiddles with her cigarette, I see the blocky outline of her thumb joint and it looks just like the outline of my own thumb, but older. My mother's were plumper, rounder and her nails more oval. There's a rectangular quality to mine and my aunt's hands. They are angular, in a hurry, hands that don't take any shit.

She puts out her cigarette on the metal lid of a bin in the street. She screws up her face. She thinks bins are disgusting and that it's better to put butts out on the pavement, but there are fines now if you are seen. Mr Todd cocks his leg and wees on the bin.

"We'd better go inside." I look at my watch.

"Come on now, Mr Todd, don't be frightened."

I scan the street for cars we don't know, or cars driving too quickly. But there is nothing, just the quiet hum of the town. I can hear some building work in the distance, a hammer and then a drill. Auntie strokes Mr Todd who wags his tail.

"We're all getting older. Even little Doll is all grown up."

Auntie is hit with a fit of coughing. She grabs the side of the bin. There's dark mucus in her mouth. I search my pockets and find an old tissue and offer it to her. She flicks it away and opens her handbag to pull out a red checked handkerchief. I put my arm around her. We're uneasy with physical contact, not like Rosie and I who are always draped around each other.

After coughing so inhumanly hard she is out of breath but pushes on through the front door of the vets, where the receptionist greets her warmly. The walls are painted a light medical green that never fails to instil the fear of God in me. There's a strong smell of cleaning products that reminds me of the mysterious scent in my own house. There's an anaemic-looking Christmas tree bending over in the corner. Being a country vet is very different to the vet concierge in London. Suzie Crowley and her now enormous swollen belly tour all over the county birthing cows and dealing with shit and piss. Hats off to her. Someone has to do it. She's the most hardworking and down-to-earth person I have ever met. No doubt she'll be able to birth this baby that no one mentions on her own, in a field if need be, with only the roar of nature and the spirits of our earth mothers to guide her.

"Suzie will see you now," the receptionist says. "Go through and she'll be along in a second. She's just dealing with an emergency on the telephone."

"How long have you had that cough?" I hold back the heavy door for Auntie and Mr Todd to enter the surgery. Auntie tells me to shush.

"Pick him up, will you?"

I bend down and pick up Mr Todd and place him on the examination table. I'm rather embarrassed by the shushing. It doesn't matter how old I am, that still induces a redness in my cheeks. My crime was to speak in front of the receptionist, but Auntie's reaction tells me that it's more than just a cough, and that she is frightened.

"I think you should think about giving up smoking," I say as Suzie arrives.

"Sorry about that, Mrs, Doll. I was just on the phone there, they have a problem up in Ballyneety and I'm going to have to drive out there after this. Something is wrong with one of the cows."

"At this time?" Auntie says. "It's starting to get dark!"

"At every hour of the day and night as you well know. I have good lights on the truck." She looks at Mr Todd, and talks to him in a soothing tone.

I realise that it's not Mr Todd who's ill. It is my aunt. I see her for the first time as someone vulnerable. Suzie uses a little light to look into Mr Todd's eyes, ears and mouth. Afterwards she pops a little treat in his mouth, which he spits out on the table. He only eats human food, but I'm not allowed to tell Suzie that. Suzie feels around his body with her gloved hands. There's a little cyst but she says that it's nothing to worry about. All dogs his age have little cysts emerging. It's if it's on an organ that it's a problem. Finally she gives him an annual booster injection. Mr Todd doesn't even flinch.

"None of my other dogs ever had a booster and they were all fine," says Auntie.

I'm going to offcr to pay, in cash obviously.

"Were you happy with the outcome of the story, Doll?" asks Suzie, opening the door for us to leave.

"Yes, very much so. They're going to be fined and the Environment Agency is watching their every move."

"It was essential for the wildlife around here. We couldn't have that happening. It was a great job, well done both of you."

"And you, there would be no story without your autopsy, Suzie. So thank you. It's down to you."

Mr Todd trundles through the door, followed by a shaky Auntie.

"Are you still working in the pub?" Suzie asks, her hands clasped over her belly like the buckle of Santa's belt.

"Yes, I'm helping out for now."

"It's got a great atmosphere in there now with you and Katherine. It's like a different place altogether. You get on well, don't you, the two of you?"

Auntie's ears prick up and her eyes sharpen.

"We haven't seen each other for years," I say, defensively. Why can't I have any elephants in the room when everyone else has a zoo full?

"Well that's nice, rekindling such a close friendship."

I redden again and Auntie can see it. I flash back to being with my mum twenty years ago, trying to suppress my feelings then and to act nonchalant. It does work, I can vouch for that. I have a failed marriage and a skip-load of terrible mistakes with men I never liked to show for those years of suppression. And I have a broken heart and an empty bed.

"You're coming to my wedding on Saturday, aren't you?"

"Of course we are! We wouldn't miss it for the world," I say.

Outside the evening has drawn in. Auntie shuffles. She seems smaller all of a sudden and balanced forward as if off-kilter. Has she been remoulded by the strength of her cough?

"Katherine Power married a *woman* in New York, you know," Auntie says with the emphasis on 'woman'.

"I know that," I say. "And so what?"

"People will talk. This isn't Dublin. Think about Rosie at school. You can't just go around doing whatever you want all the time."

Inside I roar. I look away into the distance, a street lamp blinks, glowing orange in the never-ending blackness. Why can't I do what I want and without interference? How come she can infer things from this and challenge what is, in fact, a perfectly innocent friendship. Why? Because we're the witches, the odd women with no men to look after them.

"Fine." There's no point arguing with her.

"Good. You're just so free that someone will always want to clip your wings."

I look at my aunt. I see a kindred spirit, but Auntie's life has been so stunted by duty and family and church and Ireland that she has never been free. She never ran away to England, or to New York, she stayed and she did what was expected of her and her life has been hard. But what would she have chosen? For a moment I suspect that she is insanely jealous of my freedom, but more than that I think she is jealous of my friendship with Katherine, and I'm not sure why it would bother her so much.

We get into the car. I lift Mr Todd onto her lap in the passenger seat.

"Maybe we could go to New York?" I fall into my fantasy, this time with Auntie joining us. I could take her to Ellis Island. We could visit our cousins, perhaps go up to Boston, or see a baseball game.

"Nah. It's too late for that. I've no interest."

Maybe true freedom is the freedom of our minds.

"You should see a doctor about that cough. What about Suzie's soon-to-be-husband? I'm sure he'd give you good advice. You could get a prescription. I could take you," and as she doesn't immediately say no I push it and suggest, "I could go in with you?"

"All right." She sits bolt upright in the car. As we leave, I turn on the radio and by coincidence it's playing 'Born to Run' by Bruce Springsteen. It's Auntie's favourite song. I turn it up full volume so that the sound begins to distort in this old car. Although it's freezing and dark we open the windows, and Mr Todd sticks his head right out, the wind streaming through his white fur, and we scream freedom into the void.

33

THE SCAPEGOAT

I wake to windows frosted on the inside. The cold melts into my skin like a minty face mask. There's a crackle at the end of my breath, and a tightness in my chest. The damp is playing hide-and-seek in my lungs. Worry is alive in my aching muscles, and in my newly formed frown lines. How much longer is this necessary? I can't keep Rosie in this house indefinitely.

We wash, shivering. We brush teeth, spit, pull our pants on, a cotton vest with a tiny bow, and a bra for me. I make a mental note to buy a new bra, this is how I know I am alive, my inner vitality hopes for better times with me tanned and bronzed in posh new underwear. I'm not sure I can ever return from where I am now. If I can set aside the shame and guilt then perhaps I can move forward.

In the kitchen I put the radio on while Rosie makes my breakfast. She's giving me toast. She's not allowed to warm hot milk on the range. It's too dangerous and she's still small, she's still just a baby to me. She eats her toast while playing with a few characters from her advent calendars. I bought her a Lego Friends one and Katherine bought her a Playmobil calendar and she mixes the two in a brand-new game that she has invented. I love that she has two calendars and a hint at being spoiled because right now she's the least spoiled child that I have ever met.

"Mummy Doll?"

"Yes," I reply slowly, waiting for the question.

"I didn't really like it when Auntie shot the rabbit."

"Oh, darling, okay, I know." I move over and slip my arm around her. We cuddle.

"Now all the bunnies feel sad. I don't want to do it again."

"I know. I know."

"That poor rabbit."

"You won't ever have to do that again, I promise."

"Don't tell Auntie I said that, though, will you, because she'll be upset?"

"No, I won't say that you told me. I'll tell her that I said it wasn't allowed, okay?"

We drive to school and I see the gardaí car passing and see him again at the school gates. Rosie's teacher comes out to meet us and after they go inside, Father Aidan comes out and locks the gates with a big key. I watch him from my car and he holds up a hand to slowly wave to me. I drive into town and find a shop that doubles as a vaping shop and a mobile phone shop. I buy a peach-flavoured vape and a pay-as-you-go burner phone.

At home I make instant coffee and light a fire. I take the phone out of its box and fiddle to insert the SIM card. It lights up Eire Ireland and just like that I am back in the connected world. I send a text to Katherine with my new number and she instantly replies.

> So I guess you won't be coming round here anymore?

I instantly reply.

No, I'll be there soon – I still need your internet.

I telephone Kelly but she's either not there, or too busy to take my call, so I leave a message with my new number on her answerphone. On the road outside my house a white truck pulls up. I immediately assume that it's a delivery for the pub, but they usually deliver in the yard at the back. It could be anything: a new dishwasher, a pizza oven, or some other equipment that Katherine is installing to upgrade the pub's services. But there's a knock at *my* door.

I open it and there's a guy in a white coat and a blue and white striped apron.

"Delivery for you, love." He walks to the back doors of the van.

"I didn't order anything," I say. "It must be for the pub?"

He opens the heavy van doors with a metal lever; a huge gasp of cold steam surges out. It's a freezer van.

Katherine comes out of the pub. "What have you bought?" she asks.

Pat is behind her; he holds the wall carefully for balance. "Are you all right, Doll?"

The delivery driver climbs up into the van.

"Pat," I say. "Are you feeling better?"

"I'm a bionic man now!" he says while the delivery driver pushes a large box to the edge of the ledge of the van and jumps down, soil crunching under his boots.

"It's for this house," the delivery man says.

There are no house numbers as such on this stretch of road. Each tiny group of houses along the main road has its own area name. We're called Holy Cross with my house loosely known as The House at Holy Cross. Next door, of course, is Power's Bar, Holy Cross.

"What is it?" I say.

"Can you manage?" asks Katherine, moving to the van to lend a hand. The box is a metre cubed and heavy. Katherine and I look at each other.

"What is it?" I ask again more frantically.

"I don't know. What did you order? You're going to need a big freezer by the looks of things," the delivery man says.

"I didn't order anything?" I say. "Katherine, did you?"

"No," says Katherine. "It's heavy. Where are you from? What shop?"

"We're the Halal butchers in Limerick City, Parnell Street." The delivery man looks quizzical, as if most people are fully expecting what he delivers.

"Is there a delivery note?" asks Katherine.

"Hang on a second." He reaches into the front cab for a black clipboard. He scans it and hands a sheet of paper to me. "Here you go. Oh, it's a goat."

"A goat?"

"What have you bought a goat for, Doll?" Pat shouts.

"I didn't buy a feckin' goat!" I shout, as Katherine takes the delivery note from me.

"Is it dead?" asks Pat.

"We're a butcher's shop so it's pretty feckin' dead all right."

"Is this the number of the shop?" Katherine takes out her phone and dials the number.

"Do you sell many of those?" asks Pat.

"Goat, yes. But not whole ones. More like a shoulder joint or something like that."

"So it's a whole goat?" asks Pat.

"It's butchered, it's skinned, but I'd say it's the whole animal, like. It'll make a change from the Christmas turkey, I'd say. Where do you want it?" He begins to shut up the back of the truck.

Katherine talks loudly on the telephone to someone at the butcher's shop.

"I don't want it," I say. "I don't want it at all. Take it away."

"It's all paid for. I can't really take it back. I've got other deliveries to make."

Katherine puts her phone in her pocket. "Help me bring it into the pub," she says, "it's real. It's all paid for."

Pat opens the door wide and Katherine and the delivery driver manoeuvre the box through the doorway and into the middle of the pub. It rests in the centre like an exhibit. Pat sits on a chair, wincing as he lowers himself down. "I've seen people roast a whole pig, or a lamb, but never a goat."

"It was 180 Euros," says Katherine. "And fewer calories than beef, lamb or even chicken."

"Who sent it?" I already know, and I don't want to know.

"It was ordered on the internet. It was paid for by bank transfer. It was addressed to Claire Halliday at the house at Holy Cross."

"Oh Jesus." I feel my legs turn to jelly beneath me. My mouth is dry, the room suddenly feels so hot.

"Who's Claire Halliday?" asks Pat.

Katherine takes a long knife from behind the bar and runs it along the packing tape on the top of the box. I shift from one foot to the other. It's a rare and weird feeling having this dead beast in a box. An unlucky omen. My heart races. I sit down by Pat for a moment and then get up again. I need a drink.

"We don't know who she is," says Katherine, lifting open the flaps. She looks inside. She's braver than me. I don't know what to expect. It's certainly a large enough box to fit something big, or someone big inside. Katherine's face contorts. "Yeah, it's a goat all right."

"How do you know?" I rush to her side and against my instincts look inside the box. There's an animal carcass in red and white, bound in plastic. A skinned head has bulging lidless eyes and a long tongue that extrudes from the mouth. My stomach turns. Sick comes up my throat.

Pat guffaws from his chair. "We'll make a farmer of you yet, Doll."

I much preferred it when Pat was stuck upstairs. Katherine closes the lid.

"The delivery note names the sender," she says, taking my hand.

"Give it to me." She hands me the note. It reads, *With love from Harry.*

"Harry?" I say in disbelief, because it can't be from Harry. Harry cannot speak, write or use the internet. Harry requires twenty-four-seven care. Plus Harry and I never spoke again after the story came out. We were kept firmly apart. And then I realise the point. It's not from Harry. It's from Andrew Marlow. The goat is Harry, the scapegoat on whom all the blame was put so that myself and Julian and numerous other journalists and employees of the newspaper could get away with our crimes.

"It's a scapegoat," I whisper to Katherine. "Harry was the scapegoat. Uncle Andy is coming here. He's coming here for me."

"It's okay. We're not going to let anything happen to you and Rosie," says Katherine.

I nod, but I know that Katherine won't be able to stop him and certainly not Pat in his high-backed orthopaedic chair.

"It's a shame to let it go to waste," says Pat. "Good meat like that would go a long way."

"Let's have a Notting Hill Carnival night," says Katherine. "I'll make curried goat."

"You can't eat it!" I shout.

"We can and we will," says Katherine. "Fuck him. We'll have Barrington Levy, Toots and the Maytalls. I'll put a board outside advertising goat curry and if he sees it he can fuck off!"

"I'm not touching it."

"You don't have to. You don't have to do anything you don't want to. But you're not going to be horrified and scared anymore. I'm not going to let you be terrified by him. We're taking it back into our control."

I nod once again.

"One love," sings Pat, and we both swivel our heads to look at him. "Bob Marley, 'One Love', just saying it's a good song for the carnival night."

THE VET

Suzie and her good doctor are lucky with the weather. The church stone sparkles against a clear blue sky. The cottages on the high street pop in complementary colours of pink, blue and cream. In the distance are endless lush fields of the deepest and most vivid jungle green. A large Christmas tree is decorated with red and green bows in the foreground. It's freezing cold but clear, crisp and frosty. I can think on a day like this.

There are at least two hundred and fifty people at the wedding. Our vet, Suzanne Crowley, is marrying the doctor from the neighbouring town of Charleville. Between them they know everyone in the immediate vicinity. The Crowley family are out in force and Peter Crowley makes a special effort to stop by Auntie, Rosie and I to compliment Auntie on her dress. The three of us went shopping to get new dresses. It is so cold that Rosie wears a striped bobble hat and matching gloves.

We are ushered into the church and onto the bride's side. With so many people around I can't help but feel particularly vulnerable. Who would question a stranger in this environment? There are guests from Canada and England. There are many faces that I'm seeing for the first time. But I scan each one to see if it might be an aged version of Andrew Marlow. It always amazes me that there are infinite variations of the human face.

I read the wedding service printed in silver lettering on thick white card. An organist plays an instrumental piece I don't recognise, and there's a strong godly smell of incense that transports me back to being a child in church grasping my mother's hand. I take Rosie's hand in mine and I smile at her. She's a good child but she's going to be bored. There's a full Catholic Mass, followed by the wedding service itself. It may be two or more hours long. Rosie stares at the statues of the Virgin Mary looking down at us, immaculately preserved in pale blue and white.

"If you make your First Holy Communion while you are here, then this is where you'll do it." I have been resistant to this idea, but just like all of my other values it is melting away, so that Rosie and I can assimilate more comfortably into our new surroundings. In London we never went into a church. I once went on my own to light candles for my mother and father. I never wanted to push any religion onto Rosie, but maybe she is missing out on spirituality, learning what is right and wrong.

"Can I play a game on your phone?" she asks, her angelic face smiling.

"Absolutely not!" I look around me. It's the people behind that worry me, naturally. I wonder who is hidden in this crowd. Could Andrew Marlow hide in plain sight amongst this crowd of wedding goers? What does he look like now? I was only in his presence for a few hours but there is no person on this planet who has made a greater impression on my life. Would I recognise him? Did my actions ruin his life? Have I saved other people from his clutches? I will never know.

I look up into the gaping roof of the church. They have such big churches in such little towns. The priest offered to take my confession once. It used to be that I could not imagine myself confessing my sins to him, but now it's beginning to feel more appealing. A short heartfelt chat with Aidan and I could be absolved of all my wrongdoing. I could start over.

Dry heat rises up through a grate in the floor. It must cost a fortune to keep this huge draughty building warm. Auntie takes a sudden, dramatic coughing fit that draws looks. It's not a healthy cough, any fool can hear that. The organist pauses, breaks a beat, and we the congregation all stand up together. Suzie begins her long ascent of the nave walking slowly, emerging from the dark recess of the church. Rosie squeezes past me in the pew to get a better look at the bride. It's delightfully shocking to see a heavily pregnant bride dressed in white.

The word, relayed to me in bits and bobs by people sworn to secrecy but namely Auntie, Katherine and Connor, is that they spent a disgusting amount of money on the hotel reception, and would have lost it if they cancelled. Although the Catholic Church does not have a rule that forbids pregnant women being married in church, the general consensus is that the priest would try and speed up and downplay the wedding, perhaps moving it to a smaller section or side-chapel, limiting numbers, and once again ruining the massive party that Suzie had planned.

I look at Suzie holding on to her proud father's arm and she really is beautiful. There's a light and glow to her that is pure goodness. She radiates healing and creation. She is Mother Earth, she shows us why every woman should be loved and respected and everyone in that church can feel it.

But over Suzie's father's shoulder I see a face I recognise. The shock hits me like a bolt and I gasp out loud. Rosie thinks that I'm moved by the sight of the bride and looks up at me sweetly and slightly shocked herself. I raise my hand to my face, covering my open mouth. It's not Andrew Marlow that I can see; it's the man from the bungalow in Ennis and he is sat next to Sean Gallagher. Sean Gallagher looks across at me and tips his finger against his forehead to acknowledge and salute me. I know what he is saying. He's saying, sell the house or he's going to make what happened in Ennis public knowledge. Rosie would know what I'd done. There would be no way of explaining what had happened without coming clean about Andrew Marlow. I'm sure Sean Gallagher might try and spin it some other way to smear my character, and turn the good people of Ireland against me, like I have done to him.

I might have to sell the house to Sean. It's what I said I would do. I guess I can move in with Auntie. I will miss Katherine. I can't imagine not having her in my life, not being able to put my head around the door to see her, but Pat is back on his feet. He wants to sell too, and perhaps she'll go back to New York. We hush for the welcoming words. Suzie and the doctor are so well known and well liked that there are three priests. Father Aidan Lynch, the parish priest from Charleville, and the old retired parish priest. They work together in their flouncy embroidered robes. Eight altar boys adorn the flanks and after all these years, it's still a bunch of men in skirts parading around telling us all what to do.

Somewhere on the groom's side a mobile phone rings. There's a ruffle as people search for the noise. Everyone thinks it's themselves. Clutch handbags snap open and shut. Auntie lifts up her bag, takes out her phone and turns off the sound and gestures for me to do the same. I'm so used to not having a phone that I had forgotten I had it, and I jerk in realisation that mine could ring loudly at any second. I reach inside to get it. The screen is lit. There is a message. It says,

> Looks like we're going to get that second date after all.

He's here. He has my number. Somehow, just like before, he is able to find my number and contact me, get right inside my inner circle, and scare me right here and right now while I hold my child's hand in church. I type, *Go to hell,* but then I delete it. I don't want to rile him. I must not engage with him in any way. This will be untraceable as it will also be sent from a burner phone that he'll get rid of as he sees fit.

The congregation sits and leaves me standing, still looking at the phone. Rosie pulls my hand.

"Sit down, Mummy Doll," she whispers.

The phone vibrates again. It's from a different number and is a video. I make sure the sound is turned down and glance at it. It's the poor man in Ennis. To my shame it's the video they made of his interrogation in his own home. Guilt catches in my throat, how could I have stooped so low? I turn it off. I silence the phone and bury it back into my bag. I look around again. Is he here? Is he watching me now? Sean Gallagher's eyes follow me. Some crook. He was supposed to take on Andrew Marlow but he couldn't even find him.

I pass the next two hours in limbo. It's pure torture not knowing who is behind me in this massive crowd. Rosie starts to play up and repeatedly asks how much longer it's going to go on for. She sits with me, and then she sits with Auntie and while there she spies a little boy, a little younger than her, and the two of them begin to look at each other which distracts her, thank God, for a good twenty minutes.

I go for Holy Communion. I haven't taken communion since my mother's funeral but I just thought, fuck it. I need something to pass the time and the queueing up the nave and subsequent walk around the entire church was a good way to have a look around at who was hiding at the back. I expected a wink or at least a hello from my friend, Father Aidan, but nothing. I was impressed by his professionalism.

Finally, when the church service is over, we trundle out into the cold. Auntie takes a light from a young chap in a shiny grey suit. He's so cold his hands shake as he holds up his lighter.

"You can't smoke inside anywhere anymore. It's like having the plague." Auntie draws on her cigarette, her cheeks scarily hollow. We head off in the car to the reception which is a twenty-minute drive towards Tipperary. It reminds me of the night that we drove here from England.

The reception is in a large hotel and Rosie spots the little boy from the church right away. He shows her a game on his mother's phone. I show Auntie my vape and she looks at me as though I were mad.

"You're smoking a pen, you silly girl." I feel ten years old again.

We eat at the same table as Peter Crowley and his son and family. Connor and his wife and children join us, Connor makes a big show of shaking the hand of Peter Crowley's son.

There are no more messages on my phone. I drain a glass of white wine.

The tables are decked with mini Christmas trees, a red tablecloth, and green napkins. I smell a real fire and the roast cooking in the kitchen. We eat turkey and Brussel sprouts.

The speeches begin. It's bad enough listening to speeches by someone you know, never mind people you don't. I laugh alone, desperate to fit in, wondering if I ever really will. I am English. I'm never aware of feeling English when I'm in London. I get a pang of something pride-like in my heart when I see a red double-decker bus go over Westminster bridge in the rain. But that's more about being a Londoner. But being here I do feel English, or rather, I believe they all think I am English and not really one of them.

At the back of the room more people are arriving for the evening. There are instruments set up on the stage ready. Sean Gallagher is here, sitting at a table with his wife but there's no trace of the man from Ennis. He has vanished. I wish I could make amends, and one day I will make it up to that man.

I look back. I realise I'm looking for Katherine. She arrives for the evening with Pat and she looks stunning. She is wearing a long black sequinned dress with a halter neck. She looks magnificent, like a Hollywood actress. People are staring. I can't take my eyes off her, but I'm so embarrassed that people can see me looking. They might be able to see what I can't even admit to feeling. She walks down the opposite side of the huge room, and then seeing us, makes her way over through the crowd.

"There's Katherine!" says Rosie. "Wow, she looks so pretty!"

I can't look at her. I turn around.

"You look really pretty too, Rosie." Katherine smiles. The children move off to play tag on the dance floor. The adults shift seats to make room. I stand up and Katherine's taller than me in her heels.

"You look beautiful," I say, embarrassed.

Katherine is popular and all sorts of people emerge to speak to her. People that went to school with her, people who cycled in the cycling club, old men who knew her father and mother. It's not long before she is called away to meet an old school friend's new husband.

The band starts up and the kids dance. People take to the floor but I'm much too uptight to be able to dance. I've forgotten how. It's been so long. The band wear matching suits and play traditional Irish music. It's as if nothing has changed since I was a child and the same songs are played by the same men. It's wonderful and timeless: it makes me feel very safe. Then Sean Gallagher taps me on the shoulder. His face is bruised, and he has a recent cut across his nose.

"Do you have a minute, Doll?"

I stand up telling Auntie to watch Rosie like a hawk. She thinks I'm a crazy 'helicopter parent'. Sean is limping.

"You're trying to blackmail me." I'm fuelled by a bottle of white wine. I'm direct, confident sounding.

"Not at all. We made an agreement. I've been waiting for you to speak to me and thought you might need some encouragement."

"Encouragement?"

"Don't you miss London?" He pronounces 'miss' as 'mish' and it makes me think of 'pish'.

"I want the recordings deleted. I don't want anything coming back on me."

"Good. The paperwork is being drawn up. I want to bring this to a conclusion. Now, you're a very pretty girl, Doll, and Rosie's a pretty girl too. We wouldn't want anything happening to the looks of either of you, would we?" He is sure of the loud music, the drink. He knows no one can hear and that this might be one of the most private conversations we have ever had, and will ever have.

"You do not come near my daughter," I say, horrified.

"Well sign the paperwork and fuck off back to England. Have a good evening." He walks away.

I have to sell. There's nothing else I can do. It's over. I can feel it coming to an end. I can't see Katherine anywhere. Connor plonks another wine on the table for me, and a vodka and tonic for Auntie. I try to make conversation with Connor's wife but I am too traumatised by Sean Gallagher's threats.

The music slows. Time has moved along. It's after ten and the band starts to play slow music. Peter Crowley takes Auntie up onto the dance floor, and Rosie pairs off with the little boy. It's cute and old-fashioned but lovely and innocent. As is the way when there's not enough men, a few older ladies start to dance in all-female pairings. I sip my drink. The music changes gear again, even slower with just the singer playing guitar while the rest of the band takes a break.

He starts to sing and I know the song. It's a Christy Moore song called, 'Ride On'. It's haunting. Katherine appears, walking towards me. We could be anywhere in the world.

"Dance with me, will you?"

She must be crazy. "Are you serious?"

"Yes. Come on." She takes my hand in hers and leads me to the dance floor. She puts her arm around me and her hand on the small of my back, and I place my hand on her shoulder. My breathing quickens. She spins me around slowly. Rosie loves it. We pass her. The kids are ducking in and out of the adults.

I can't dance. There's no space in my head or heart for dancing but somehow she bends me, she softens me, she warms me and makes me pliable. And then I'm not looking anywhere but straight at her, and she is looking right into me. I feel her breath on my face. She pulls me to her. My breasts brush against hers. We twirl around and around. It is the most gorgeous moment of my life.

Her chest is heaving, her eyes looking at my mouth, and then into my eyes. She moistens her lips. I want to kiss her. I know that I want her and she wants me. She swallows. I'm dizzy. I kissed her eighteen years ago and I've never forgotten it. I've thought about her all that time. I realise that we have stopped dancing right in the middle of the floor and we are standing there holding each other.

"I can't…" I need to go. I break away. She doesn't want to let go of me. Auntie is watching with a foul look on her face. "I think it's time for us to go, Rosie."

"I don't want to!"

"Come on now, it's been a very long day."

"Let's go so," Auntie says, delighted to have an excuse to smoke outside. She eyes me suspiciously. Are we so alike that I can have no secrets? She knows everything and it's too late to stop it now because Katherine and I both know how we feel. I take Rosie's hand and we leave. I don't look behind me. I don't look for Katherine. I can't do anything for us, not now, not with everything going on.

35

THE CONFESSION

Father Aidan comes to the house. He is wearing a shiny green tracksuit with no dog collar. He looks more like a youth from an estate than a parish priest. He smells of dark musk and flowers, a new Christmas aftershave gifted by one of his flock. I think, *Christian aftershave* and that makes me laugh. Perhaps I am nervous.

We sit in Katherine's 'outside gym'. Her bicycles, a road bike and a spin bike, sit front and centre, pristine and as ornamental as a crucifix. This is her church, festooned with cycling paraphernalia and big speakers. The only living beings that she likes in here with her are the feral cats that live outside, that slink around and sometimes drape themselves in the upper corners of the former milking shed. I'm more of a dog person, but I love the way that Katherine cares for these untamed beasts. She doesn't get much in return, just the satisfaction of providing for them.

From a plastic carrier bag Father Aidan takes out a cream humeral veil with an embroidered cross. He wraps it around his shoulders, shrugging himself to get the thick material into the correct position. I turn on an electric heater that Katherine keeps out here.

"It would have been better if you could have come into the church, but this is fine," he says. I check around me once again to ensure that no one can hear us.

"I don't even know if I believe."

"Sure, neither do I," he says. "You know my brother died unexpectedly when he was only twenty-one years old, and if that had not happened then I don't think I would ever have become a priest."

"I'm so sorry, Father, that must have been awful."

He blesses me. "You know, Doll, the question is not about believing in God, it is about humanity and how we find the strength to live, and that is through love."

"Did you write that?"

"I just thought of it."

"It's really good."

"In the name of the Father, the Son and the Holy Spirit, go ahead, Doll, with your confession." My thoughts come from somewhere untapped. I don't believe it and yet I know what to do. It comes from a part of my brain on which my Irish Catholic cultural identity is tattooed. I make the sign of the cross.

"Bless me, Father, for I have sinned. It has been, well, around twenty-seven years since my last confession."

"Twenty-seven years?"

And I confess to it all.

"May Almighty God have mercy on you, and having forgiven your sins, lead you to eternal life. Amen…" and he continues his prayers of absolution, washing me clean of my sins. He doesn't have to. He leads me in my Act of Contrition and gives me a penance of saying a decade of the rosary every night for a week. I don't even know if I want forgiveness, I don't know if I deserve it, and yet here I am, as pure and as innocent as a child once more.

DOUBLE THREAT

I am in my own house. It is the middle of the afternoon and I was just about to leave for the school nativity play. I am with the thin man with the moustache from the drive to Ennis. He sits on my sofa with his legs spread astride like a poisonous spider.

"We only need five minutes," he says.

He is with an accomplice, a man that I don't recognise. He could have been in Ennis with us, the memory is blurred. He is stocky and has a thick neck. The cup of tea that I made him looks tiny in his huge hands.

"I don't even know your names," I say, awkwardly. I'm not immediately frightened for my own physical safety but their lack of warmth and lack of friendliness is certainly intended to intimidate me.

"We're both called Gary," says the thinner man on the sofa. He clutches a brown envelope containing, what I imagine must be, documents to transfer ownership of the house to Sean Gallagher or whatever corporation they act for.

"Both of you?" I ask, disbelieving.

The stockier man drops his full cup of steaming hot tea in the centre of the room and it smashes violently on the floor, the ceramic mug bursting into sharp pieces. I shudder and jump out of my seat to clean it up. He grabs my wrist and pulls me down.

"No you don't," he says. "You can do that when we've gone."

"Your signature," the thin man continues, "must be witnessed by a solicitor and we have enclosed the details of the solicitor within this envelope. You are to take these documents into his office in Limerick and he will make the necessary arrangements. He will be closed from Christmas Eve so you are to make your way in before then to avoid any further delays."

The stockier man releases me and I pull my hand tight into my chest, rubbing my wrist.

"Doll, are you clear on what you need to do?" asks the thin man.

"Yeah, I get it. Can you please leave now?"

He stands and the two of them crowd into the hallway and out onto the road. I slam the door behind them.

37

THE HUSBAND

A block of sun, shaped like a large wedge of hard cheese, cuts through the window and across my face. It's an unlikely and unexpected joy. It is the winter solstice. The shortest day of the year in the northern hemisphere, and marks the point in which the days begin to brighten again, unrecognisably at first. I love the thought that light is working away behind the scenes.

There's a knock at the front door and I turn over to lie prone on the floor of the lounge. The carpet is musty. I've hoovered and cleaned but the years have not been kind to this carpet. It's older than me, and thinner than me. It's not good enough for Rosie. She could get asthma, or allergies. I'm hiding. I now have an aversion to people knocking on the front door.

The knocks come again, faster and louder.

"I know you're in there," says Katherine.

I've been avoiding her since the wedding, and that is hard when you live next door with not another soul around. I have to sell my house. I may have to go back to London. What is not in my plan, nor was ever in my plan was her to be here when I came back to Ireland. Now I've got all these feelings. I wasn't expecting it and I'm not ready for it. I'm sad about the timing.

"I have to tell you something right now, Dolores," she whispers through the letter box, "and it's not about the other night if that's what you're worried about."

I prise myself off the floor. I straighten my jumper. I've taken to wearing huge mohair sweaters to keep warm. My feet are in oversized fluffy socks and slippers. My hair, at least, is washed. I unlock the door and there stands Katherine. She's wearing work-out gear, tight black leggings and a zip up hoody sports jacket. She eyes me up and down.

"Are you cold? You need to go out and move around, and then you'll feel warm when you come back in."

"How can I help you?" I ask curtly.

"I…" she begins to say and shakes her head. I shake mine too and hold up a hand. I don't think I can cope with hearing anything else right at this moment. I can still feel her touch on my back, her body against mine. "There is someone here to see you."

"Who?" I lean forward and look over her shoulder. There's a hire car parked outside the pub. "Who?"

"It's not *him*, him."

"Really?" I say, massively relieved. "Who then? It's still bad, Katherine, I can tell by your face."

"It's your husband."

"Fuck."

"I recognise him from your mum's funeral."

"Fuck." I lean against the wall.

"He knows you're here and he knows you're in. Will you come?" She reaches out and holds my wrist. It's still sore from Sean Gallagher's henchman.

"I'm sorry. I didn't call him."

"It's none of my business if you did. He's Rosie's father. He has a right to see her," she says.

"I have no interest in him, in that way. I'm not running from him either. I don't love him. It's over."

"It's none of my business, Doll." A cold breeze cuts through us and she rubs her hands together.

"But I want you to know that I didn't call him, that I would never have invited him here."

"I've got to go, I've got things to do."

I am jealous that Katherine has got secret things to do that don't involve me. I worry that it's booking flights back to New York, or phoning her ex-wife and begging her to take her back. I already miss her and myself together, bumbling around during the day, drinking coffee, listening to music and chatting about our lives. But I am so good at getting people hurt and I really don't want to get her hurt.

Still in my slippers, I walk into the pub. David is sitting in the same chair Julian was, and when he sees me he tries to stand. He's very tall and awkward and so his knees hit the table and a little trickle of stout wobbles down the side of the glass and onto the table.

"How's Rosie?" he asks desperately, sitting back down. She is the only thing that he cares about, her and his work.

"She's at school, she's doing well. She's loving it here," and as an afterthought, "she does miss you." It's cruel to say anything less, and it's true, she does.

"I miss her so much." He picks the pint up. He's watching me carefully. I think back to the day before we ran away to Ireland, when I confided my fears about Andrew Marlow's release and he laughed at me. I showed him a message from Andrew threatening me. I can still see David's condescending face. He'd told me that I was 'just a mum', and that no one was after me, and that I was living in the past. He'd said that Andrew Marlow was looking for a pay-off, his beef was with the newspaper, not a 'has-been mediocre journalist' like me. I threw a vase at him. I smashed it against the wall, some expensive thing that David had insisted we buy. And rather than support me, David told me that domestic violence worked both ways. He threatened to call the police about me. I knew I had to go and get away from him, finally.

"Do you want a drink?" he asks.

"No, thank you," I say, the pub looks different with him in it, more ugly and basic, broken and colourless and dull with him and without Katherine. It's all coming to an end.

"You look cute," he says.

I'm not cute though, am I? Yes, I'm a mum, yes, I'm in a woolly jumper but I have a razor-sharp mind, a curious intellect and enemies left, right and centre.

"Why didn't you tell me that you were coming?"

He shakes his head quizzically. "Didn't your aunt tell you?"

"My aunt?" What the fuck has she done?

"I thought when she suggested reconciliation, and that she act as mediator…"

"Reconciliation? Mediator? My aunt said that?" Pat coughs behind the bar, and hobbles away out and into the kitchen. "You can't stay with me."

"I'm staying with your aunt, actually."

That fucking snake! How could she? She has no idea who she is dealing with when it comes to David. She's only met him once before and of course his behaviour is always perfect with relatives, his friends, and anyone outside the family home.

"Julian is dead," I say.

"I know. It's devastating. He had mental health issues. You just never know what's going on in someone's head."

"He didn't kill himself," I say. "Andrew Marlow is free. He's sending me notes and photographs again."

"Right," he says dismissively.

"He's here in Ireland. He's hacked into all my accounts: my bank, my email."

"And how are you, Doll? Are you still taking your medication?"

"I don't need any medication. I never did. I got rid of my phone, David, because I was receiving so many untraceable threatening messages that you dismissed. You didn't believe me. You didn't back me. I want a divorce and full custody of my child. I need you to be reasonable and understand that we can't be married anymore."

"You sound paranoid again," he says, mock-doctor. I want to strangle him. He is so entitled. He's a master of deflection. "You should hear yourself," he continues.

"I can hear myself," I say, and he raises his eyebrows. "Julian came here to warn me. He sat right where you are sitting now."

"That's what I always liked about you. You're a clever girl, plucky. Rosie gets that from you," he says.

"Rosie is so much more than me. I'm going to protect her. That's my only job in life now."

"If you come back to London with me after Christmas, I will not tell social services about your mental health problems, your drinking, or your illegal activities at the newspaper."

"I need to go to the police about Andrew Marlow. And I can't do that if I'm subject to your gagging order."

"Julian came here? Is that the house next door? It seems smaller than I imagined. It's not in the best shape, looks fit for demolition if you ask me. The whole area seems much darker than I thought it would be although I suppose I'm not seeing it at its best. You never brought me here, Doll, in all these years."

"You never wanted to come. You said it was a bog, a backwater. You said my family left me to deal with my dying mother on my own and that they didn't deserve me. You did. That's what you said, many times. When I wanted to bring Rosie to see my aunt, that's exactly what you said. You made me choose between a holiday in Greece and coming here. Ridiculous. I don't know why I let you get away with it for so long."

"Did I? I don't remember saying that. I'd never say something like that. I'm not that kind of man."

"David, wouldn't you be happier with some new young girl that you can bully instead of me? I'm done."

"I want to look after you, for Rosie's sake too. I don't want you having another breakdown or episode."

"Oh fuck off. Are you recording this? And if not, why even say it when we both know it's not true."

"There's no need to be like that, Doll."

"How long are you staying?"

"You've been working, I see. You haven't touched your bank accounts, credit card, your car is still on the driveway in London. How have you been surviving?"

"Don't fuck it up for me."

"What?"

"Don't you dare!"

"I haven't done anything."

He was a very good litigator. His cases never ended up in court. A call here, and a threat there, and he always managed to solve problems, bring them around to the corporation's way of seeing things.

"You must admit, Doll, it looks pretty fucking crazy, you running off here like that, stealing my child, taking her out of school, taking her to a different country, she doesn't even have her toys, it's cruel. And for what? Because you imagine some bogey man is after you when it's all just in your mind. I've been advised to invoke the Hague Convention for what you've done, although I wouldn't do that to you. I want to help you but you must admit that you've really lost it this time."

His incessant passive-aggression doesn't scare me as much as it used to. When Rosie was very small I started to notice his control. On my own with a baby I didn't have much power. Our getting together all happened very quickly. It sounds pathetic but I was so happy with Rosie that I let it slide. I did what he told me and I was free with Rosie most of the time. He left early in the morning. He had late dinners during the week. He was exhausted from work on Saturdays and slept until noon, and that suited me fine. David negotiates every action. There is no yes and no. If you ask for one thing you end up agreeing to three other things you never wanted. He plays life like chess. He tries to make me feel vulnerable by showing, through sleight of hand, the things that he could take away. Taking Rosie, or the threat of controlling access to Rosie, is the only thing that he has left over me. There is nothing else that I care about and I hate him for that.

"If you come home, I will sort out the legalities with the corporation and we will formulate a plan to have a restraining order taken out against your stalker."

"He's more than a stalker, David. First he maimed Harry and now he's killed Julian."

"As you allege, Doll, but I warn you that sounds crazy. And you don't have any evidence. Don't forget that the corporation has your HR record: your behaviour, your drinking at work, your mental episodes, going on benders on company time, numerous sexual relationships breaching our code of conduct."

"That was years ago, it's irrelevant!"

"You signed a non-disclosure agreement that you are still subject to."

"Fuck your agreements! What it comes down to, David, is whose side are you on? Mine or the corporation's?"

He takes a moment to think about this.

"Yours of course. You are my wife."

"Then start fucking acting like it. I am not part of the newspaper. You saw to that. You made sure that I was sidelined, you and Julian, and I am so glad that you did. You are Rosie's father and you've got the choice, you've got the power to let her mother be killed by Andrew Marlow, or sent to prison, or be free to live her life. And one day Rosie is going to know everything, and she's going to ask you about what you did. We're here in

Ireland because of you. Because of your gutless loyalty to your job. You can try to spin that, but Rosie will know the truth, and she's going to fucking hate you when she grows up."

There is silence in the pub. Somewhere in the back Pat smashes a plate. It's a rare treat when David is silent. It usually means his brain is cycling, trying to find ways to wriggle out or spin information into even more of an entrapment. But he can't argue about the love between a mother and her daughter. I look at my watch. David drains his pint and looks down at the floor. I'd have never looked at him twice in my better days. But he gave me Rosie.

"Do you want to collect Rosie from school with me?"

"Yes."

I've often found that the biggest arseholes are completely vulnerable underneath their scaly exteriors. I guess that vulnerability is attractive to some women but I find it repulsive. Suddenly he seems so hurt and self-conscious. It's part of his act.

At the school gates I am aware of other parents looking at me and this mystery English man. They are putting two and two together. Rosie carries a huge cardboard structure, her school project of building a house in cardboard. It's the last day of school before Christmas and she is bringing the project home. Her coat hangs open and I can see the glint of glitter on her red Christmas jumper catching in the street light.

It is already dark as she comes out through the school gates and it takes a moment for Rosie to realise who is with me. When she does, she screams. She drops her school project, which crumples to the ground. She runs into David's arms and the two of them start crying. I am a bitch. My stomach turns. This is for life. He's in my life, for life. I can't run; I can't separate them. I'm just going to have to find a way to live with him as part of my world.

3 8

THE HOSPITAL

Auntie puts her lipstick on in the same habitual motion that I have been watching my entire life. She puckers her lips at herself in the mirror. She's all that I have left of my mother. They were so different, and yet so very much the same.

David and Rosie sit at the table playing Monopoly. I loved this game when I was small and it's the same edition that I have played hundreds of times with Connor. There are still little scraps of notes with 'I Owe You' written on from thirty years before. Ryan Tubridy plays on the radio. Mr Todd snores loudly from the best lounge chair, his paw waving in a dog's dream. Auntie's rifle is safely secured back up on the wall, and not locked and loaded and ready to shoot rabbits with Rosie.

It's a perfect scene. Auntie's tree is in the hallway but she has made me help her arrange threadbare tinsel around the curtain fixtures and kitchen cupboards. Soon my cousins will arrive. They are already on their way, on the boat and on the plane, and I will have to share her again. But it's me that Auntie has chosen to take her to hospital, and me who is her confidante about her health. No one else knows, not even Connor.

I take the fast road into Limerick City. It feels risky, but everyone knows where I am now anyway. There's a drama about paying for parking. We have to telephone a number and pay with her credit card. It takes ten minutes and Auntie is eagle eyed and sharp. She's nervous about seeing the doctor.

She saw the vet's new husband in Charleville. He took blood and sent them off. He didn't like the sound of Auntie's cough. She was given an appointment at the hospital straight away.

The oncology wing is in a vast new four-storey building. What strikes me about hospitals, after spending so much time in them with my mother, is the walking. I would sit there listening for particular footsteps that I recognised as certain nurses. Each set of footsteps was different and unique. I hear our own. My aunt's tip-tap in her best shoes. She's light and so the tap is light. Mine is much more muffled in Nike trainers, more like a snare drum with plenty of treble.

Auntie's blood came back with high markers that concern the doctors. The doctor in Charleville is concerned. And the doctors here, that we have never met yet, are concerned too. A medical examination, a CT scan and a chest X-ray are going to make us very concerned, I dare say.

Auntie looks so vulnerable in a red plastic chair in the waiting room. I sit right next to her, our elbows touching in our winter coats. There's a droopy Christmas tree, some tinsel and a nativity scene made by local children with a shoe box for the stable and fluffy cotton-wool sheep. There is a picture of the Sacred Heart of Jesus, my mother's favourite religious picture. It was never the toxins in the lough, it was the cigarettes.

"Why did you invite David?" I ask.

Auntie's eyes widen with the shock of receiving a direct question. I know she'll be appalled that I would ask her when she is the centre of attention.

"For Rosie, for Christmas, and you could do with a chance to sort things out now that time has elapsed." Her hands are clasped together as if in prayer.

"But you don't know anything about David. You don't know about the hold, the control that he has over me and what it took to get away from him."

She is mortified as my voice rises and that other people in the waiting room, or a nurse or a doctor might hear us.

"Keep your voice down."

"I think you did it out of spite because I'm close to Katherine."

"So you admit it then?"

"Admit what? There's nothing to admit. She's my friend."

"Your mother never liked her."

"What's it got to do with my mother?"

"Katherine wanted to go to London to study sports."

"Sports Science with Business at LSE." I remember clearly what she meant to study, and that she had got a place. She was meant to stay with us while I went to City to do Media and Communication, which I did, and afterwards, journalism.

"Your mother told her she couldn't come. She telephoned, and the following week she got the green card in the ballot, so it didn't matter anyway, she went to America."

"My mother telephoned Katherine and said she couldn't come to London? It can't be true."

"She didn't want that for you. And she was right. You'd never have had the life you've had, had your career, got married, had Rosie. You'd have been ostracised, lost your family."

Her eyes fill with tears. She fiddles with the vape I bought her, desperate for a hit of nicotine. Who is she talking about? Me, or herself?

"I could still have had all of that, and I would have been happier than I am now." A door opens and a doctor steps out into reception. He calls my aunt's name and she stands righteously, the defender of my mother's ignorance, here to inflict further misery on me. But I am older, I'm wiser now.

In the car on the way home we travel without music, just the whoosh of cold air as we pass through the countryside. He's not meant to say, but the radiologist has seen a mass on the lung. He's told her that it's treatable, an operation most likely to remove those cells and then treatment afterwards. She's to stop smoking immediately. She puffs on the vape and the car fills with a cloud of sweet peaches.

"Why aren't you happy in your life?" she asks. "The man that sent you the photographs of Rosie? He's nothing to do with Sean Gallagher, is he? Or with the story, or the dairy?"

"No, he's not."

"Who is he, then?"

"He's a very dangerous man. He's followed me from England, I believe. I think he means to punish me for something I did years ago."

"What did you do?"

"He thinks I ruined his life."

"What does David say?"

"He doesn't believe me, he thinks I'm mad, depressed and seeing things that don't exist. He says I should be medicated, high on something so that I can't think straight."

"Why would he do that?"

"He still works for the newspaper and they don't want any of this to come out because it makes them look bad, because it was an illegal investigation. He's chosen his career over me and Rosie."

"Phone hacking?"

"Yes, and I can't leave David because he's threatened that if I do he'll give evidence against me to the courts and I'll lose custody of Rosie."

"He's blackmailing you. You should have told me, Doll."

We drive in silence to Auntie's house with no more secrets between us. It's dark when we arrive and we see David and Rosie playing happily through the window, Mr Todd sat at their feet.

39

DO YOU KNOW CLAIRE HALLIDAY?

Connor joins me in the car. He'll only be a minute he assures me, sitting stationary on Auntie's driveway. A video is circulating, something that he must show me, as it has been seen by various people. He is coy, holds his body rigid, there is a tremble in his fingers.

A lurching jump of panic spreads through me. Is it me? Is it about me? He sees my discomfort.

"It's not you," he says, pressing play. The video is dark. There's a rumbling sound, white noise, looming in the background.

"I can't see, it's too dark," I say, taking the phone from him. It comes into focus. A darkened room, with a light white mass in the middle of the shot. The camera pans in to reveal that it is a person. The man from Ennis? But no, not the man in Ennis. As soon as he opens his mouth I know who it is.

"You'll regret this," the man says, pronouncing this, 'thish'. Unmistakable, it is Sean Gallagher bound to a chair with a black eye and a bust nose. He cradles his arms in a bloodied white blanket.

Another voice speaks, an English accent. "I'll ask you again," he says, and his hands lift Sean Gallagher's head toward the camera. I have a horrible feeling that the video is for me. Sean stutters and shakes. There is a tear in his eye.

"I told you, I don't know her," mutters Sean.

The man releases Sean's head and it wobbles back to the centre. Sean looks petrified. It's a look I once longed to see on him, but now that I do I wouldn't wish it on my worst enemy.

"Do you know Claire Halliday?" the man asks, confirming that it is Andrew Marlow. Andrew Marlow has Sean. This is bizarre. And confirms that he is here in Ireland.

"Who? I told you. I don't know anyone called Claire Halliday." Sean shudders.

"Why were you asking questions about Andrew Marlow?" asks Andrew Marlow.

"I've never heard of him," Sean says.

"That's bollocks. I've seen a video of your people asking after Andrew Marlow. Torturing a poor old man. Why?"

Sean sighs and lifts his head as if he has no energy left at all. "You're Andrew Marlow, aren't you?" he asks, breaking a smile.

"Okay, so you don't know Claire Halliday, but I bet you know Dolores O'Rourke? They're the same person. Did she put you up to it?"

"You already know? That bitch in Holy Cross. The journalist. She wanted you dealt with. It has nothing more to do with me. Number plates were traced to the old man's house," Sean says.

"What did she want you to do to me?"

"I don't know. Stop you in your tracks. Make you go away."

"She wanted you to kill me?" Andrew asks, furious.

"Yes," says Sean.

The recording stops.

"When was this created? Is there a time stamp? Sean had a bust lip at the wedding." Connor chews his top lip nervously. I need to carry a knife, a bat, even a gun? I need to be able to defend myself. Rosie is safer with David right now.

"Doll, who is Andrew Marlow?" asks Connor.

I can't tell this story again. I should never have come here. I am putting everyone at risk. I am selfish and I have no morals.

"Andrew Marlow is the devil," I say.

40

―――

KATHERINE POWER

I sit and wait knowing that Katherine will come. Rosie is with her father and my aunt, in a house full of my cousin's children. She is safe. This is the first time in months, maybe in years, that I don't have to look after her. I choose a dress, and then I take it off and change into jeans. Let's face it, it is freezing in this draughty house and anything other than a jumper seems too contrived.

I drink a glass of red wine and listen to the muffled bass echoing through the wall. If I survive the next few weeks then I won't ever live next door to a pub again. But here, in this part of my life, I love it. I love the way I never feel alone. I like hearing people's voices when I put Rosie to bed. I light a fire in the kitchen as I do a lot now while Rosie does her homework and I cook in the evenings, but now Mr Todd dozes in front of it, enjoying a break from a house full of cousins.

You only get one life. It is better to spend it with someone that you love, and overcome the difficulties your being together might cause for other people, than to be alone or miserable with someone that you hate. My most important person is Rosie and Rosie loves Katherine. Who knows where this is going, or where

239

I am going. I type a text to Katherine and then I delete it. No, actually, I'll call her. I dial her number and she answers straight away.

"Can you come over for a minute?"

It's late on Notting Hill Carnival night and the music is playing loudly. I love the bonkers entrepreneurialism of this special evening only two nights before Christmas, because, well, there's a spare whole goat knocking about in the freezer. Barrington Levy and Bob Marley make me remember Ladbroke Grove. I get a pang of homesickness. As much as I wish I was Irish, as much as I want to be one of my Irish sisters, I am a Londoner, and I stink of it. I can't change my spots. It's in my DNA. I stand by the back door. I wait. Through the wall I can feel the vibration of the bass. It's a slow tempo reggae song. 'Silly Games' by Janet Kay is oozing through the wall when I hear her knock.

I open the door. It's freezing and I see Katherine shiver. The night is pitch black. From the back door a tepid security light illuminates the middle of the yard.

"Everyone loved the goat curry," she says.

I am trying to work up the courage to tell her. But what if she thinks I am damaged, too much baggage, a bad mother, a cheating wife with no moral code and no ethics. I am part all of those and part not.

"Why are you looking at me like that?" she asks.

I take her hand, touching her skin sends sparks through my fingers. It's like when we were dancing at the wedding. There is a charge between us that has always been there. I think she feels it too. I can hear her breathing quicken. I pull her inside the house, and close the door and I lock it decisively, out of fear for what lurks outside and to keep Katherine here, inside, with me. We are face to face, our bodies touch. In courage or madness I have to tell her how I feel.

"I…" I begin, and stumble over my words. I've rehearsed what I might say in my head so many times. "I'm in love with you."

There is silence and then the fire crackles.

"I think I've always loved you," I continue.

She seems surprised. She shouldn't be, I believe I'm an open book but no one ever agrees with me about that. But then her hands are touching me, my neck, my face and my lips and I think I might explode, and she holds my head in her hands and she kisses me. It's a long deep kiss, like she's inside me, healing me, warming me. She tastes like the flesh of a peach. I might drown in her arms, and never come back up for air. When she pulls away she drops one hand on my chest and slides the other around my waist.

"I can feel your heart beating," she says.

"I'm so nervous."

"I always wished that you had come with me to New York."

I can't believe that we have wasted all this time. She kisses me again. The fire casts a low red glow across the room. Our shadows move as one. I close my eyes. She slips her hands inside my jumper, running her fingers over my goose-bumped skin. Every inch of me is alive to her touch. I feel like I have been in pain, and have sacrificed so much and she is my panacea. She is my reward, my luxury and my necessary food.

"I've dreamt about this moment so many times."

"I think we're being given a second chance," says Katherine, and I dearly hope so.

She slides her hands up my sides lifting my jumper and pulling it off my body, and she bends and kisses my stomach. My breath is quickening. I hold up my arms willingly as she takes off my top. I push her away for a moment to slow us down and for a second, she thinks I want to stop, but I don't and I take her hand and lead her upstairs, the sound of reggae music pumping deep bass through the wall.

41

CHRISTMAS EVE MORNING

Katherine's arms are around me, her body pressed up behind me. I can't believe that she is here, that this has happened. I relax back into her. Her skin is white in comparison to mine, which is always olive, even in winter. I link my tan fingers with her white fingers. She wears a big emerald ring set in platinum on her forefinger. No wedding ring, but I sense a groove where she might have worn one for a decade or so, just like me, wearing a ring for the wrong person.

I hold her hand up to the light of the window, creeping in around the edges of the curtains. The cold is biting against my face, I can see the frost plastered to the window outside, condensation drips inside. It must be a few degrees warmer than it has been in the last few days. I kiss her hand and she moves.

I can't believe that last night happened. I have no idea if I've snored, or worse. I am naked. I need to get out of bed to let Mr Todd out for a wee but I don't want Katherine to see me, and I don't want to awkwardly cover myself in a sheet. It's also freezing cold. I stand up brazenly.

"Stay," she whispers, but I have to sort out Mr Todd. I'm surprised he hasn't come upstairs. When I open the bedroom door there's an unexpected breeze. I feel it whip around my ankles. I grab my towelling dressing gown. I descend the staircase. Mr Todd doesn't greet me at the foot of the stairs. When I've looked after him before he's slept in the living room, but always been alert and awake, waiting for me or Rosie to come down.

Could I have left the door open? I was sure that I had locked it. But with everything that happened with Katherine perhaps, in that moment, I forgot. Where's Mr Todd?

The kitchen door is wide open, allowing an arctic wind to rush inside and fill the house. It's the weirdest thing. The net curtains sway. The air, already cold, is alive with the scent of outdoors. Even if it was left unlocked it was on a latch, wind couldn't blow it open. No, somebody would have had to open the door and leave it open. Perhaps Katherine came down when I was sleeping to let the dog out, or to pop next door for something that she had forgotten. The cold is sharp. Where's the dog?

I take a pan and spoon and stand outside in the yard banging them together. I scan the fields and the road that leads up to the dairy. The wild cats that Katherine likes to feed prowl the outbuildings, hanging from the beams in the abandoned barn, their limbs long and lazy. Katherine's spin bike sits stationary opposite her speaker system. Her gleaming road bike sparkles next to it, freshly washed and oiled, leaning against the old pitted wall. There's nothing missing; nothing has been stolen.

"Mr Todd! Mr Todd!" I shout.

Pat hobbles out of the back door of the pub, straighter and more confident than I have seen him.

"You've lost your dog?" He lights a cigarette. He's meant to have given up smoking.

Suddenly there's the tearing of little feet scratching against the yard and Mr Todd rounds the corner and bounds up to greet me.

"He tried to get away from this place, but he couldn't," says Pat.

"Thank God!" I say. "Naughty boy! Where have you been?" I pick him up and he's wet and dirty. My aunt would be devastated if anything happened to him. And I would be killed if I let anything happen to him.

"I'm not a loser, you know," says Pat, drawing on his cigarette, the cloud of smoke joining with the early morning mist.

"I never thought you were."

"I want to get away from here. I'm in recovery. I don't want to be in a pub anymore. I want to move to the city. But I need to sell in order to do that."

"That's good, Pat." Does he guess that his sister is in my bed? "Did you see anyone out the back here, Pat? I can't figure out how Mr Todd got out."

"No, and I've been keeping an eye out for you."

I am unexpectedly touched, I wasn't expecting Pat to know, or even care about my problems.

I bring Mr Todd inside and feed him. I give him small premium pouches of lamb and vegetables. It's the only dog food he'll eat, being so used to the meat and potatoes that Auntie cooks him alongside her own dinner. He's the only person that she has left to cook for.

I check the lock on the door again. It is terrifying that it was open. Never in my life have I slept in a house where I left the back door open all night, especially not now when I've been so vigilant. Even when I was drinking heavily, when my mother was dying and I didn't know where I was or what hour of the day it was, I never left a door swinging open like this. I'm a Londoner; I'm streetwise. I know how to look after myself. I don't take risks and I don't make mistakes with my basic safety.

My phone beeps with a message. I am petrified that it's from Andrew Marlow but it's from my beautiful Rosie, sent from Auntie's phone, telling me that she's okay and asking if David can come back to the house to spend Christmas Eve with us. I reply:

We'll see.

If Andrew Marlow had been here and opened the back door, then presumably he could still be in the house. I take a carving knife from the drawer and check behind the curtains, in the long press, under the sofa, and behind the chair. Mr Todd noshes diligently at his food. I clear the area and start up the stairs. I check the bathroom, pulling back the shower curtain. I check Rosie's room, under her bed and in her wardrobe. And then I am back in my bedroom and Katherine is lying naked in my bed. Burning embers of the fire still glow red.

"Come back to bed," she says and I comply, resting the long black-handled knife discreetly on the bedside table. Her body against mine is gentle and warm.

"Did you let Mr Todd out during the night?" I ask, as she kisses me.

"No," she says, "you know I'm a cat person."

I push her gently away, but not wanting her to stop.

"The back door was unlocked. Mr Todd was outside."

Katherine sits up abruptly. We venture downstairs and check all the locks.

We don't care who knows about us. We'll never regret this night. We have been waiting for it for almost twenty years. All I ever wanted is here in my arms. I don't think that you can really love someone until they love you back. In that moment it becomes real. I trace my finger along the outline of her jaw. I have to pick Rosie up at noon.

There's a knock at the front door. Who now?

"Ignore it," Katherine says, moving onto her side to hold me down, but I can't ignore it. I wrestle myself free. I pull on the jeans and the jumper from last night; they're icy cold from the floor. I glance outside to see the outline of Pat's head. I go down the stairs. Mr Todd gets up from his bed by the fire and stretches lazily, satisfied by his lamb breakfast, exhausted by his adventures overnight. Patches of his fur have dried in muted grey.

"It's your brother," I call up to Katherine.

"Tell him I'll be along in a minute."

Somehow I sense that Pat is always around now and I find it reassuring. His smoking outside, which I don't mind, is an extra pair of eyes, alert to those who stalk me. I open the door.

"Pat."

"Doll." He pushes me back into the narrow hallway. "Be quiet now so he doesn't hear. There's a bloke here for you. Don't panic but I think it might be trouble."

There is a noise upstairs as Katherine jumps out of bed. "You're not going," she whispers down, over the banister, frantic.

"Blond hair?" I ask.

"Shaved head. Lean. English accent. Dodgy eyes, I don't like the look of him," says Pat, and I tend to believe that publicans are acute judges of character. I know what must be done.

"Jesus Christ." Katherine is barefoot on the stairs, zipping up her jeans.

"We don't have much time," says Pat. "Katherine, call the police, I'll stay with Doll. We'll keep him occupied until they get here."

"In the pub? No, you can't!" Katherine tries to hold me back, to stop me from going.

"He's not getting past me." Pat puffs out his chest. He's a big man.

I put on my shoes.

"You've only been on your feet for a week."

"We've no choice. Hurry up now or he'll leave. Let's get him arrested," says Pat.

I know that Pat is nearly fifty years old and Andrew Marlow would only still be around thirty-three years old, in his prime. Pat wouldn't stand a chance.

"I really don't want you to go in there, Pat. I'll go in on my own and keep him talking."

"Let's all wait for the police?" pleads Katherine.

"He'll leave," I say, knowing him well, knowing that every second that we delay right now would make Andrew Marlow suspicious. I've come to learn that there are good nerves and bad nerves. Good nerves spur you on to go in for that first kiss, give you the cheek to ask that question no one else will, good nerves give you the confidence to walk into someone's own house to snoop on them. Bad nerves, on the other hand, tell you that to get through the horrors of the coming moments you need to draw on a strength you didn't think you had. It's the panicky, claustrophobic sensation that you get when you're waiting to have a tooth pulled, or waiting for your mother to take her last breath. You can't go around it, you can't avoid it, you have to go through it, and somehow, unbelievably, we do.

"Let's go," says Pat and I follow him out. I know who it is in there waiting for me. I have waited too, anticipating this moment for many years now. I never thought it would be here, in the place of my childhood holidays, a place of peace and calm. I've shattered that too, that memory is irrevocably changed, coloured by what is happening right now, what I have made happen.

Pat still has a pronounced limp but he's a big burly fella. He only needed his hips replacing because he was so physical in rugby union. He was a back row flanker. He and Katherine were both stand-out athletes. He was once called up to train with the Irish national side, people boast that he played with the finest doctors and lawyers in Ireland but he was a notorious drunk even then. His antics even made rugby players blush.

There was a specific incident in Dublin, not long after their father died, and Pat was sidelined. He only played in Limerick after that despite being, perhaps, one of the best players in the county. Yet another unfair disappointment for the Power siblings.

"I'll go alone. Stay here with Katherine, please?"

"No, I'm coming with you, there's no time to argue," he says, and the two of us leave through the front door. Katherine has got her mobile phone, and is making the call to the police. I can hear her quietly talking to them as we slip away. Parked outside the pub is the same Mercedes Jeep, but with difference licence plates, but it looks the same as the one that ran me off the road. We could stab the tyres, and let the air out, but there's no time to be so calculated. The pub opened at eleven o'clock for Christmas Eve drinks and seasonal music is playing jollily to only Andrew Marlow.

I see him. He's at the bar, his back to me. He is tall and slim. My legs turn to stone, I can't move. At least Rosie isn't here. She's tucked away safely with David and my aunt in a busy, happy house. For a moment Andrew Marlow could be a cousin or someone that I'm friends with, waiting for me. Two men push in past me, saying, "Merry Christmas, love." Thank God they are here. Pat moves behind the bar and he bends to feel along the shelves where I know a baseball bat is kept.

"How are you, lads?" Pat says to the customers.

"Grand, thanks, Pat. Merry Christmas."

Their words, and their drinks orders blend into the background as Andrew Marlow turns to face me, and I swear he inhales, gobsmacked, his breath taken away momentarily by the sight of my face. The sockets of his eyes are dark and hollow. The slack make up of his shoulders and leanness of his build are familiar to me. He wears the same blue tracksuit that I have seen the man running in several times around the area. He has been here with me, watching me. He saw Julian Harper visiting me to tip me off and followed him back to England and disposed of him.

"Would you like a drink?" he asks as 'Fairytale of New York' starts up. He is deranged, in dreamland. What is he thinking? What does he want? To kill me? "This reminds me of how you and I met, in the Red Lion in Chatham."

I nod. I move as if on castors across the floor towards him.

"You look exactly the same, but you were called Claire, then." He softens his eyes and opens his mouth dreamily, as if on drugs or heavily medicated. I remember the pattern of his speech: the drawl, the drawn-out inflection. "I didn't want to wake you up too early. Did you have a nice time last night?" His face changes and becomes more pointed and reptilian.

I stand and face my nemesis and close-up he is real: his chin has stubble; I sense the static electricity of his tracksuit. His voice is flat, a Thames estuary accent that is spiky and menacing. He sounds like a Dickensian villain. I'm not used to this accent in the midst of so much sing-song Irishness.

"What a surprise." I sound quite posh compared to Andrew Marlow.

"A surprise?"

"I wasn't expecting you."

"I have dreamt about this moment so many times."

Horrified, I think back to last night and I remember I said that to Katherine, when I kissed her. I said those exact words.

"I'm not homophobic or anything. God knows, I've been in prison long enough to recognise loneliness and boredom. Some young guy walks into the rec and boom, you have a crush for a few weeks. Whatever, it doesn't mean anything. It's only sex."

Pat is listening. He and the two chaps at the bar heard Andrew Marlow, the way an admission like that would prick the ears of other men.

"I did my own investigation, Doll, and guess what I found?" He takes a step forward towards me.

In my peripheral vision I see Pat bracing, reaching behind the bar to retrieve the baseball bat. It's so ordinary, this scene, this song, it is so everyday that I feel as though I'm watching this take place outside of myself. At the same time I imagine him tying a rope around Julian Harper's neck. I imagine him pointing out Harry to prison yard thugs.

"Please, I'm sorry," I say, pathetically.

"I looked for Claire Halliday and she didn't exist. I couldn't believe it. I thought we had a connection. I felt it. She, you, had just lost your mum. I felt like you, as Claire, understood me."

"I'm so sorry, Andrew. I regret what I did to you. If I could go back and undo it I would."

He takes another step towards me.

"Do you know the worst bit?" he asks, while behind him Patrick Power is rounding the end of the bar with the baseball bat in his hands. The two customers are downing their drinks and turning to face the scene. This is it. He's going to be taken down, for better or for worse, by Pat here and now.

"My so-called friends at the pub trashed my mother's house. Everything was looted. I lost it all. Her photographs, her cutlery, her clothes. Junkies came in and used it as a crack den. They shat in her bed, and pissed on her carpets. In winter they set fires to keep warm and forgot about them and my house burned down. Everything, my entire world destroyed."

I freeze in the face of my own cruelty, my stupidity. Tears now flood my face; I am drowning in my own guilt and how everyone, absolutely everyone must suffer because of me.

Andrew Marlow is heading for the door, suddenly he is leaving. 'Fairytale of New York' is only just finishing. It happened so quickly, yet the conversation went on forever. The police will never get here in time to stop him.

I sniffle. "Please, wait, we can talk more."

Andrew Marlow looks around and laughs in my face. "I'm not stupid."

He turns on his heel to go, the jeep outside makes a tinkling sound as the doors unlock. But Pat is ahead of him, bat in hand. Pat fills the doorway.

"No you feckin don't, you're not going anywhere, you'll not get past me." Pat holds his ground, stopping Andrew from leaving, keeping him in the pub.

I think it's the speed and sheer aggression of Andrew Marlow's attack that scares me the most. He springs at Pat taking him, and me, completely by surprise. He headbutts Pat. It's so fast. A couple of teeth fly out of Pat's mouth and like dice they bounce off the table and onto the floor. Andrew doubles up and headbutts him a second time, and his nose splits with a crack and blood spurts out in a straight line.

Pat falls onto the floor, a huge beast of a man felled like a shot buffalo. He clutches his face. I catch sight of Andrew, his face splattered with Pat's blood.

I want to rush at Andrew Marlow, but I fear him now more than ever. I see his face, the face of evil speckled in blood. The two customers hold out their hands to reason with him. They might wade in, in a usual pub fight, like the one between Connor and the Crowley boy. There's an honour to it, a relief in the break up, knowing that both men have displayed their masculinity and are now free to make up or storm off in disgust. Not now though. The two men here are terrified. Andrew Marlow is an animal. He picks up the baseball bat, laughs, looks at us, and then brings it down hard on Pat's hip. To me it looks deliberate and spiteful, and Pat shrieks out in pain. Andrew throws down the bat and runs out the door. I go to Pat; he is screaming and writhing in agony.

"Call an ambulance!" I shout.

One of the customers foolishly starts to follow Andrew Marlow out the door, but it's too late because I see the car come to life and speed away, throwing up black dirt in its wake.

"I've got the licence plate," he says.

"You're going to be all right, I'm so sorry," I say to Pat. I am running out of sorrys.

CHRISTMAS EVE AFTERNOON

I'm at my Auntie's bungalow with Rosie and David. Rosie knows nothing but word is spreading far and wide amongst the adults. The pub is closed and Katherine is in hospital with Pat. He has sustained a broken nose, two missing teeth and a fractured hip again, at least we think this is the case, but we await more news from the hospital. The irony and the cruelty is not lost on anyone.

A small article has already appeared in the *Limerick Leader* online about a horrific Christmas Eve attack on a publican. My newspaper has called. A news editor covering Christmas, not Kelly as she's on holiday. But I am finished. There's nothing I can write to explain the misery and cruelty that I have inflicted on these poor people. If Katherine ever wants to speak to me again, I will be very surprised. My heart aches for her.

Pat wanted to help, wanted to repay a kindness, perhaps for his sister, I don't know. But he could not stand up to the wrath, the sheer embodiment of anger that rages inside Andrew Marlow.

It's so beautiful here. I watch my Auntie's fields slip away into the rich, dark waters of the lough in the distance. This is what I am thinking as Rosie giggles on my lap, and then jumps off to deliver a present to her second cousin. They are all back now. For reasons of safety rather than for reasons of space, David will come back with Rosie and I to the house tonight. I must keep Rosie safe. But how? Where can I send her? Who can I trust her with? For all of his faults, David is her father and he will do anything to protect her.

At one point I thought I could send Rosie with Katherine back to Dublin, or even America while I faced off with Andrew Marlow, come what may. But I will never be able to hurt him in physical hand-to-hand combat. I won't touch the sides. What have I got left? I need to be home and back in the house, locked up and ready before it gets dark. It will be so quiet without the pub rumbling in the background on the other side of the wall.

The police arrive at Auntie's and we assemble in the front room, the best room that we rarely go into. With my cousins back for Christmas – except for the one in New York who has, quite wisely on reflection, decided to stay in America this year – there's ten additional adults plus Auntie, Connor, Connor's wife, me and David here. In addition to this, there are twelve children between the ages of six and twenty-two. So that means there are twenty-seven people in the bungalow and Mr Todd, of course, who is in foul form at the lack of attention from Auntie. He takes himself to Auntie's bedroom and hides under the bed against the wall.

Auntie takes her rusty rifle down from its perch on the wall. She says she needs to 'protect' herself and others. The cousins talk her out of it and rant about how dangerous it is, so she cleans it with a duster and puts it back above the mantelpiece.

While we talk to the police, some of the others prepare food in the kitchen. There is to be a Christmas Eve curry, a help-yourself chicken dish in mild or hot options served with white rice. Tonight half of the family will sleep at Auntie's, the rest at Connor's house, and Connor himself, plus my cousin Annie's husband, an Englishman named Greg and their son, Paul, will come back to mine with David, Rosie and me. I don't know how we will fit in. I don't care. There is a welcome escalation of police interest now and we will have some security from their presence.

The bungalow smells of peat, the fire burning solidly. The otherworldly smells of turmeric, garam masala and chilli start to fill the hallway. A cousin brings in a tray of tea and cups and places it on a coffee table in the middle of the room. She begins the complex job of pouring and distributing the tea. Rosie asks to play on my phone. Playing on phones only started on the trip to Dublin with Katherine and now look what we've started. When I tell her no, she goes to play with the other kids in another room.

"No need for tea, really, I'm stuffed from lunch," says the garda. He has travelled from Limerick City. He sits in the best chair while the younger policeman, our local garda that I had seen only a week or so before, stands behind him. He has rosy cheeks and a plump, well-fed look which makes him appear rather festive.

"This was a serious assault. We are actively looking for the suspect, Andrew Marlow. We have joined up with British police and an Interpol Red Notice is in effect, so if he tries to head back to the UK we'll pick him up at the border. We're all looking for him."

"He won't go back to England." I know him; he'll stay here until he has finished this job. We have reached the end game of a plan that has been brewing inside him for a decade, and now he has nothing left to lose. I play with the autumnal coloured tassels on one of Auntie's best cushions. She's had them for years, since I was a child. How innocent I was when I used to come here on holiday.

"To complicate matters," says the garda, "Sean Gallagher reports that he was attacked by a man a few weeks ago and says that you are involved in this."

"What? Of course not."

"We suspect that it's Marlow. But there's also the matter of a man in Ennis reportedly beaten by you and some men last month."

"That's not what happened," I say.

Connor's eyes widen.

"Don't answer that, Doll. Back to the danger in hand right now, sir, have you spoken with the UK parole board?" asks David. "I have telephoned myself, and I've spoken to the Metropolitan police."

"We have, but as you well know, it's now a public holiday for three days. Andrew Marlow's parole officer confirms that he requested special dispensation to travel to Ireland to visit his sick grandmother."

"That was a lie," I say. "He hasn't got an Irish grandmother."

I know almost all of this already, and have been incubating it privately, turning it over and over in my mind. Now that everyone knows everything I only feel relief. Was it so bad, what I did? Wasn't I only doing my job? In the pursuit of keeping a danger to women and girls off the streets?

"He has been travelling because he has been attending appointments, he has missed some, but I think we'll find that he has been back and forth for the last couple of months."

"And where is he now, then?" asks David. "Where do we think he stays when he's here, I mean, someone must know, this is the countryside, it would be obvious, him driving around in a huge Mercedes Jeep."

"We have gardaí looking for his car all over Limerick. The car has already been traced to Ennis, County Clare."

"They're cloned plates," I say, despairing.

"So, Doll, this perpetrator, Andrew Marlow, let me get this right, you falsely alleged in a newspaper article a decade ago that he was involved in the murder of his own niece," asks the garda.

"Through marriage, she was his niece through marriage," I say.

"It was a type of honey-trap, a sting if you like, that you set up," the policeman elaborates.

"Don't answer this either, darling," says David, reaching out to place his hand on mine.

"For perspective only, please, Doll, we are not interested in investigating historical crimes in another country. We are only interested in apprehending him now, tonight, and for the safety of you and the community in this parish."

"Yes, that's what happened, more or less."

"For feck's sake, Doll," says Connor, draining a shot of whiskey and slamming the empty glass down on the fireplace. "You feckin' madwoman!"

"But he went to prison, so the courts did convict him of something; what exactly?" asks the garda.

"His initial conviction was a Category C production and distribution of indecent images of girls under the age of sixteen. There were six girls aged between fourteen and sixteen. And then his sentence was extended twice for a series of aggravated assaults while he was inside," says David. "He put Doll's colleague into a coma, and their boss killed himself only last month, in possibly suspicious circumstances."

"You're saying Andrew Marlow also killed your boss?"

"Julian Harper is dead, and Harry has brain damage sustained in a prison attack," says David. "I think it's fair to say that although he was not involved in the murder of his niece, he is a danger to society, a clear and present threat."

"Well, this is a fine mess you've got us all into this Christmas Eve," sighs the garda.

"She was only trying to do her job, which is more than I can say for you," says Auntie. "He went to prison for having child porn on his computer. She's not here to be judged, you need to find that bastard before he hurts someone else. He's a crazy psychopath."

"Just to be clear he wasn't convicted of child-porn criminality, it was production and distribution of indecent images," says David.

"To me it's the same thing," says Auntie.

"It's the same thing," agrees Connor. Mud sticks.

"I couldn't be more sorry, and I regret coming here now. I'm sorry about the chap in Ennis. I didn't want to drag anyone into this. I honestly didn't think he would be able to follow me here because of his probation restrictions. I thought Rosie would be safe."

"She'd be much safer in London, I told you that," says David.

"You didn't believe me, David. You told me I was mad. You stopped me from going to the police because of how it would reflect on you and the newspaper. You tied me up in knots, making me sign gagging orders, covering it all up. Well, it's all out in the open now!"

David coughs and shifts embarrassedly on the couch. "We'll go back to London at the earliest convenient moment," he says to the police.

"We can't let you go anywhere right now, sir. It would be too risky for you to travel on your own. We can put you in a safe house up in the country."

"No! It's Christmas Eve, for God's sake," shouts Auntie, breaking into a fit of coughing.

"We can give you police protection over Christmas. There'll be an officer outside your house twenty-four hours a day."

"We'll get a couple of the lads to go back with you as well," Auntie says.

"What about this?" I ask, holding up my mobile phone, the one that took me so long to get because I knew that once I did, I would receive the same messages again. The phone displays a message that reads:

You are next.

"We'll pick him up, Dolores, don't you worry about that. Stay safe now. He'll make a mistake soon enough and when he does we'll bring him in, and he'll be straight back inside in the UK."

Annie, puts her head around the door and asks if we want more tea. She eyes me suspiciously. She's been like this since she got back from London. She's jealous of my relationship with her mother and she feels guilty that she's far away. She knows nothing of my aunt's illness. She's unable to talk openly with Auntie: there's too much baggage, too much that is skirted around and left unsaid. We live twenty miles away from each other in London and haven't seen each other since my mother's funeral.

"Have you seen the dog?" Annie asks the room.

"Mr Todd's under my bed," Auntie says.

"He's not, Ma, we can't find him anywhere."

Auntie gets up to go and look for her dog.

43

CHRISTMAS EVE NIGHT

We drive back to the house in three cars: mine, Connor's, and a police car that is going to stay with us until the resolution of this mess. The sun has just set and the sky darkens from orange squash colour on the western horizon to dark purple in the east.

I have to keep Rosie with me. She is all that I'm worried about. Katherine returns from the hospital. I see the car, and later she goes out into the outhouse, puts on music and cycles her spin bike at excessive levels. My small house is full. The boys and Rosie eat curry from the pack-up that we have been given. They have playing cards at the ready and the boys have a stash of cans of Harp lager. The policeman sits in his car outside. The doors are all meant to be locked, but I can't leave Katherine out there on her own on Christmas Eve. I nip out into the back and see her for a moment.

"How is he?" I ask, as she spins on her bike. The music is blaring, so I shout louder. "How's Pat?"

She brings the bike to an abrupt halt. "He's alive, Doll, no thanks to you."

"I'm sorry for all of this."

"I begged you not to go in there."

"I'm so sorry."

"He's going to need an operation. There's a fracture in the hip socket. He hit him right where he was vulnerable. He must have known Pat had a new hip. He knew exactly where to land the blow," she says.

"There's something else. When he spoke to me, he repeated something that I had said to you last night. It might be a coincidence but it didn't feel like one, it felt like he was looking down at me. Like he's been watching us."

There is a moment's pause before Katherine asks, "Is there an *us*?"

"I think you're wonderful, Katherine, but that's got to be up to you. It's *your* brother I've nearly got killed. I don't want anything to happen to you. Come inside with me."

"Is David in there?"

"Nothing has changed, he's my ex. We've got to pull together."

"Without David's gagging order do you honestly think it would have ever come to this? He should have backed you to go to the police in London."

"Come inside. Please. I beg you."

Katherine gets off the bike and holds my hand. We move against each other, our bodies touching. We cross the yard and I go into the house and Katherine pops back into the pub to leave lights on and retrieve a bag of clothes, presents and toiletries. The blackness has set in. Night has arrived like a ghost. We are expecting a visitor. We are expecting Father Christmas to arrive during the night.

"Here she is!" Connor beams. "The party has arrived!"

"Are you all right, fellas? Merry Christmas!" says Katherine, squeezing into the kitchen.

"Katherine!" shouts Rosie, and runs to embrace her.

"How's the big fella doing?" asks David, awkwardly over-familiar, and she gives them a rundown of Pat's injuries and the likely date for his next operation.

Connor opens a bottle of wine. Greg shuffles the cards and deals them out. We play along like this, a wind getting up outside, blowing things around making noises in the yard that make me nervous. We put on Christmas music to drown them out. Greg's son, Paul, looks on his phone to show Rosie where Father Christmas is on his sleigh. We're all trying, rather pretending, to be festive for Rosie's sake. I take a glass to the policeman outside, who, quite rightfully, refuses and so I offer him chocolate which he accepts.

It is weirdly atmospheric and Christmassy being squashed in the house. All that's missing is the snow. And soon enough it is time for Rosie to go to bed. We have sleeping bags and a camping mattress for the lads. David is keen to put Rosie to bed himself, and we decide that he will sleep with her in Rosie's bedroom and they can fall asleep safely together. Her stocking is hung there on the fireplace waiting for her gifts.

"And Katherine can sleep with you, Doll, in your room," says Connor, winking. "I'm taking the sofa."

"I'll go back next door to my own bed," says Katherine. But everyone shakes their heads unanimously.

"None of us will sleep thinking of you alone in there."

"He's hardly going to come back," says Katherine.

"We don't know, do we?"

"It's just the two bedrooms, is it?" asks Greg. "We thought we might at least have a bedroom."

His Christmas trip to Ireland is ruined and now compounded by having to contemplate sleeping on a cold floor in a strange house. If he doesn't get his head kicked in by Andrew Marlow then he should count himself lucky.

"Just the two bedrooms," I say.

"What's in the loft?" he asks, because if this was London we'd be considering a loft conversion, isn't that what everyone does?

And it comes to me in a lightbulb moment. "I've never been in the loft." I turn to Connor in his capacity as the estate agent. "What's in the loft?"

"What is in the loft?" Katherine repeats.

"Rosie, David into bed, please, now!" I say. "Santa is coming!"

Rosie runs up the stairs. David is there already in red plaid pyjamas. I tuck them both in.

"Listen out for him, Mummy Doll, I've left bells by the fireplace."

I close the door to Rosie's room and stand on the landing, looking up at the loft hatch. He couldn't be there now. He couldn't. He couldn't have ever been there. The thought is just too sick.

"Fetch a ladder," I bark rather bossily, my mind is spinning. Katherine makes to go next door to get a stepladder.

Paul springs up the stairs. "I won't need a ladder," he says, hoisting himself up onto the banister rail and reaching to open the hatch. He shuffles it over to one side and it's black up there, I mean really dark, but somewhere in the back a light reflects, there's something, a flash of light.

"Be careful," I say, looking up. We're all nervous. We're all shrill with nerves, anxious with a shared frightened energy.

"Oh fuck it," he says, and he shoots up into the loft in one movement. Impossible for someone like me but easy for a fit twenty-two-year-old like him.

Katherine is still struggling up the stairs with the ladder. "This must be yours," she says. "It's not ours. It was propped up against the side of your house. I've folded it down. It's pretty long." The lads move downstairs to help her.

David opens the door to shush us, sees what we are doing and retreats silently to comfort Rosie and try to get her off to sleep.

Paul's legs dangle down from the hatch and he flicks on the light from his mobile phone.

"Holy fuck," he says.

"What?" I feel sick.

"You better look for yourself."

Katherine and Connor open the ladder and lean it up against the hatch. Connor goes first, and then I follow.

It's completely dark. The timber of the roof folds gently inwards and there is hardly room to stand. Under the eaves at one end there's a khaki green sleeping bag, ruffled and recently used, sitting upon a tattered sleeping mat. Paul puts his hand inside the bag.

"It's cold, not warm."

I crawl over on my hands and knees and smell it. I can't remember what Andrew Marlow smelled like, but there's an unknown manly odour on the sleeping bag. It is shiny and shaped like a caterpillar in mid-walk. There are energy bar wrappers discarded around the makeshift bed. There's a black bucket. Connor sniffs it and recoils, screwing up his face.

"Piss," he says. "Stale piss."

I feel faint. He's been up here. He's been up here in the house with Rosie and me this entire time.

"There's a little window over here," says Paul, and he pushes it and it opens into the fresh night air.

"Jesus Christ," says Connor. "Can you fit through it?"

"I could, yeah, just about," says Paul. "But there's a drop outside."

"That's exactly where the ladder was," says Katherine, standing on that very same ladder, her head poking up through the hatch. She turns to speak to Greg down below: "We should tell the gardaí. Get the garda from outside, will you? He better have a look at this."

In the stomach-churning shock we fall quiet, mesmerised by

the little nest in the loft. In the silence we can hear David's voice reading Rosie a story in the room below, snuggled up in her bed.

"Night, night, Daddy," she says, and we can hear her voice as clear as day.

44

CHRISTMAS DAY

We pass the night in traumatised awakeness. The lads sleep in my bed, the three of them together, and Katherine and I hold each other on the sofa. I check on Rosie and David every hour, sometimes peeking through the door, sometimes going in and rearranging the covers around their faces. The garda outside swaps shifts with someone else. The fresh one walks around the pub and house with a flashlight, checking doors and the outhouses. We wait like hunted animals, fenced in, hens in the henhouse while the fox prowls about outside, our scent tantalising his nostrils. But the fear in me has gone, replaced by anger and disgust. If Andrew Marlow approached our house we would tear him apart with our teeth like a pack of angry dogs.

Then, before first light, while the lush green fields are still shrouded in icy mist, I hear Rosie upstairs.

"He's been!" she shouts, and plows down the stairs. "Mummy Doll!"

"Merry Christmas, baby!"

"Mummy Doll, look! Look, he's been!" she says, examining the chewed carrot and oats leaving a trail from the chimney across the floor. She picks up a little silver foil tray. "He ate the whole mince pie! Look!"

"How the heck?" I say. "I didn't hear a thing! I didn't wake up at all! Did you?"

"No!" says Rosie.

"Did you hear bells? Or, or a reindeer?"

"I didn't hear anything, only Daddy snoring!"

I'm never going to be able to get her back into sleeping in her own bed on her own again. All the good habits and the good intentions that I had worked hard to instil in her have vanished since arriving in Ireland. Will any of us ever sleep soundly again?

"I'll put the kettle on," says Katherine, getting up and walking to the kitchen. She wants to be inconspicuous, she thinks she's intruding on Rosie's Christmas, on our family Christmas time, but she couldn't be further from the truth.

"Look what was in my stocking." Rosie holds up a box of two miniature steering wheels.

"I wonder if there's anything to go with those steering wheels?" I point to a large box. Rosie forages in the presents.

"This one says, 'Katherine'."

"Give it to her," I say to Rosie. "It's from you."

"Okay." She jumps up and runs into the kitchen.

I love it that Rosie loves the giving of gifts as much as she loves opening her own presents. It's a weird Christmas for her but I am determined, all of us are determined to make it as perfect as we can for her. I know that gripping onto Christmas should be the last thing on my mind, but it is, along with keeping her safe, and catching this bastard. Katherine comes in with two steaming cups of tea and a box of chocolates.

"You're allowed chocolate for breakfast on Christmas Day, isn't that right, Mummy Doll?" Katherine hands me a hot cup of tea.

"Absolutely!"

"She called you Mummy Doll!" Rosie laughs. Everyone loves

the ring of it. Katherine tears open the Christmas paper, golden and shiny. The cycling top falls out of the paper. It's bright red, and I got it from a specialist cycling shop in Limerick City.

"It's Rapha," says Katherine. "I absolutely love it. It's so cool."

For a moment I have exactly my heart's desire right in front of me. Christmas alone with Katherine and Rosie would be the most perfect Christmas that I could ever wish for, but who knows if I will ever get it, so I squeeze Katherine's hand, and I commit this moment to my memory. If now is all I get with Katherine then I want to remember it. She hands me a little wrapped box. She and Rosie have handmade labels with robins on them, the kitchen table was covered in them. They have drawn pictures, glued them to card and cut them out with pinking shears. This is the gift that I am most excited to receive, but I wish we were alone, certainly not with David lurking in his pyjamas. It's a long silver chain with a large silver wing pendant. I love it.

There's more noise upstairs, the lads are waking. David comes down first, beaming. "Merry Christmas!"

Katherine makes him a cup of tea, and then another round for the three lads upstairs, who come down in last night's clothes and squish together on the sofa. David leans over and presents me with a box.

"I'll open it later," I say, but he insists that I open it now and I slowly loosen the Sellotape, the ribbon and the bow. He has not wrapped this. It's been wrapped by someone in the shop, probably a woman in duty free. The box is red velvet and inside is an expensive-looking charm bracelet, with roundels in red glass hanging from it. I don't want to seem ungrateful but it's not my style. It is perfect for the type of woman that David wants to be married to, but not for me.

"Merry Christmas!" Connor bellows into the front room. "Are we all still alive?"

"We are." Katherine smiles.

"Merry Christmas, Uncle Connor," shouts Rosie.

Katherine takes tea outside to the policeman.

"I could do with a fresh drop, Katherine," begs Connor as she returns.

"Merry Christmas to you too!" she says, walking back into the kitchen and flicking on the kettle. Rosie rips off the paper from her Nintendo Switch, an expensive gift from Santa, and handily bought by David in the duty-free shop.

"Wow!" she says. "Can we play it now?"

"I'll have to get back to my own brood, but everything's okay, right?" asks Connor. "He might never show up again, we might have scared him off."

"I doubt it," I say.

David delights in opening the instruction booklet of the games console. Rosie comes to sit on my lap. She is still warm and sleepy. She doesn't look as happy as you'd think she'd be.

"I didn't get my wish from Father Christmas, Mummy Doll."

"Why not, baby? I thought this was what you wanted?"

"It's a good toy, I do like it a lot," I put my arm around her, "but I wished to go home. I made a wish to Father Christmas that we could go back to our house in London."

Right then, I know it's time to go. I know that the game is up. It's time to face the music. I can't keep running. I flick up my eyes to the kitchen where Katherine is brewing tea.

"Then we'll go back home. I promise."

"Really?"

"Yes, really."

"You really mean it, Mummy Doll? You're not just saying it?"

"We'll go home, I promise."

"Really?"

"Yes," I say, and we're both crying now. I'm crying for everything. For all the mistakes that I have made. For being a bad mother. For taking my child away from her home, her toys, her father and her friends. I'm angry with myself for putting her at risk. Allowing her, still now, to be at risk.

"When, Mummy? Not ages away? Soon, tomorrow?"

"Not tomorrow, we have Christmas to enjoy first."

"The day after then?"

"We'll take you home for the start of the school term. When's that? January 5th or around then. A week and a bit."

She throws her arms around my neck and squeezes me so tight that I can't breathe, but I love it.

"I'm going back to my old school!" She jumps up and runs into the kitchen. I mean to tell her to be quiet for the time being, that it might upset Katherine and Auntie if we leave, but it's too late.

"I'm going home with Mummy and Daddy!"

As Katherine turns, I can see the disappointment in her eyes. I choke back my guilt. I didn't promise her anything. She has a life, a wife (an ex-wife) in New York. What would she really want with me? He has heard us; Andrew Marlow has tainted everything. He has been visiting the loft in this house. I have no idea when, or how many times he has climbed up and squeezed silently through that little window. But I feel sick at the thought of him up there as Rosie and Katherine innocently went about living their lives.

Katherine opens the back door and brings in a huge present. I can see it's a bicycle through the wrapping paper.

"Oh, a bike! Thank you!" Rosie jumps into Katherine's arms. How am I going to get that back to London?

"You can send me a picture of you riding it in London."

45

A HAWTHORN

We wave off the boys in Connor's car. I feel oddly safe, standing here on the main road outside my house, outside the pub in daylight, with a police car parked and a garda watching over us. We are in charge. We can do something. Perhaps the family Christmas dinner at my Auntie's bungalow might be a welcome relief, perhaps even fun. My contribution is a prawn cocktail for twenty-seven people. I am serving it in throw-away bowls: iceberg lettuce, Marie Rose sauce, cucumbers and eight kilos of prawns. Perhaps we will be all right after all.

As Rosie and David step inside the house to get ready I grab a moment with Katherine to explain.

"You can settle up, pay your tab before you go," she says, pulling away from me, but I take her arm and hold her wrist gently.

"Come with me," I whisper.

"David's pretty happy."

"It's for Rosie's sake. Will you come for Christmas lunch? Auntie is expecting you."

"I'm going to the hospital. I'm going to sit with Pat."

"Later then, I'll see you tonight, when you get back? I don't know how much longer we're going to be able to stay."

"What's the point? You're married. Your husband is right there, next door. We live in different countries, on different continents. You are being stalked, it's going to end up messy, even if they catch him now, today, it'll end up in court. How can you even care about *us* right now?" She tugs her wrist free.

It shocks me. In the moment of silence my eyes fill with tears.

"Because I love you," I say, desperately. Her head cleaves to mine and our foreheads touch and I try to kiss her right there on the road but she pulls away. I just want to touch her, feel her skin on mine. I'm frightened that if I mess this up, I am going to lose her forever.

"Connor's back." She nods up towards his car coming back around the bend.

"He must have forgotten something."

Connor's car circles back slowly and he blows the horn, winding down the window. Steam or cigarette smoke wafts out. Greg and Paul are still in the back, silent and looking pale.

"You'd better come, Doll," says Connor. "We've found the dog. He was hanging from a hawthorn tree just up the lane there. I took him down. He's at peace now."

We take Mr Todd up to auntie's bungalow.

"No, no," Auntie weeps.

"I'm so sorry. I'm so sorry," I cry. She lets out a wail, and her body stumbles. The family rush to support her.

Annie throws daggers at me with her eyes. "How could you have done this?" she whispers. "You silly bitch, bringing *your* problems to our mother's door."

I hear the boys say: "If that fucker comes round here" and "we'll take out a car and look for him, and by God when we find him, he'll know about it" and "first Pat and now Mr Todd. We'll fucking do him for the pair of them."

My God, what have I created? I am no longer one of them. I am not a woman of Ireland. I shame them for bringing this trouble to their door. I feel so English with my London accent and total disregard for these good people. I'm not one of them. If I don't know whether I am English or Irish, then who am I?

I am Rosie's mum. That is who I am.

"I have to get back to Rosie," I blurt out, panicking.

"Boys, get the shovels," Auntie rasps out, turning practical, "we'll bury him in the back field facing the lough. He always loved to run down that way."

Peter Crowley turns up in a beaten-up four-by-four truck and blocks the drive. He takes off his hat to examine Mr Todd.

"Ah, Jesus!" he says. "The poor little fella."

"Please," I say to Connor, "will you run me back? I have to get back." I pick up my phone and call David and there is no answer. The same for Katherine. It just rings through to voicemail.

I have a horrible feeling.

"And there's a crazy maniac on the loose?" asks Peter.

"Doll has brought all this trouble to my mother's door," shouts Annie. "She got the dog killed."

"Enough," says Greg to his wife, but I deserve it.

"She's caused nothing but trouble since she's been here. She's been an attention seeker her entire life. She's dragged that poor child out of school, away from her father."

"She single-handedly stopped the dairy in its tracks, don't forget the good she's done for this community," says Peter sternly. "No one else could have done that."

"Well tell that to Pat Power sitting in the hospital waiting for his next operation," Annie says.

"For a man to come after a woman, chase her to another country, to send threats, to harm animals, there is no excuse for that, Annie, no excuse at all, whatever she has done in the past."

"He's been up in the loft at Doll's house," says Greg. "Watching them. It's really creepy."

"Feck the police, we need to find him ourselves," says Peter.

"It seems like Doll picked the wrong crazy bastard to phone hack," another cousin mutters.

"Leave her be. Doll loved Mr Todd," I hear my Auntie snap at her daughters as the procession begins around the back of the bungalow. She stops to cough up her guts. "I'll be with you again soon enough, my precious boy."

"Please, all stay together," I plead as they disappear around the side of the bungalow, but they don't look back except for Annie.

"Feck off," she says under her breath as she sticks her two fingers up at me. I want the ground to swallow me. This is awful.

"I need to move your truck, please, Peter," says Connor.

"Sure, the keys are in it. I'll be around the back with Mrs helping with Mr Todd. I'll be here for a while," says Peter.

Connor gets into the truck to move it and turns over the engine. He seems to change his mind. There's another rental car in between us. He calls me into the truck.

"I'll just take you in this," he says. "I don't know if we should have left David on his own with Rosie."

I get up into the passenger seat.

"We better get back quickly," I say. "It's what, a mile? There's police outside. It'll be fine, won't it?"

"The pub to Ma's house is one and a half miles. I've walked it enough times."

He reverses onto the main road despite the blind bend, crunching the gears. It's a dangerous manoeuvre but my heart can't beat any faster than it already is.

"I've got the paperwork for Sean Gallagher, and I'm selling the house. I'm going to give away the money to make amends. I'm going to split it between you, Pat, Katherine, the poor man in Ennis and Auntie."

He puts his foot down and the truck's rear portion lowers to the ground and screeches as we bounce along the road.

"You don't have to do that, we're family."

"No, I do have to. I've made such a mess of things. In case anything happens to me you split that money, and make sure the fella in Ennis is compensated. Promise me?"

"Fine, whatever, I promise."

"I never intended this. I swear it. I thought we would be safe here. That we could live quietly for a while."

"Don't feel so sorry for yourself."

"I should've known he'd take the dog."

"You certainly picked the wrong man. He seems hell-bent on revenge."

"I wish I could go back and undo it."

"He'd have probably killed someone by now if he wasn't in prison, so you've done people a favour. Although you can never prove what you've stopped from happening."

"I hope you're right, Connor, but we'll never know for sure."

"Jesus, I've been out so long, my wife will think I've been seeing another woman."

"I wish it were that simple," I say.

As we round the last bend we notice straight away that the police car that has been stationed there for the last twenty-four hours has gone.

"Where is it?" I ask, not expecting an answer.

"It must be round the back," says Connor. "They'll be checking the yard." Connor drives the old truck past the buildings and takes a left around the corner of the pub and an immediate left into the yard.

There's no police car.

"Something's happened," I say. He hanged Julian Harper, and he hanged Mr Todd, and he's put Pat Power in hospital. I jump out of the truck and run into the house. The back door is wide open. A wind rages through the house blowing the curtains. I am screaming.

"Rosie! Rosie!" I go from room to room. I can feel myself sobbing, my breast heaving up and down.

"Rosie! Rosie!" I go up the stairs. Connor's behind me. He mounts the banister to push open the loft hatch and check up there.

"They've probably gone with the police. We didn't think of that," he says.

I pick up Rosie's pillow and let her scent fill my nostrils. But my breathing is shallow and I can't get my breath. My vision seems squeezed; I feel faint.

"Doll. Doll. Doll." Connor shakes me and then gives me a swift, sharp slap across the cheek. He hasn't done that for thirty years, we used to do stuff like that all the time.

"Katherine," I say. "Let's check next door. Her car is there. She was going to go to the hospital."

We dash out of my house and into the pub, which is open and silent. No music, no customers. But Katherine would never leave it open while she was alone upstairs. She's spent too much time in New York and especially with everything that's going on. I go upstairs, where I never go, and go in a room that looks like something from the 1970s that must be Pat's room. Katherine's room is immaculately tidy with a stack of books by the bed, a diary that I would like to read, laptop computer, all her stuff – everything is there, including her mobile phone with a notification of a missed call from me.

"We need to call the police," I say and dial the number of the local gardaí, but as I do a message pops up. It's from an unknown number, another burner phone of Andrew Marlow's.

We are at the lough.

I hear myself wail; I feel the vibration of my screams through my chest. Connor bursts in.

"What the fuck is it?"

"He's taken them to the lough."

"Show me."

"Look. It's from him."

"How do you know?"

"Well, they haven't just gone for a fucking walk to the lough on Christmas morning. They were sitting in their pyjamas thirty minutes ago, playing Nintendo, and now they are gone, and all the doors are open!"

"Let's go, we'll call the police on the way."

RETURN TO THE LOUGH

He's got my child. He's tricked the garda into leaving us unmonitored.

The realisation comes to me, suddenly, that my father dying, and my mother dying, and everything bad that has ever happened to me is nothing compared to this. He has my Rosie.

We get into Peter Crowley's truck. I have the phone to my ear waiting for the gardaí to answer. The way Connor has parked means we have to reverse onto the main road, the flatbed part of the truck sticking out into the unknown.

We should drive into the yard and turn around but we are both so hyped on adrenaline and sheer panic, we don't. Because he doesn't know the truck and is used to driving an expensive automatic Connor stumbles getting it into gear. He's a pretty boy, not a fixing stuff kind of guy. He tries again, there's a raw screeching noise and we lurch backwards.

"Oh fuck it!" He slams his foot down into reverse and we sail into the road backwards with the intent of doing a three-point turn, I guess.

"Wait!" I shout but it's too late and suddenly, there's a god-awful smash and a deafening noise as we hit something.

Connor's face bounces off the steering wheel. It's an old beaten-up truck, full of pointy surfaces. I have my seat belt in my hand. I hadn't yet put it on. Neither had Connor. I am thrown up into the air, I hit the roof, and feel the tug of my muscles straining with whiplash. There's a sharp pain up the back of my neck, and in the side of my ribs by my right breast, my elbow fires with intense pain.

The truck goes up into the air, and then comes to a rest diagonally across the main road. My fingers, my shins, and my ears, everything burns. I struggle to get my breath. I've been winded by the impact.

"My leg, my leg," cries Connor. He has a deep cut on his nose where he's hit it against the steering wheel. It's a crooked line of dark red blood, and I can see his nose is broken. But he doesn't mention it, he just screams about his leg, and I look down and it seems bent up underneath the steering wheel.

"You're going to be fine," I say, my vision woozy, feeling dizzy. "I think you've hurt your leg but it's not too bad."

"I think it's broken," he gasps.

I grope for the door handle and tug on it. I open the door and turn and vomit onto the road.

It's a black four by four and I think that it's the car that took me to Ennis. They must have been travelling at speed because Peter Crowley's truck has indented a huge V-shape laceration into the front bonnet where steam now rises.

The windscreen is smashed. A person has hit it. They haven't gone through, such are the safety features on expensive vehicles like this.

I am so frightened that my child is in this car.

I take the handle and open the door of the passenger side.

On the far side away from me, the driver's air bag has failed to open. I can't see the man's face for blood, but he's in a bad way.

I know him. It's the thin moustached man. The one who works for Sean Gallagher, the one who told me to sign those papers, or else!

The bigger chap, the other Gary, turns to me, tears streaming down his face. An airbag has cushioned his impact, there's not a mark on him, bar the tracks of his own tears.

"I don't think he's going to make it," he cries, pulling at his pal's collar to loosen it.

"Could you not see us coming out?" I ask, bewildered, possibly concussed.

"Call an ambulance!" he screams. "Gary, Gary, wake up!"

A second car approaches behind us. It's a Nissan in a soft metallic green colour. The car slows and the door opens. There is screaming, blood-curdling screaming coming from the back seat. I don't want to look, but I have to. I am walking in a fog in my mind. Get with it. Sort this out. Get to Rosie. Save Rosie.

"Are you all right?" asks the driver, and I see that it's the doctor from Charleville. Thank God. There is screaming coming from the back seat where Suzie, the vet, is lying on the back seat with her knees bent and legs open.

"Is anyone hurt?" shouts the doctor, getting out of the car.

"Oh God! She's in labour!" I say. They must have been driving to the hospital.

"The labour has come on fast," he says as Suzie moans again.

"How long are the contractions?" I ask, as if I would know better than the combined knowledge of a vet and a doctor.

"Every minute," she screams. "Is that my uncle's truck?"

"Connor's driving," I say.

The doctor is on his phone speaking to the ambulance service. He keeps them on the line.

"Suzie has a few minutes yet before the baby comes, what have we got?" He runs to the black four by four, and then to Connor in the truck.

"The baby's coming, there isn't going to be time to get to hospital." Suzie sighs in the pause between contractions.

"Come into the house," I say. "Please, another car could fly along this road." I help Suzie out of the car and support her to walk slowly across to the house and into the lounge. I dash into the kitchen to get towels.

Connor is ghostly pale. The doctor gets his bag and gives him a shot of something and Connor's teeth unclench. The muscles relax in his jaw.

"Get Rosie," he murmurs over and over. The cars fill the entire road so that nothing can pass. The truck lies diagonally across the junction facing back towards the pub. There's no time.

I want to help Suzie but I have to get to the lough to save my own child. I can't walk down, it will take too long. Could I run it? How long would that take? I make one last call to my aunt. I tell her that Andrew Marlow has Rosie down at the lough and that I'm going there now. I tell her about the car accident and she sends the family to come down to help Connor, the vet and the doctor.

"I have to get Rosie," I shout to the vet who is now bearing down on all fours on my front room carpet. The Christmas tree lights twinkle. I race through the house, out of the back door and into the yard. I unfasten Katherine's racing bike from its fixtures and mount it before cycling out of the yard, past the crashed truck and four by four, over Holy Cross and down the lane that leads to the lough.

The road throws up mud and tiny stones. I hear the grip of my tyres, the stony whirr of my bike as it picks up speed. Brambles and leaves reach out to touch me from the hedgerow. I turn at the first bend and get a good look down into the lough itself. The water is moodily dark. The visitor centre is shut up. There are no cars. It is still Christmas morning, after all.

But what is that floating in the lough itself? A dark round boat. In fact, it's a coracle, the old-fashioned traditional Irish fishing boat made from stretching an animal skin over a skeleton of lightweight willow. And is there someone in the coracle? Someone small? I know straight away that it is my Rosie drifting in the middle of the lough in the flimsy boat. Yes, she can swim but if it capsized she wouldn't know what to do. She wouldn't stand a chance out there in the cold, dark water.

I pedal harder, faster. If I go to the far bank I could swim out to her and pull the coracle in. Should I go into the water? Or would that be dangerous too? I could go to her in another boat. But why is she there and where are the others?

As the road swings around and opens up into the car park and visitor area, I see Andrew Marlow in full view, not at all hidden. After everything, all of the threats, the secrecy, and the online disruption this seems scarily theatrical. He's planning something big. I drop the bike and walk toward him on foot. I don't think he's seen me. By road there is only one way in and out, and that is via Holy Cross. He has set up here so that anyone who comes down that road will be led to him. In the distance, in the other direction, I can see Auntie's bungalow, and I can see the large red pipe from the dairy that Rosie and I took samples from all that time ago.

Andrew Marlow stands over two bowed figures who are kneeling on the floor. Both have their hands tied behind their backs. David is upright, while Katherine has fallen onto her side in the dirt. David is still wearing his pyjamas and his feet are still bare, now red with cuts and scratches. Andrew looks canine, a ferocious, feral creature. There's a stringiness to him, a putrid ranginess so you never know when he might just lurch forward and bite off the end of your nose. He plays dirty, he fights dirty. I'm no match for him in that regard, very few would be.

Out behind them in the distance sits the coracle balanced on the choppy waters, and within it my innocent little daughter.

"You took your fucking time!" Andrew Marlow says, waving a pistol in the air. "I was beginning to think you weren't coming."

Katherine, hearing me, shuffles to sit back upright and she turns to look at me. There is a gag in her mouth.

"I'm sorry."

I wonder if I should keep him talking. I need to buy time for the police to arrive. Even then, though, what happens when he sees them coming down that road? If he's out here so openly with a gun and two hostages and my child floating unstably in an old boat, he's not standing down easily. There's no talking him down.

"Come and sit here with your friends," he says.

"My daughter, please let me get her."

"She's fine. I pushed her out there so she'd be out of the way."

"Please, Andrew, what can I do to show you how sorry I am?"

"Nothing."

"We should go back to London and get you a lawyer and press charges against me and against the newspaper. Do this all properly."

"Press charges. As if! It's the system."

"You'll be entitled to compensation for everything that you have been through and wrongfully accused of."

I step very slowly closer to them. David has a black eye. It's already swollen and shiny purple like an overripe plum.

"Fucking media," Andrew spits.

"It was wrong, and I'm sorry, and if you pursue this in court then we can make sure that it doesn't happen to anyone else. I promise you I will tell the truth about everything that I have done, regardless of the repercussions."

"British media need a story to fucking implode themselves and that's what they are going to get."

"No, now you need to tell your side of the story."

"Who to? The story is that you all fucked me, you ruined my

life for no reason, and so I fought back," he says. "That's what they'll report. You messed with the wrong person. You should have chosen someone weaker."

"It doesn't have to be like this."

"And then people will be inspired to fuck the British press, burn them down, like they burnt my mother's house down. You're a puppet. You're not important to them or me, but you are the one who is going to be made an example of."

I was a puppet, a willing puppet reporting back to Julian Harper, the greatest ringmaster of them all, reporting in to the top bosses, who conducted the whole thing with gusto, with leagues of little Davids collecting signed agreements and non-disclosure agreements and paying out sums of money to buy people off and shut them up.

"But I'm a mother now, Andrew, and that's my little girl out there, and I want to make sure that she is safe."

"I would never hurt her. I'd never hurt a child."

Hard to believe with his actual convictions.

"I need to get to her and make sure that she's safe."

"She could have been my own child if you and I had made love that night."

The image makes me feel sick. I find it hard to imagine now that Andrew would be capable of consensual sex.

"Please let me row out and get her then."

"Not yet," he says. "Wait until I've finished. You know I went to the hospital looking for you? I couldn't believe that you had just vanished when we had such a connection."

"I'm sorry, Andrew, I was doing my job."

"Do you think in other circumstances you could have liked me?"

"Yes," I mumble.

"You liar. I saw you with her! You still lie. You made up that name for me, Uncle Andy, a paedo kind of name and it has stuck to me like rotten shit. I've had it sprayed on my house and spat in my face, that's on you that one, I know it is. Harry told me that part was one hundred per cent you."

"No, then! No, I would have never given you a second glance, nor you me. You would have never liked the real me."

He stands up straight and rolls his shoulders back, widens his stance and spits onto the floor like a cowboy. Then he lurches forward and strikes me across the face. It's a fierce blow, the strongest I have ever felt, and I ricochet onto my backside a few metres away, my head ringing. I touch my face and there's blood. Perhaps he used the butt of his pistol. I feel a deep, intense pain across my cheek and right eye socket.

"Doll, you choose, it's David or Katherine," he says. "You have your love. Or, you have your child's father. You have your own happiness or your daughter's happiness."

A choice between David and Katherine? This is crazy.

"You have to choose, or I will choose for you. You can have a minute and no longer."

I notice both David and Katherine are starting to shake. David turns his face pleadingly towards me. He's the biggest coward I know. He wouldn't think twice about making a choice. It crosses my mind that a fresh start without David wouldn't be a bad thing, but Rosie doesn't deserve this and besides, he is my friend. We've been through thick and thin. Birth, death, marriage and soon, divorce. I don't want him dead. I couldn't live with myself, and I don't trust Andrew Marlow. I don't trust anything he says. I just have to get Rosie back.

"David, do you know that this one here, the barmaid, has been shagging your wife? Did you know that?"

David makes a noise and trembles in his bindings.

"Let me row out to Rosie, please, and then I will make a choice, I promise." She isn't a strong swimmer. I should have taken her to the swimming baths more often.

"David, when you visited me in prison, I thought I was going to be looked after," Andrew says.

What was he talking about? David visited him in prison?

He continues: "But no, you threatened me, and told me that if I made any allegations about being hacked, being burgled, being misled and being deceived, then I would be taking on the full force of the newspaper corporation and that I would end up back in prison for life."

"When? When did David visit you in prison?" I ask.

David is shaking, pleading, making little insipid noises.

"Only last year, Claire, when he knew my parole was coming up. He paid me a visit and warned me off. He took away any chance of a fair trial and now this is the only vengeance I have left. You've got your husband to thank for all this."

David is trying to shout and scream through the ragged bandana shoved in his mouth and is shaking his head.

"You wouldn't believe the dodgy shit that David gets up to. Or would you? Up to his neck in it. Right, mate, your time's up." Andrew pulls the metal shaft on the pistol up and down, I guess to load it. It makes a fast, harsh metallic sound. David pisses himself, a dark stain appearing on his Christmas pyjamas.

"You were right, Claire, you were right about me all along," Andrew says, widening his stance.

What can I do? I can't jump him. He'll shrug me off like a bug. This can't be happening. I pray that Rosie cannot see this far back to shore.

"I'm so sorry," I say.

"Yeah, you little bitch, you ruined my life. I'll make the choice for you, make it easy."

"No, please."

"You let me take the blame for things I hadn't done. You misled me, reeled me in to trust you. You spied on me. Right, stand up, fella, let's get you on your feet."

David staggers to stand up, his loose piss-stained pyjamas covered in mud from the shoreline. Katherine whimpers and shakes her head. She's trying to tell me something.

"I'm so sorry. What I did was wrong, and if you let David live then I will spend my life making this up to you," I say, I don't have much left to offer apart from myself. If he wanted sex to spare their lives, then I would do it. "We can work something out."

"No, you won't, you slag, you can't stand the sight of me. You're petrified, I can smell your fear."

Katherine shivers. No, not shivers, she's trying to tell me something and that is when I see, up in the rising bank of grass, my aunt.

Rather than go to the car crash at Holy Cross, she has quietly walked from her bungalow on her own, over the fields, to the edge of the lough. She's around forty metres away. Andrew Marlow, for all his cunning, doesn't know that she is there. She is behind him.

In the distance Auntie widens her stance, and lifts the shotgun up to her eye. She takes a slow, deep breath, holds it, her lips pursed, and pulls the trigger.

A single bullet rips through Andrew Marlow's left shoulder, the padding on his jacket seems to spring open with a sprout of cotton. But David drops to the floor. It looks like the stray bullet has pierced David somewhere I cannot see.

Andrew looks down at his perforated shoulder. The bullet has passed through and into David. Andrew is surprised, still not realising what's happening. Ever efficient, my aunt does not like wastage or risk, so she uses her first shot as a place finder, and the second, immediately after, to kill.

Andrew's forehead bursts open like a scarlet spring tulip. For a moment he looks at me in utter disbelief. Then he topples forwards like a felled tree, faster and faster until he lands face first in the earth of the shoreline.

Behind him, in the distance, Auntie sinks to her knees. Her job is done. I move quickly to feel Andrew's pulse. I don't know really what I'm looking for but he's not breathing. I take his gun and throw it into the long grass far enough away in case he comes around, which he is not going to do, or in case it fires off or something. Next, I pull the cotton from Katherine's mouth, and she takes a huge breath.

"Undo me." She wriggles her hands. I turn her over and fuss with the knot. Eventually I'm able to release her hands.

"Is he dead?" she pants.

"Yes, I think so."

"And David?" She turns to David who is lying on his back on the muddy sand, his arms out by his sides. I take the bandana out of his mouth and his breathing is shallow. Katherine pulls his T-shirt up over his stomach and there is a hole where the bullet has pierced him and blood begins to leach out of him. Katherine presses on his stomach. I take off my coat and hand it to her to stem the flow. I take off my top and trousers, and I stride out into the lough. My aunt kneels on the hillside like a young girl in summer.

I put my aching face under the water and I swim for my life, for Rosie's life, faster and further than I have ever swum before. I do not feel the cold. In the distance I hear sirens coming down the road from Holy Cross. I stop a moment to look back and see Katherine bent over David busily working on him.

I can't see her.

I can't hear her.

I take a mouthful of water, and cough it out, screaming, "Rosie!"

I hear a little girl's whisper. "Mummy."

"Rosie, I'm coming," I shout, giving every last morsel of energy that I have left. Before long I can hear Rosie calling me louder, her voice curls over the waves on the wind.

"Mummy!" she shouts.

I reach the edge of the coracle and she leans over into me. She is distraught, crying.

"I'm here. Lean over the other side while I flip myself in," and I do. I have no idea how I am able to scale the small side of the boat so easily, but I do it in one go and I'm on the floor of the coracle like a caught fish. I lie there in my bra and knickers on the bottom of the boat with my daughter clinging on to my cold, wet, exhausted body.

"I'm scared. What's going on? Who's that man? I heard a gun. What was Auntie doing up there on the hillside?" Rosie's tears emerge and through big gulping sighs, she hiccups. She can't catch her breath.

"Naughty Auntie," I say. "She shot herself a big rabbit this time."

"Your face, Mummy Doll." Rosie kisses my face, her arms and legs wrapped around me like a baby koala. I shiver with cold, my teeth chatter but I do not care. My child is in my arms. She lives, she cries, she will be fine, in time.

"Mummy's here, no need to be frightened anymore. I won't leave you again. It's over." I look up at the sky as the grey clouds stretch and break apart, finally revealing a glimpse of blue sky beyond. We lie on the floor of that spinning boat for some time, locked together, holding each other until they come and get us. I'm happy here, we're safe here, just Rosie and I.

I do my community service on Hampstead Heath. Among the descending fields that make up the area we pick up trash and place it in bin bags. We have waded into the ponds to remove shopping trolleys. It's nothing flashy nor sordid, we keep the heath clean, I wear a high-vis jacket, I breathe in beautifully clean London air, and I hear the comforting hum of the city all around me. I've made some of the best friends in my life.

I received three hundred hours of community service. I nearly fell off my chair when I was sentenced. Not so much because I had escaped a custodial sentence, but because there wasn't really a crime to answer to anymore. With no one to press charges against me there was no crime. I wanted my punishment. I handed myself in to the police and explained what Harry and I had done but there was no case to answer.

After considerable wrangling with the newspaper, they dropped legal action against me, personally, for breaching their NDA. My circumstances had also changed. With my husband now disabled I was his and Rosie's carer, and so the court looked on that favourably. I couldn't be taken away from either of them, and neither could Rosie be taken from me.

I am all right for money. And I've even made a few quid from my book. It's not a bestseller, but it has done well enough. When I went through the courts it meant that I could go on the record about what I knew of unethical and illegal media practice, and once that testimony had been given it became unlikely that I would later be sued by anyone involved. I pay my penance (Father Aidan would be pleased to know) by telling the general public about the hacking that I have seen and been part of. Many newspapers dispute my account and make me the villain which, of course, I am.

Am I sorry? Yes, I am. Was I wrong about Andrew Marlow? No, I don't believe that I was. I knew there was something off about him and I am able to sleep at night, because I had him locked up and he is no longer able to take out his violence on anyone. When we take evasive action we never really know what would have happened had we not, but I am a mother and I am glad Andrew Marlow wasn't out on our streets for all those years, and I'm glad that he will never be able to hurt anyone again in the future.

My local bookshop is a dark and dusty narrow space that I have loved for years and years. It is an honour to occasionally do a book signing there and answer people's questions. I sometimes get given a hard time by a smart alec but I take it. I guess I'm easy to hate. I haven't been back to Ireland. If they have any sense, they will never let me back in.

We had the house rearranged so that David can have the ground floor. I can't leave him now he's like this. In spite of everything, I've promised Rosie that I will look after him. But I also promised myself that I would look after and love me. David has a physiotherapist called Dannielle who has been irreplaceable in his recovery. I encourage her to come as much as possible. I can see a spark between them. I want him to be happy. I still want to be free.

It is the height of summer. The middle of July just before the school summer holidays. The grasses on the heath are growing high. The meadows are beginning to brown. The ponds are full of swimmers and down on the track, St Frederick's Primary School have noisily had their sports day. I take off my high-vis vest, my work for the day is done, and say goodbye to my team. I walk up to the top of Parliament Hill and see all of London screaming out to me in the blazing sunshine, buckling in the heat.

I look east down the hill toward the dog swimming pond and lo and behold I see my three loves coming up to meet me. Rosie has a kite. We usually fly it from this spot but it's too muggy, there's no breeze. Rosie wears parachute trousers and a cropped top. She's ten. She really is a big girl now. She's even stopped sleeping in my bed which, after everything that happened, I thought would never happen.

In front of her runs Kielty, our little black puppy. She sees me and goes crazy, jumping up, kissing me, licking me, wagging her tail.

And behind Kielty walks Katherine Power. She was crazy and trusting enough to come with me when I asked her, and God only knows I'm lucky because if the roles were reversed I don't know if I would.

"You missed a bit," says Katherine, pointing at an empty can on the path. I thank her and laugh. I've been to the shops to buy a bag of snacky bits as a picnic, with cans of mojito and fresh chicken strips for Kielty. The three of us sit, with Kielty jumping about us and over our legs, and we look out over London as the summer sun sits high in the sky. I thank God, even though I don't believe in him, for everyone that I have in my life.

Later that night, Rosie stays in and watches Saturday night television with David and his physiotherapist. Katherine and I get the Tube across London to North Greenwich. The O2 is a carnival of light. I take Katherine's hand and we walk into the concert. The crowd roars as Depeche Mode come onto the stage. We are two women in black band T-shirts. We are young and old all at the same time, our regrets are behind us, we have the future. We have all the time in the world.

Margaret O'Shea, the environmental activist and campaigner, has died in Limerick aged 77 years. O'Shea rose to prominence for exposing the Lough Goren pollution scandal alongside her niece, journalist, Dolores O'Rourke. O'Shea was acquitted on all charges related to the self-defence manslaughter of convicted sex offender Andrew Marlow in 2018.

In her formative years, O'Shea turned down a prestigious scholarship to the National College of Art and Design in Dublin in 1967 to marry her beloved husband, Martin O'Shea, from whom she was widowed in 2002. She died peacefully at her home in Ballymaura surrounded by family. She leaves seven children, and eighteen grandchildren.

THE END

ALSO BY HELEN TREVORROW

In The Wake

New Brighton

AFTERWORD

PLACES AND PEOPLE

This is a work of fiction. Names, characters, and places are fictitious. The setting of Limerick is inspired by my beloved childhood trips to visit my family in the area, but geographical details have been imagined suiting the geography of the plot. Likewise, all characters are completely fictional. I was inspired to create the character of Auntie in honour of all the strong, brilliant women who raised me, and those that I am inspired by in life and in fiction. On occasion I have re-used names of places and family names to bring the plot to life, but none of this story is based on real people or real places.

ACKNOWLEDGEMENTS

With the greatest of thanks to my daughter Ruby who is my world and it is a privilege to be your Mum. Thank you to Louise for saving my life, continuing to do so and I am so proud to love you out loud.

Thank you to my agent, Andrew James and the fabulous team at Bloodhound, Betsy Reavley, Tara Lyons and my brilliant editor, Abbie Rutherford. Thank you to my friends and early readers who helped me to shape this book; Richard Skinner, Alison Marlow, Giles Fraser, Kelly Allen and Patti Cohen.

I undertook extensive research in writing this book so thank you for your insights and expert knowledge; Suzanne Plunkett, Dan Waddell, Erin Cowley and 'Ryan'. Thanks for inspiration to Liz Ivens and my cousins, The Colls, and many people in the media I have met over the last two decades.

Thank you for all your continued support in my writing to the St Bernards Convent girls and Langley Massive. There are too many people to name but I appreciate you all and all of the positive vibes that you send.

I find this story shockingly prescient having written a narrative about a mum on the run with her child, finding love and surviving a difficult situation. Life has mirrored art since finishing the first draft of this book. I would like to say thank you to everyone who has supported me over the last two years of challenges. I am very grateful to have you in my life; Mel, Joy, Lauren Deighton, Brighton Squirrels Netball team, Ria, Karen, Dr Pippa, Alison, Sophie, Dannielle Bull, Kerry D-J, Mia, Lena,

Cazza, Kerry, Owen, Tracey, Daisy, Aidan, June, Jonathan, Matthew, Jade, Adele, Kwali, SJ Watson, Rosie.

A NOTE FROM THE PUBLISHER

Thank you for reading this book. If you enjoyed it please do consider leaving a review on Amazon to help others find it too.

We hate typos. All of our books have been rigorously edited and proofread, but sometimes mistakes do slip through. If you have spotted a typo, please do let us know and we can get it amended within hours.

info@bloodhoundbooks.com

www.ingramcontent.com/pod-product-compliance
Lightning Source LLC
Chambersburg PA
CBHW061521210726
48287CB00006B/1769